# Whispers

## in the Dark

# LeTeisha Newton

# Whispers in the Dark

I was captured...

That's just the beginning of my tale. I've survived Purgatory, abuse, and near death. In that abandoned farmhouse I nearly lost everything, but Jacob saved me. We were trapped in this hell together, giving each other the strength to hold on. I fell into darkness with my captor's son.

Until I left him behind.

She was perfect, my Alana. Brilliant and full of pain. She understood my darkness and fueled the fire. When she left, I waited patiently to find her, and in her honor, I killed men who took away from innocents.

Then I found her...

She's deadly now, a killer too, and perfectly mine. It was beautiful to behold, but she belongs in a cage. My cage. She'll love me again, or I'll expose her dirty secrets for the world to see while going down in flames with her.

*In darkness, it's most definitely till death do us part.*

# Contents

# Other Books by LeTeisha Newton

### *Dark Romance*
Vanquished
Going Under
Midas (Truculence Book 0)
Collared (Dark BDSM)
The Lost Series
One Hour Girl
Scarred
Phenomenal

### *Military Romance*
A SEALed Fate Series
Protecting Butterfly
Protecting Goddess
Protecting Vixen
Protecting Hawk
Protecting Hearbeat

**Paranormal Romance**
Claimed Trilogy
Taken Trilogy

**Romantic Suspense**
Corporate Hitman Trilogy

# Dedication

To Jessica,
the one who passed the reins.
I did it with LBM,
and  you matched me with WitD.
Thank you.

# Acknowledgements

First, and always, I'd like to thank my editors. Ella, your notes were amazing, insightful, and much needed. This book is what it is because of your thoughtful reading of it. Thanks, *chica*. What a wonderful addition to my powerful team!

For Tiffany, I don't think I have the words for you. I swear you've saved me. *Saved me.* Thank you for being my friend, my editor, and accepting that you can completely bash me on the head (friends don't let friends write stupid shit), and yet clean my words up in ways I couldn't have imagined (my favorite hashtag has become #MyEditorIsBetterThanYours). Or for making me go sit down and rewrite an entire blurb because, you know, tenses!

To Laura, well, there is a special place for people like you in heaven. You took me out of comfort zone (way out) and sat my ass down and basically said get it done. I did, and it was better than I expected. And the end result? Wouldn't have happened without your expertise. Thank you, again. You are amazing.

To Anne and Ashley, you guys are my first line of defense. You ladies are wonderful and dark. The best in the world. What in the hell would I do without you? I'll keep sending words as long as you're willing to read them.

To Deena Rae, hold my beer.

My Book Bitches, thank you for providing a safe place. Your laughter, support, and love are indescribable. It's so wonderful to have found you, and I wouldn't have it any other way.

And lastly, my Vixens. Love hanging out with you in our group (because it stopped being mine long ago). You help keep my head on straight, wow me with your engagement, and keep me on my toes when I ask the crazy posts with wicked dark content.

# Taken

## Alana

*What's past, is prologue.*

**—William Shakespeare**

I raided the cupboards for something quick and easy to make and grabbed a package of blueberry Pop-Tarts to throw in the toaster. As I waited for them to finish, I figured I'd broach the topic of the father-daughter dance with Dad. Every year, Northside Prep held its annual dance to raise money for the after-school programs. The dance was the talk of the town as the girls ran out to buy their dresses and make appointments for hair and makeup. Me? I got to wait for the dad who never came. This year, I wanted to be the same as the rest of the girls; I wanted him to choose me.

"Hey, Dad, the dance is this weekend. Can you get away from work for a few hours and go with me?"

He looked up from his laptop, eyebrows drawn and a faraway glaze to his eyes. Aaron and I had dubbed this Dad's "deep thought" expression. Usually, it ended up with one of us in trouble or disappointed, unfortunately.

"What day is it, Lani Girl?" Dad was the only one to call me Lani Girl. I loathed nicknames, especially the horrendous "Al" Aaron kept insisting on calling me. For Dad, I was always his Lani Girl, no matter how much he loved my name Alana Rose.

"Saturday night. The dance starts at eight o'clock," I replied, hopeful. Always hopeful.

"I'm sure I can get away, sweetheart. Let's go."

"Oh, Daddy. Thank you, thank you, thank you." Running around the counter, I gave my dad the biggest hug I could.

"How about I take you to dinner before the dance too. Just the two of us?"

I squeezed him harder. "I'd love that. I've missed you so much."

"I've missed you too. I'm sorry I've missed so much lately. Saturday night is all yours. Dinner, the dance, anything you want."

As he planted a kiss on the top of my head, I thanked him once more before grabbing my Pop-Tarts and heading upstairs to get ready.

I turned my iPod on and danced to Fergie's "London Bridge" as I made my way to my closet to pick out an outfit. I chewed on the last bite of my Pop-Tart as I sorted through my pants until I landed on a pair of dark-blue American Eagle jeans. I completed the outfit with my tan Ralph Lauren boots I'd received a few weeks earlier for my birthday and a burgundy tank top. Styling my hair in a messy bun, I grabbed my book bag and took one last look around my room to make sure I didn't forget anything. I had a habit of leaving behind my homework almost every time I left my room.

With one more stop in the kitchen, I threw my arms around my dad and kissed his scruffy cheek as I thanked him again for agreeing to go to the dance. Moving on to my mother, I gave her a kiss on the apple of her cheek. Saying goodbye, I popped my earbuds in my ears and let James Blunt serenade me with "You're Beautiful" as I headed in the direction of Northside Prep. I had to pick up the pace so I wouldn't miss the first bell. Lost in my own world, I jumped when a heavy hand came down on my shoulder. I turned around to see who it was, thinking it could be Ryan. Instead, a tall man stood in front of me. My five-foot figure was small next to his; he had to be over six feet tall. With wire-framed glasses and dress pants, the man looked harmless enough despite his basketball-player height. He reminded me a lot of our eccentric neighbor, Mr. Edwards. His dark hair blotted out the sun, and his nose, crooked as if had been broken before, caught my attention between steel eyes. He could be hot, but something about him was wrong. Buzzing nerves crept down my arms. *Get away from him, Alana. Run.*

"Do you have the time?" His gruff voice shocked me to the core. The roughness to it was almost biting.

I offered him the time and backed away. Adrenaline raced through my blood and kicked my heart into a gallop as a cold chill raced down my spine. Continuing my walk to school, I refused to turn and look back, even **though** I knew his eyes were boring into me. Within a few steps, his hand landed heavily once more on my shoulder, but before I could scream, his other hand came around and covered my face. As the world blurred, I noticed the rag in his hand. The slightly sweet smell filled my nostrils and I swayed, only to be caught before I fell. I was weightless, floating in the air, and then I crashed to the ground and darkness claimed me.

"Wakey, wakey, little girl."

Hot breath hit my face with the whispered words. Disoriented and sick to my stomach, I couldn't wake up fast enough or bring the world into focus. The loss of my bearings made my stomach pitch.

*Where am I?*

"Wake up. Wake the fuck up. Open your goddamn eyes!"

I shook my head, attempting to clear the fog, as a smack blazed across my face. A cold trickle of fear rushed up my spine. I recognized the voice. The man in glasses who'd stopped me on my way to school. Afraid to open my eyes, I turned my head away from his voice, but surprise filtered through me with a sharp pain spreading over my cheek as his meaty fist connected again. One tear escaped as I bit my lip and opened my eyes before another hit could come my way. He held my arms viciously, digging his fingers into my biceps, and my breasts were smashed into his chest. I could barely touch the floor on my tip-toes.

"Ah, there she is. Hello, sweet girl."

His voice was beyond creepy. Refusing to respond or look him in the eye, tears choked me, and my cheek burned from his strike.

"Aren't you a stubborn little one? But oh, so precious. Look at you, sweet cheeks. You're sure going to be fun to break in. Those stunning looks of yours must've driven the boys crazy, but don't worry, you'll never have to worry about them again. You're mine. All mine."

Terror shook me to my core, and I whimpered. My heart throbbed, pounding so loudly I knew he must have heard it. Mouth dry, and tongue thick in my mouth, I stared at him. This man was a monster, and Lord knew what he planned to do with me. Against my best judgment, I couldn't stop the words from pouring out of my mouth.

"I want to go home. Please, please, please let me go home. I won't tell. I promise I won't tell. Let me go. Please." My voice cracked over the last word. I wanted my mom back. My dad. Even my brother. Anyone. I didn't want to be *here*.

"Isn't it the cutest thing? You think you have power here. Well, you don't. You're nothing but a slave."

There was recently an abduction case on the news. The newscaster shared tips from law enforcement on how to deal with being taken. Didn't the police say to make yourself real to your captor? To get them to feel something? Humanize yourself.

"My name is Alana Masters. I'm only eighteen. I've done nothing wrong. I'm a normal teenage girl. Please don't hurt me. Please. Please."

A change came over him; those must have been the wrong words. Where he looked like a normal man before, his eyes darkened with evil and his face filled with rage.

"Of course you've done something wrong, little girl. You're like the rest of those bitches. Flaunting your ass in front of me. Teasing me but never giving me the time of day. You're a manipulative little whore. You begged for this. You begged me to take you and make you mine, you fucking bitch. Don't worry, *whore*, you'll learn your place before I'm done with you. I'm going to fuck you up and make you scream. Make you regret turning up your little prim and proper nose at me, cunt."

His eyes glazed over, lost in his own world. He no longer looked at me. His gaze went through me, and I wondered who he was thinking of. Who did he remember? Frightened more than ever, I wanted to go home. But somehow, I knew the nightmare had only begun. Grabbing my face, the monster brought my face to his. Looking me right in the eyes, he spoke, and every word cut me to the bone.

"*You are mine.* Your body. Your pussy. All mine. I am going to train you, mold you, and break you. And if you ever, *ever* dream of escaping me, remember this: You are Alana Masters. Your parents are Alan and Barbara Masters. You live at 3412 West Monroe Street, and you have a younger brother. If you step one foot out of line, little girl, I will kill them all. Their blood will be on your hands."

When he pushed me away, I landed on the harsh, cold cement. I was in a large cage, maybe about six-by-six, with a mattress full of stains— the smell of urine wafting from it—lying on the floor in one corner and a bucket in another. A loud clang made me spin. He locked me in here. Sweat trickled down my back, and my clammy hands wouldn't allow me to be fooled into believing this wasn't real. I had been taken. *I'm going to die here.* How'd this happen to me? What had I done wrong? I wanted out *now*. Back with my family, my dad, my mom. But the grit on the ground and the soiled mattress were all I could see through the watery film in my eyes.

"From now on, you will call me Master." He turned and headed up the darkened staircase, leaving me behind as the tears flowed freely down my face.

"Don't worry, you'll eventually have cried so much you won't be able to cry anymore," a voice said from the darkness.

"Who's there?"

"My name is Celia. And I'm you, months from now. Welcome to Purgatory."

# Chapter One

## Jacob

**B**lood and spit.

It drizzled from her still-red mouth. I didn't like it. But I did. It confused me. I fucking loved the way her insides dripped on me, pooled into my navel and sloped down further. But it made me sick too—twisted in the head for liking her pain and misery. Pretty little Tanya, my father's favorite for a while. But now he had a new girl; he had to make room. I don't know if I loved the idea, or if it terrified me, but it didn't stop me from being here, enjoying her pain and the slickness of her bodily fluids. Although I found pleasure in this, nausea rumbled through my belly at the same time. Besides, I didn't have a choice but to be in this room, just like her. My father controlled everything, even the life and needs of his son.

Suspended above me, Tanya swung in silence on little meat hooks—the ones Dad had pushed through the bolts installed in the delicate flesh of her back. She'd screamed. I stayed silent. And then I came all over my dirty, stained sheets, my hips twitching and flexing as I humped into my hand. Because Dad asked me to, yelled at me to, and beat me if I didn't.

*You like treating them like whores. That's all they are, son. Whores.*

So I did. Palmed my cock, jerking, twisting, and pounding until the sickness over watching his little toys in pain didn't make regret eat at me. Until their screams sounded more like pleasure to my ears than agony. Then, I took a step further into the darkness, exactly like he wanted me to.

For a time, this toy belonged to me.

She was pale and dark-haired, too dark for my taste, but she had other qualities. When her eyes weren't swollen shut, they were the prettiest gray I'd ever seen. And she teared up so nicely. Now my father was done with her, about to toss her away, but I wanted her a little longer. It was what he expected out of me.

"That's my boy," was all my dad said. He stared at me for a few minutes, his brow furrowed, an eerie smile on his face. He wanted to make sure I enjoyed it. Dad wanted me to need this shit to live. Maybe I did. Maybe I was more like him and less like the man I hoped to be. But then, I didn't know any man but my father, so it was stupid to try. My father walked away and didn't say anything as he shut Tanya and me in the room together.

My toy didn't cry or shiver away from me, and it irritated me. My father taught them to be afraid, to bow down. But she didn't, and it made me angry. So angry. I released my cock and jumped to my feet. It bobbed in agreement as I curled my fists. The bite of my nails into the palm of my hand was surreal, but it planted me firmly in the moment. My father had taught me how to deal with unruly toys: deliver a beating so she would know who was Master and who was the slave. The first hit went a bit wide, grazing the top of her head, but the squeak of the chains welded to the hooks was sweet. I swung again, harder this time, and caught her right on the cheekbone. Enough pain made anyone give up, I'd learned. She moaned. Better. So much better. I laughed until my stomach ached, and then kept pounding until her flesh was black and blue, ripping her little puncture holes and making her bleed all over.

Fucking served her right.

*I hate myself.*

I was my father's son—born and bred in the blood of his victims. And the sins of the father would be mine too. As her warm blood slid down my skin, I laid back underneath her. Forgetting the hate, the sickness, only pleasure swelled now. Her blood met my twisting fingers, and it made me so … *wet.*

"Yes," I gasped. Perfect. So hot. So good. It was sloppy and dirty. Nasty and filthy. And it turned me up so high, my little teenage heart almost thudded out of my chest. But there it was, the final moment, the weightlessness in seconds where I was only pleasure.

My cum mixed with her blood and spit.

Pretty. Ever prettier when covered in our mixed fluids.

The sins of my father most definitely belonged to me, but I couldn't stop them now.

Her body hung frozen-still long before I saw what I'd done. For the first time since I'd stepped into this final room, the death glade, I could see it. My father had built this concrete room to be solid and soundproof. The windowless room was dark and gloomy, deep underground. A single, bare bulb swung overhead, yellow and dirty in its age. Father had put in four different stations where he killed the toys he didn't want anymore. Tanya hung in station one, the Hooker's Place.

The next station held a large, glass tube about ten feet high, with manacles attached inside at the bottom and to the top, underneath the lid. The chains connected to the iron bracelets could be adjusted from the outside to make up for the height of the victim standing inside the tube. Once one of the toys was strapped in and the lid locked down, water would be slowly pumped in from a hose attached to the top. The Witch's Redemption. The device was my father's favorite to use. They screamed for hours while they were in there, begging for him to free them, but he never did. Not until their bodies stopped twitching.

The Bitch's Punishment was right next to it. My father had fashioned a working guillotine he used to quickly break the women who irritated him the most. At first, I found it odd my father gave the worst slaves the quickest deaths. Wouldn't it be better to have time to watch the piece of shit die, to enjoy their demise? But, to my father, a quick death amounted to the greatest insult. He didn't even want them, even in death. They were unworthy of his final act of need.

The last station was where my father began everything, and where I, too, had my first taste. The cold, metal slab had ties for the wrists, chest, head, and then stirrups for the feet. I'd lost my soul to a toy as she bled out into dirty, white buckets from the deep gouges in her wrists. I masturbated and finished long before she died, and my father stayed with her for hours afterward, but I didn't stay to see. I threw up every time I remembered it.

A whimper pulled me from my thoughts, and I looked up at Tanya, hanging motionless and dead. The whimper came from me. The ache in my chest swelled outward until I swallowed the tears. I spun and ran from the room, pounded up the stairs, past the sounds of the crying new slave in the above-floor cells, and into the house. My father wasn't in the main kitchen, thankfully, and I breezed through to my bedroom. In seconds, I stripped off my jeans and was running to my adjoining bathroom.

My father said every man needed his own time and space after he dealt with a toy. I welcomed it now. I turned the water as hot as I could stand it and climbed in. My flesh burned, and the steam choked me, but not as much as the wracking sobs I fought to keep silent. I'd killed her. With my own two hands. Covered in in my own semen and her filth, I enjoyed it. My father and I were the same. My tears pooled with the muck at the bottom of the shower as I fell to my knees. I would never be clean enough.

My father told me my regret for killing toys was on account of my weak constitution passed down to me from my mother. I was stupid and sickly, but he'd fucking make me into a man if it was the last thing he did. But my mind couldn't keep up. It was fractured. Lost. One side of me needed these victims. The side he'd beaten into me needed their blood, screams, and deaths. The other side of me mourned their loss, wondered if they missed their families, and cursed the day my father had even come across them.

But I was as bad as him. Nothing would ever take away the hell I'd caused or the fucked-up shit I'd done over the last couple of years. How could God forgive the Devil's son? I was a piece of shit, worse than the slaves, yet I held their lives in my hands.

"I wish I could die."

It was a worthless whisper, from even more worthless lips, but it didn't stop me from praying for it.

"You done sniveling in the shower, boy?"

"Yes, Father."

"You handled the toy well. She was getting too broken in. You have to deal with them like horses, son. A stallion gives the best rush, but after a while, you've snipped his balls and taken all the fun out of him. He won't buck even if you try to make him. He won't try to bite you and will follow your every rule. When he gets too compliant, you've taken everything he could have been. It's better to put him down. Do you understand?" He glared at me as I sat down at the table, the smell of blueberry Pop-Tarts wafting to my nose.

Those were my favorite.

My father got up and grabbed the sweets as they popped from the toaster and brought them back to the table. His dark eyes scanned me before he slid them on a plate and handed them to me.

"I understand," I said.

"Once you're finished eating, we need to get rid of the body and clean up down there. If you want to have your own toy, you have to know how to care for her. And I've brought you a real pretty one to learn on."

My heart thundered in my chest. I couldn't stop the happiness coursing through my veins at the mere mention of my own slave.

"You caught me one? Really, Father?"

"I just said I did, didn't I?" The irritation in his voice dampened my joy.

"Yes, sir."

"I got this toy because you are ready to capture your own yet. She's a looker, with perfect blond hair and bright eyes. She has probably fucked plenty of guys before with the body she's got."

A blonde. I'd always wanted a blonde. They were the prettiest girls in the whole world to me, with fair skin that easily bruised. And he got me one. All for me.

"Can I see her?"

"Not yet. I need to break her a bit before you can handle her. But she will be a good first toy for you once she learns the ropes."

"What's her name?"

"Alana. Alana Masters."

Alana Masters. My first toy. A blonde. Perfect. So perfect. I smiled wide.

"Thank you, Father."

"Good boy." When he smiled back at me, the darkness inside of me—the monster he'd made sure I was born with and cultivated every day—waved in greeting. Morals clung to thinning threads of my fear, but the monster would still rise. Right now, it stretched and unsheathed its claws, eager to use them.

"Did you fuck the toy before you killed her? I saw the marks on her throat. A tough way to kill anyone, and you held on, but she was dry between the legs."

I swallowed. "No. I was already in the process of masturbating when she didn't make enough noise for me. I was so mad I beat her until she was bloody and then finished before killing her."

Lying to my father was impossible. He could smell it in the air, the perfect predator. When he narrowed his eyes at me, I knew I had incurred his wrath.

"You haven't fucked one yet. They're whores, boy. You fuck whores until they're useless. You beat them until there is nothing else to beat. And then you destroy them like the filthy animals they are. How many times do I have to tell you this?"

"I understand, Father. You also told me a man gets his needs as he sees fit. I like to beat them, hear them scream, make them cry. It turns me on, their tears and blood all over me. I like it, I enjoy it."

"No man turns down the chance to get laid unless he's a fucking fag. You a fag, boy? Huh? Is that what you are?"

"No!"

My words fell on deaf ears. My father was already on his feet and lunged at me. His fingers wrapped around my throat faster than I could get away. I couldn't breathe. The Pop-Tarts in my stomach tasted sour as I struggled to breathe, to fight back. But he was too strong. He cleared the table, sending everything crashing to the ground with his free arm, before slamming me on top of it. Then he was jerking at my belt, wrenching it from my hips.

"I didn't raise a fucking faggot. But you want a man, hmm? Don't want to fuck like a man should? Let me show you what it's like."

My mind went hazy and black dots swam in my vision. I was barely there as my father flipped me over, pressing my face into the rough table. At least I could breathe, but it was only to gather enough air to scream. With my pants around my ankles, my boxers ripped away, I was exposed and bruised to my soul.

He ripped me in two.

"Take it, you piece of shit. Hmm? Take it all."

I don't know how long I screamed. Or when exactly my voice wouldn't work anymore. I don't know how long it took before my tears stopped coming because there weren't any left to shed. Or even how long it took before I realized I was as much a toy for my father as the women in cages. Sooner or later, he would destroy me as easily as he did them. I would never be like him, no matter what he did to me. But I'd survive, by whatever means necessary, and then I'd find a way out.

I would do anything to never know such agonizing pain again.

# Chapter Two

*Alana*

Celia Whittaker was reported missing last fall. She was a beautiful brunette, with freckles dotted along her cheeks and a bright smile. I remembered seeing her photo on the television for weeks and on the front page of every paper. The Whittaker family kept searching and tried to keep hope alive with candlelight vigils and flyers everywhere. I could still remember the horror reflected on my mother's face the afternoon Celia's disappearance was broadcast. For weeks on end, she prayed for her and the Whittaker family. Now, my poor mother was living the nightmare firsthand. It made me sick to my stomach to think of what she was going through, what my dad and Aaron were going through. With so many kidnapping stories in the media, I never imagined I could become a statistic, a victim.

"I know you. You were on the news." Catching a glimpse of hope on her face, I continued, "Your family misses you. They're looking for you." As soon as the words left my mouth, the small light in her eyes evaporated.

"My family is dead," Celia whispered back, emotionless.

"No. Your mom was on the news a few weeks ago holding another candlelight vigil for you."

Her family never gave up believing their daughter would come home, but as news trickled out, searches were stopped, and the people of our community did. And now I was staring at the girl lost to everyone. No longer smiling brightly, Celia was despondent and sorrowful. It was a heart-wrenching sight. Where Celia was once healthy, she'd lost a lot of weight and her skin had taken on an ashy pallor. Looking at her was like looking at a ghost. But I knew the truth. It was a glimpse of the future. *My* future. Celia had been missing almost eight months and no one had found her. How long would I be kept prisoner alongside her?

"Impossible," she replied angrily. "My mother has been dead for over three months. Master killed her when I tried to run."

Thinking of her words, I remembered how the man threatened me with the death of my family if I didn't listen to his demands. If Celia attempted to run and her family was still alive, would he really kill mine? Or would he torture me with the news of their death, for his own sick pleasure? Would believe him? Celia had lived with this man's torment for months, thinking she was the reason her mother was dead. No wonder she lost all hope.

"Celia, I swear to you, your mom is alive. She's never stopped looking for you. They'll find you. They'll find us."

"You're awfully naïve, aren't you? What's your name anyway?"

"Alana. Alana Masters."

"Well, Alana Masters, I am Celia Jane Whittaker, but I guess you know my name already," she said with a sheepish shrug.

"What is this place, Celia?"

"This is Purgatory. Or at least I've heard him call it Purgatory. Girls come and go. Some stay months, some only last a few weeks. I've been here the longest."

"How did he take you?"

"I was coming home from a soccer game. Dad was in surgery and Mom was home with my sister. She had chicken pox. I decided to walk home from the game with some friends. My friends lived on the same street, so after walking them home, I continued to my house. I had this really creepy sixth-sense thing, ya know? Like someone was watching me. All of a sudden, I got grabbed from behind and the next thing I knew, I was waking up here."

So close to home. Exactly like me. "I'm sorry."

"Me too."

"I was walking to school. I was so worried about being late after being up all night talking on the phone. I was super mad at my brother too. He got on my last nerve. But mostly, I was happy. We've got this dance coming up at my school and my dad agreed to take me. I wasn't even paying attention when he grabbed me. He looked so normal, so harmless."

"Looks can be deceiving. He's the Devil. Purgatory is his own special brand of hell and torture. And if you step one foot out of line and do something wrong? Well, let's say he's quick to punish."

"Punish? Punish how?" The memory of the sharp sting on my cheek where he'd slapped and punched me earlier chilled me. I wondered how much worse it could get. After a bit of silence, Celia confirmed my terrified thoughts.

"He's got a room. A torture room. When girls misbehave, they're sent there for punishment. It's not pretty, Alana. It's painful. I haven't gotten the worst of it, but some girls have. Some girls have gone in normal and come out insane after what he does to them. They've gone mad, Alana. Mad."

"How many have there been before me?"

"Three since I've been here. Probably even more before me."

"Where are they?"

Celia didn't answer; she didn't have to. Her face said it all. Letting out a whimper, my fear manifested itself all over again. How naïve had I been to think the man would let me go? He'd had Celia for months and who knows how many other girls before her. Would I ever make it out of here alive? Would I ever see my parents or Aaron again? Ryan would probably be beside himself wondering what happened to me. We'd almost gone to the next step, to express the love we shared, and it was all gone. I wanted him to hold me again. Anything but the hell surrounding me now.

Panicking, I shut my eyes and covered my ears, not wanting to hear anything else Celia had to say. Sinking into a ball on the mattress, I tried to control my breathing. *Breathe in, breathe out. Breathe in, breathe out.* I had to remind myself over and over again to inhale. In the midst of my panic attack, the tears came pouring out. Wiping my face, I leaned over and threw up until the bile stung the back of my throat and nothing was left. Crying harder, I tried to make myself as small as possible, wishing I could disappear. I cried for hours until I fell asleep with dried tear tracks down my cheeks, fear in the pit of my stomach, and the stench of vomit wafting through the air.

When I awoke, my body ached, and I curled on the piss-stained mattress, tracing the edges of faded brown spots. Would I be relegated to this? Stains left behind long after he was done with me? I probably would. My captor controlled this domain, and no matter how hard I may fight him, he'd win. How did I win? Could I? I buried my face in the mattress and choked on my tears. My throat ached, and the scratchiness behind my closed eyelids taunted me.

*Tears won't make it better, Alana.*

But I couldn't stop them anyway.

"I'm sorry, Alana."

I didn't react to Celia. I couldn't prepare for what had never happened to me. Not like Celia. I wasn't ready. How could I be? Hearing a noise, I turned my attention to the door, thinking the man had finally come off his throne and decided to swallow me whole. Shaking, I prayed he'd take Celia. It was horrible, but I didn't want him to touch me. But to my surprise, it was not my captor. Instead, it was a boy my age. Brown eyes, brown hair, and standing perhaps six-foot-tall, he had broad shoulders and sharp features. He looked like the man who took me, yet different. Softer, maybe, and gangly in his youth. Creeping toward my cage, he spoke no words. The silence between us was deafening but comfortable, as if we knew one another. Kind eyes scanned me a moment before he lifted a finger to his lips. Celia nodded, and I was confused. Who was he? The darkness in his eyes, the fear, I could relate to it. Before I could speak a word, he did.

"Don't be frightened. I'm Jacob."

Jacob. It was a simple name, but one I could hold on to in this place, like Celia's.

Celia frowned at him. "Why are you here?"

Jacob winked at her, and my heart stuttered in my chest when he tossed her a lopsided grin. What the hell was wrong with me? When his gaze swung back to me, I shrank away. I didn't want him to see me like this, and whatever he held in his hands wrapped in a paper towel terrified me. Was this a test?

"I wanted to meet you, Alana."

My name on his lips froze me. "You know my name. How do you know my name?"

"My father, the bastard, is the one who did this to you."

I wanted to be frightened. I wanted to protect myself. The other part of me wanted to rage at him. If he knew about me, why hadn't he come before? Why now? Instead, I looked at this as an opportunity. I wasn't sure for what yet, but I knew I could somehow work this to my advantage if I played it right.

"What do you want from me? Do you want to hear me scream? Is your father going to be there too?"

It all came tumbling out, a temptation, a fear, a challenge. I wanted to know what would happen to me. His face morphed— his lips curled and narrowed, anger glinting in his eyes. I knew my comment angered him, and perhaps I shouldn't have spoken. A part of me was afraid of what he could do, but the other half wanted to keep fighting, to *feel* something. I could fight him, I may even be able to break free.

"Don't you ever fucking compare me to him. I may be a lot of things, but I am *not* my father!"

"So I'm supposed to believe you want nothing from me? You have to want something!"

"I don't want anything you wouldn't be willing to give me, Alana. When you submit to me, when you give yourself over to me, I want it to be because you want to. I want you to want to bleed at my hands, have me inside you. I want you to crave it. I want you, Alana, but the difference between my father and I is I won't force you."

His words didn't do much to soothe my fears, but some of my anxiety faded as the truth rang in the air. I knew I should fight back against his words; they were still threats, though they were gentler than his father's. I feared what would happen if I pushed too hard against him. My life was a strategy game; I needed to keep the upper hand.

"Okay," I whispered. I gave him what he needed, now I wanted to know more in return. "When will he come back?"

"Soon. He doesn't stay away from new toys very long. I can't stay here, or he'll catch me."

"What will he do to me?"

"What he does with all the others. Kill you after he's done having you."

"No! No, no, no. We need to get out of here. Can you help us?"

It was a risk, what I was asking, I knew it. But the threat of dying spurned me on. If Jacob could help, I'd take what I could get.

Jacob shook his head. "Not yet."

"Why?"

"Because I'm not strong enough to," he said. "But I won't let him kill you, Alana. I promise."

"You can't make a promise like that."

"I just did."

He made it sound so simple. As if he hadn't promised to not let me die at the hands of his father, the man who'd raised him. And the funny thing was, I believed him. I had every reason to be afraid, to not trust the son of a monster, but I did.

As his hand passed through the bars, I wondered what he was trying to do. Thinking he was trying to touch me, I backed further away from him.

"It's okay. It's some Pop-Tarts. I thought you might be hungry."

"Pop-Tarts?"

"Yes. Blueberry. They're my favorite."

"Mine too."

I saw the surprise register on his face and was happy to have caught him off guard. The Pop-Tarts looked delicious. Was it a day ago I ate one in my home for breakfast?

My expression changed almost immediately to a blank slate, and the boy noticed.

"What's wrong? Don't you like it?"

"This was the last breakfast I had before your father took me."

"Oh. I'm sorry. I can take them. I'll get you something else."

"No. No. This is fine. Thank you."

Taking the Pop-Tart from his hand, I inhaled the sweet aroma. Immediately, I bit into the treat Jacob had given me. My taste buds exploded under the taste of blueberries and frosted goodness. Licking my lips, I took another bite and then another. I couldn't get enough of the Pop-Tart. Maybe it reminded me of home. Or I could act, for a few moments, like I hadn't been taken. Practically inhaling my treat, I could hear the boy, Jacob, chuckle. He'd given one to Celia, too, and she smiled up at him.

"S-so-sorry," I stuttered out, wiping my lips with a swipe of my hand.

"Don't be. I figured I was the only one who loved them as much as I do. Did."

"Did?"

"I guess both of us have bad memories associated with Pop-Tarts and my father." Jacob's face hardened, no trace of the chuckling boy from moments prior.

"I'm sorry."

"I should be the one apologizing to you. My father is keeping you prisoner."

"That's true, but you are the only one to show me any type of kindness since Celia. This is … nice."

He smiled again, and I found myself smiling back. "No problem. I've got to go, but I'll be back."

He slipped up the stairs on silent feet, taking the paper-towel evidence of his visit, and my gaze followed him until he disappeared through the door.

I looked at Celia, incredulous. "Is he for real, Celia?"

She sighed. "He's his father's son, but I don't know if he has a choice. When I have to clean upstairs, sometimes, I see him get beaten."

"He's trapped like we are," I said.

"No, not like us. He doesn't have to stay in a cage."

"There are different types of cages," I whispered.

And maybe I was making excuses for him. He sort of reminded me of Ryan—cocky and sweet wrapped up in one because he hadn't really come into his own. It was out of place here, his kindness, but I appreciated it.

"Don't get your hopes up," she said.

"We can't lose hope, Celia."

"This isn't a place for hope. It's a place to survive until you die. Jacob is supposed to fuck the toys, did you know? His father wants him to be like him. Hasn't been able to knock a toy up and have her survive to delivery."

"What do you mean?"

"He wants heirs, little boys who will grow up like him."

"So what's different about Jacob?"

"You heard what he wants to do to you too. Only difference? He'll ask you first. There is no way out of here."

I didn't want to accept she was right. I didn't want to give up on getting out of here. And maybe it was silly to hold on to Jacob as a chance, but I couldn't help it. I had to find a way to get out, and if it meant letting Jacob believe I would go along with what he wanted from me, so be it.

\*\*\*

Later, the darkness surrounded me, and I believed I was back home in my own bed, with my family, and this was nothing more than a nightmare. Unfortunately, from the second I opened my eyes, I could tell this was not my room. I was still locked in the cage, kept a prisoner.

"Alana … Psst … Alana," Celia called out.

"Yes?"

"I wanted to warn you. The man will be doing checks soon. He does them every morning."

Muscles stiff from a restless sleep on a hard mattress, dread filled my stomach at the thought of him coming back. As I tried to stretch my aching limbs, my hand flew to my cheek, the remaining sting reminding me of his palm smacking against it. I didn't want to see the evil reflected in those eyes ever again. I never wanted his hands on me. Summoning all my strength, I stood and gathered my resolve to not let him affect me. I may have been his prisoner, but I was still Alana Masters. I was not his. Despite what he thought, I was my own person.

Whistling echo through the air, the door above the staircase opened and the man came walking down the stairs, a tray in hand.

"Be quiet and agree with everything he says. Okay, Alana?"

I couldn't bring myself to respond with the terror rising in me, so I nodded my head.

"Good morning, girls. It's a beautiful morning outside." He chuckled before he continued, "But I guess you wouldn't know, huh?"

Every bone in my body shook in fear at his sadistic laugh and the evil grin on across his face. I was absolutely terrified of this man and what he could do to me.

"Celia Jane, I hope you've been a good girl while I was gone."

"Yes, Master."

"I trust you told Alana how things work around here."

"Some of it, Master."

"Good girl, Celia. You'll be rewarded tonight."

From the moment he walked in, Celia had completely changed. Where she'd been serious and determined moments before, she now looked submissive, eager to please. Answering only in short sentences, Celia addressed him as Master each time. I remember his parting remark from yesterday and wondered if that was how I was really supposed to address him. It made me cringe thinking about it.

"Breakfast is served, ladies. I'll be down in an hour to collect your plates."

I was confused. Utterly confused. He'd taken me—stole me from my parents and everything I knew and loved—yet he could act like everything was sunshine and daisies and offer us breakfast like he hadn't kidnapped us. And to top it off, he was ignoring my presence, overlooking me as if I were nothing but a piece of trash.

Unlocking the cages, he placed our meals on the floor. When he was finished, he turned and began to walk up the steps. He looked over his shoulder, directly at me, his eyes black with rage and his words echoing in my head. "Training starts today, Alana. Eat up if you want to live through it."

After he was gone, I looked down to find a bowl of bland oatmeal and a piece of toast sitting before me. A banana was to the side of the plate as if it had been added as an afterthought. Far from appetizing, the meal began to turn my stomach.

"Eat it, Alana. If you don't, it will make things worse. Trust me."

No, I wasn't going to take this. I couldn't. I picked up the tray and threw it as hard as I could at the bars of my cage. He could eat it.

"You shouldn't have done that," Celia cautioned.

"I'm not going to lie down and take this," I argued.

"I tried to warn you."

"Oatmeal was never a favorite of mine. It was always more of Aaron's, my brother's. Aaron would have Mom buy the flavored kinds, and whenever he wasn't eating his Cocoa Puffs, he was shoveling in mouthfuls of peach or apple cinnamon oatmeal," I said, filling the space. Oh God, Aaron. Yesterday I was so mad at him and wishing I would never see him again. They say to be careful what you wish for.

Tears clogging my throat, I tried to hold back from crying. Much as I tried to keep the fear at bay, I could not. I had gone from innocent and free to captive. My world as I knew it was irrevocably changed, and I knew the worst was yet to come. The terror overtook my mind, images flooding through it of what this man could do to me. Would I ever make it out of here alive? Thinking of my inevitable death and of the nightmare my parents must be going through, I leaned over and emptied what little I had in my stomach.

Hearing the door, I scrambled to sit up as the man's heavy boots hit the stairs. Forgoing the glasses and dress pants, he was dressed in black jeans with a tight, black thermal shirt clinging to his body. Seeing the well-defined muscles set me on edge thinking of the power he could assert over me, the pain he could inflict. Holding back a sob, I scooted as far back on the mattress as I possibly could. The fear of never leaving became much greater as he set his black-as-coal eyes on me.

"Alana, Alana, Alana," he began in a malicious tone.

He shook his head, spying the oatmeal but stepping the goo anyway. My stomach leapt up into my throat and my heart began beating faster.

"Your parents are looking for you. They're sick with worry. Their poor, precious Alana … missing. You take a mighty fine picture, young lady. It's all over the front of the newspaper this morning. Little Alana Masters, presumed missing, last seen leaving for school. Your parents will be on the news today, seeking sympathy and begging people to find their precious little girl. I'll let you in on a little secret. They'll never find you."

Fear turned into anger as he mocked my parents' pain. How dare he talk about them? How dare he act so nonchalant about the fact he stole me away from them? *He* was the one causing their panic and pain. His cruelness knew no bounds. Celia was right. This man was the Devil.

"They will find me!" I yelled.

"Yeah? You think so?"

"They won't give up on me."

"You have fight in you, girl, and I like that. More to beat out of you," he hissed at me.

"I'm not—"

"Careful, cunt. You wouldn't want me to punish you."

As tears streamed down my face, the man looked positively gleeful for taunting me so cruelly. He was getting off on seeing me in pain, seeing my tears. He was one sick son of a bitch and I had yet to see what else he could do to me. He looked like the kind of man who took pleasure from kicking puppies and picking fights for the hell of it. And he kept it all buried underneath a disguise of wholesomeness. He opened the cage and climbed in with me, pressing me back against the bars. The cold metal bit into my skin.

"It's time, little girl."

"Time for what?" I understood too late my mistake when he lifted his beefy hand high in the air and swung, sending me down to the mattress. Nerve endings sizzled along my cheek, and my eye throbbed in my skull.

"What did I tell you to call me?" His beady eyes narrowed in on me.

"Master." What else could I say? My body crawled with nerves and pain, my face hot with the reminder. I bit the inside of my cheek until it bled to keep from screaming at him.

"That is how you should address me at *all* times. If you do not, you will be punished with a whipping. Twelve lashes from my belt should make your gorgeous ass the perfect shade of red. The only reason I'm being lenient and not beating your ass bloody is because your training is beginning today."

"T-To-Today?" I stuttered.

"Right now, to be precise."

The terror gripped my heart and wrenched at it. He backed out of the cage, a cruel look on his face. Once he was right outside my cell, he stopped.

"Get your ass over here right now. You have until the count of three. One … Two …"

Scrambling off the soiled mattress as fast as I possibly could, I sprinted over to the monster waiting for his next demand.

"Take your clothes off, little girl. All of them."

I shook my head. I wouldn't strip for him. I stood tall, fingers clenched into fists at my sides. I couldn't force myself to give in, despite the fear. Could I live with myself if I did?

He approached me slowly, stalking until he stood before me. "You take them off, or I fuck your pretty ass right here. Would you like that?"

*No!*

With shaky hands, I lifted off my tank top, wringing it in my hands before letting it drop on the floor. Moving to my jeans, I tried to unbutton them, but my uncooperative fingers shook.

"Hurry up! Hurry the fuck up."

Finally getting them unbuttoned, I rushed to get them pulled down. Letting my pants drop to my ankles, I was left only in my bra and panties.

"All of it," he snapped, growing impatient with me.

No one had ever seen me in my underwear. Nor had they ever seen me fully naked. I wasn't a prude, but Ryan and I were waiting until homecoming to take our relationship any further than some heavy make-out sessions and groping. With fear clawing at my insides, I took a deep breath, unhooked my bra, and pulled my panties down, leaving me completely bare to the monster's leering eyes.

"Good girl. While you're training, you will only be naked. Once you can prove to Master how good you can be then, and only then, will you be given clothes." Taking a whiff of the air, his lip curled. "In the meantime, you smell absolutely putrid. It's time to groom you to perfection, little girl."

The look in his eyes turned more devilish, if that were even possible. He began leading me away from Celia and Purgatory until we stood at a door at the far end of the room. Walking through the door, my eyes immediately fell on a large bathtub centered in the middle of the room, a shower in one corner and a toilet in another.

With a smirk on his face, he called me over to the tub. I stood, shaking, as he filled it with warm water. The steam from the tub filled the room, and I had to admit the thought of being clean again tempted me.

"Ah, you can't wait to be clean, can you, little girl? But before I allow you to have a bath, I think you need to do something for me."

"Wh-What, Master?"

Unzipping his jeans, he took out his erection. Of all the times Ryan and I had fooled around, I never saw him fully exposed. Fear washed over me once more as the man gripped himself in his hand. His shaft wasn't very long, but it was thick. Turning my head, I clenched my eyes shut, refusing to look at him.

"No, no, no. Don't do that. Don't close your eyes. Open them up, sweet cheeks, and get on those knees of yours. I want to see how good your little whore mouth is."

I shook my head, but he gripped the back of my head and pushed me down until my knees hit the cold cement floor.

"Open your fucking mouth, whore."

Too scared to open my mouth or eyes, I wasn't prepared for the hit that followed. Pain exploded across my face. Heat from the sting spread as I cupped my cheek. Grabbing me once more by the hair, his hand landed on my jaw, prying open my mouth. One minute, I was on my knees, terrorized. The next, my mouth was full to the brim and my eyes were flying open in time to see the man's hands land on my cheeks. Beginning to fuck my mouth,

I choked on him. Eyes watering, my throat constricted, air supply dwindling. In reaction, I bit down.

"You fucking cunt!"

He punched the side of my head, sending stars dancing across my vision, and stuffed his shaft deeper. Cutting off circulation, he choked me until I released my grip with my teeth, eager to take a breath.

"Should have been a good girl."

He took time stringing me between breathlessness and gagging. My jaw ached, and I couldn't catch a decent breath without keeping my mouth open wide in preparation for those rare moments of oxygen.

Shame overwhelmed me. I was sick to my stomach thinking about him filling my mouth. I had never done this. I didn't want this. But that monster didn't care. My pain was fodder for him to get off. Fucking my mouth harder, my throat grew raw, and I struggled for breath. He was using me like a dirty toy, treating me as if I were nothing but a prostitute. When I thought it couldn't get any worse, the man groaned as his seed coated the back of my throat, making me gag around him.

"So good, precious, so good," the man rasped out in pleasure as I shuddered in disgust. "Get up and into the tub."

Without a word, I scrambled into the bath, falling against the porcelain. Timid and submissive, exactly how he wanted me. After what I had gone through, I needed to clean every inch of my skin. I needed to sanitize his touch from my body. As I sank deep into the water, all I could think about was drowning myself. How slipping underneath the water and letting it overcome me would be better than ever having to live through this. I never wanted to have that vile man's *anything* anywhere near me again. But as he began washing my back, my heart wrenched. This was only the beginning. With a man this cruel, things would only get worse.

# Chapter Three

## Jacob

My father had taken everything from me—my manhood, my power—but I'd snatch it all back. I needed to. Today, when I got to have Alana, I'd be more than his sideshow. I'd rule, and maybe then my soul wouldn't be so weak and twisted.

Everything inside of me ached. I tried my best to ignore it because then I'd have to remember washing the blood that had dripped from my ass in the shower. I'd be forced to recall my father had taken another first from me, and there was nothing I could do about it. I ignored the bruising around my throat from his hand, the ache when I walked. On top of the pain, my *father* would be training her. She was more beautiful than I'd imagined—sweet and pure. She … made heart throb in a way I didn't understand when I was near her. Maybe I was sick? But I liked it. I liked her. My father didn't deserve to put his filthy hands on her.

I fucking hated it because I knew there was nothing I could do to stop it.

I knew it would begin with her being stripped and cleaned after she learned she was never rewarded without doing something to earn a reward. I wouldn't lie and say it didn't make me mad as hell to know my father would have some part of her first. Always the first. The bastard couldn't allow anyone to go before him. I knew this, perhaps more than I ever thought I knew before. But I didn't want him to touch her at all. I never gave a shit about the toys. I'd learned young having them was a fact of life. It was how women were supposed to be treated. So why did I want to touch Alana in ways that wouldn't hurt? I didn't know, but I did know I needed to pacify my father long enough to figure it all out.

Like a good little soldier waiting for orders, I hung on his every word. I sat at the kitchen table in black jeans and a close-fitting, black t-shirt—working wear, my father called it—and waited for him to summon me. Evidence of last night's events was erased from existence. There were no shards of glass or plates on the floor. The water that had spilled from my father's cup was mopped up and long dried. Even the centerpiece, a vase with white lilies, was back in its place. I hadn't helped with the cleanup. I hadn't been able to stand longer than the time it took to crawl back into my shower. I wondered if Father made the older toy, Celia, clean up the mess while I went to bed.

I wish it had been Alana instead.

Even that didn't clean the memory from my head. Staring at the room in perfect order made my insides raw. I wanted to scream and rage, destroy everything around me. Because my world was fucking shattered. It was twisted and fucked up. I was controlled by a demon who wanted me to be his perfect spawn but made it fucking obvious I wasn't worth more than the nut that had created me.

He completely erased the worst experience of my life as if it had never been. As if life went on.

I wondered if the girls trapped in the cages felt the same way. They were stuck in this hell, frozen in fear and the unknown, but life didn't stop. Did they feel that, though their families might miss them, *their* lives went on? They weren't tortured or raped. They weren't out searching for them every minute of every day. No, they had to go to work; bills were still due. There were times they could laugh at someone's joke and enjoy a good movie to get their minds off the fact that right at that moment their little girl might be suffering some sort of torture. They always scream for their mommy and daddy. Always. And those parents never show up. Because their fucking lives move on.

Because the kitchen had to be cleaned, the world was still spinning, and their death wouldn't stop that from happening. No human's death was that significant. No matter how important they may think they are. Those thoughts made it impossible for me to even rest my hands on the table. I couldn't stomach touching the areas where I'd sobbed last night in agony. There should be some sort of stain. Some sort of imprint to bear witness to what I had gone through. But there wasn't. It was perfect, clean, like it was when I sat down to eat my Pop-Tart. I hate this house. I hate my father.

Fuck, I hate myself.

But like those toys, I could do nothing about it, and there was no one searching for me. My mother was one of my father's first toys. He practiced on her and slowly learned his craft until she was helping him capture other girls to save herself from the pain. When she died, I bore witness to it. Held her hair out the top of the tube as it slowly filled with water, and Father wanted to see her face the whole time. I'd never really known who she was. He told me afterward, and I hadn't cried. I'd been raised by the many toys that had come and gone. I didn't miss them when they were disposed of. There would always be another.

I picked at the skin on the side of my thumb, calming my nerves. I didn't want to be in the kitchen anymore. I wanted my father to hurry the hell up so I could take Alana away from his hell. I'd be called Master. Maybe I'd gain back some power with her. And she'd be thankful to not be abused by my father. I'd be kind and show her that life could be better. I didn't know any other way to train a woman, but she wouldn't fight me like she would fight him. My cravings were fucked-up, I knew that in my soul. But maybe, through her, I would gain my manhood back and grow in strength. Maybe, just maybe, I'd be okay after I went through this year with her and then ended my father. Then we could find someplace in this world.

I knew the fruitlessness of my wish, but I would try anyway. Throw myself completely into what he needed from me and wish it wouldn't break me in the end. The door to the basement swinging open got my attention.

"Good morning, Father," I said, standing.

"Good morning. It's good to see you up and ready to go. We have some things to discuss."

My father walked out of the kitchen but not toward the basement. I followed him, wondering where he was going. Most of the time, we ignored the other ten rooms on the first floor of our home. They were decorated and filled with furniture, TVs, and weapons to keep us protected if someone were to come knocking. But the sheer amount of land we resided on would stop too many from snooping. Upstairs was reserved mostly for cleanup and sleeping. There were eight bedrooms, the largest two were on opposite sides of the manor, and my father and I occupied those. Outside, we had sheds for our tools and barns for animals that needed to be cared for before slaughter and packaging.

Although none of it really mattered much.

Father always had money, and things were continuously provided for. Now, though, there was a new toy, and her training would begin in earnest today. There was no reason for us to be anywhere but the basement once she was properly cleaned and readied. So, as we reached the large tool shed that also acted as a barn for some of the animals, unease spread through me.

"Jacob, do you know where I got your name?"

"From the Bible, Father."

"Yes. He was the younger twin of Esau. When he was born, Esau came first, and Jacob was grasping his heel. Did you know the original definition of Jacob means 'to supplant?'"

He still hadn't looked at me as he shifted around some bales of hay until four were on the ground, making a square. He then lifted three on top, sideways and stacked, so it made a little platform. I watched him, getting an eerie sense I should run, but I couldn't make my feet move. They rooted me to the spot as my father calmly spoke to me. He headed into the tack room and came back with some rope and gloves, handing me a pair.

"I didn't know my name meant that, Father." I sat down on the bottom level of hay and put the gloves on before my father handed me the rope and some oil for it.

"Yes. Though he was blessed from the beginning to rule his brother and become what would be known as the Father of Israel, he was a deceiver. He took what wasn't meant for him, as he was the second-born. The second. Not the first. He shouldn't have been rewarded for being worse than the first. Esau was the hunter, the warrior. He was stronger and more rooted as a man. And because he loved a woman and gave respect to the old gods, he was passed over. Because of vindictive spitefulness, he had his birthright taken from him."

I looked up at my father, unsure of what to say or how to take his change in mood. I always thought my name was biblical, never more than that. It was my name and I answered to it. But as my father's cruel smile came into sight, I wondered if there were something more to it.

"I realized you are closer to the meaning of your name than I ever thought."

I gripped the rope tighter, pressing the oil into the threads. My heart stuttered in my chest and my mouth went dry.

"Father, I—"

He struck lightning-fast. There was a nasty crunch to my nose, and then my eyes were watering uncontrollably. I couldn't see past the tears as I waved my arms around, trying to find purchase. Instead, I found my father. As he hauled me to my feet by my shirt, my knees buckled. Not knowing what I had done, I still sputtered out an apology.

"You were born, son. You were born weak like your fucking mother. And then you hope to be better than me. Take what rights belong to me. Like you deserve to be my heir. To be *me!*"

The rope I had oiled was wrapped around my wrists, the threads digging into my gloves. The inner flesh on my wrists cracked and split, blood oozed. Then my father threw the other end of the rope over the high beam above our heads. He left me bleeding on the hay and pulled the end of the rope until I was lifted off the ground, hovering above the second level of bales.

He looked at me hard. "What did I teach you about suspension?"

"T-too long and you can cause permanent damage to the shoulder blades. Or hands because the circulation is cut o-off."

"Let's see how fucking long you last, shall we?"

There was no way I could fight against his punches. He angled them, standing on the first row of hay to get to me easily. When he liver-checked me, I gasped for breath, swinging on the ropes to get away. I didn't give a damn about my hands or the pain to my numbing shoulders. I wanted it to stop, to get it over with. His punches rained down over my chest, diaphragm, stomach, and around my sides. Then he caught me in the lower back over and over. My torso morphed into one long, throbbing pain. I spewed my breakfast down my shirt, bled steadily from my nose, and could barely catch my breath.

My eyes were open, but I couldn't see anything. The barn was fuzzy brown and smelled of sweat and desperation. My vision grew hazy, darkening around the edges as I held on. Sight wavered and floated, the light winking in and out, but it was there. I was still awake, grunting with each punch. Twisting with each dig into my side.

"You know I fucked her mouth good and long. She gagged. She's a pure one all right. Had probably never seen a man naked in her life."

Something cracked, deep inside. What slithered out was small at first. Oily and twisted, it pushed through my insides. It burned everywhere it touched, like a hot poker jamming inside of me with every breath. Then it burrowed into my heart, wormed its way through the sinew, and squeezed the life out of the red flesh until it was all black and dripping with raw anger and twisted needs.

A monster of pure rage and hatred formed.

"She was mine, you fucking bastard. Mine to control. *Mine!*" I screamed. That deep, demonic voice didn't sound like it should have come from me, but it did, and getting it out tasted sweet.

"You think you can talk back to me, boy? Hmm? I'm going to fuck that blonde bitch until she can't stand anymore. And then I'm going to fuck her again. I'm going to beat her until she can't stop calling me Master, until she's begging me to put her out of her fucking misery. And then I'm going to get her on the slab and cut her veins open one by one while I'm stuffed inside of her. And then I'm going to keep her. Twist her and fill her with seed, until she gives me the son I should have fucking had, not some faggot who bent over and gave me his ass."

I roared, curling my body up and lifting my feet off the ground. The total weight on my shoulders made them burn, but it was good. God, so fucking good to be hurt like that. I laughed, a deranged, crazy sound that curled through the barn and stopped my father in his tracks. Then I lashed out, kicking with all my might right into his chest. He went flying and slammed into the wall before sliding down to the floor.

I knew it was short lived—this anger, this sense of power— but he wanted to fuck with what was mine. What should have belonged to me. I wanted her, needed her, because there was something that finally belonged to me.

"Strong, but not fucking strong enough," my father growled at me. "You're no longer a man, but maybe if you'd fought like this last night, you'd still be one."

Then he was releasing the ropes. I screamed as blood rushed back into my shoulders, but I didn't get a chance to release my hands. He grabbed the rope still bound on my wrists and dragged me out of the barn. Rocks and gravel dug into my back and the top of my ass as he pulled me. The stairs slammed into the small of my back, sharp pains ricocheting through me as he pulled me up the onto the porch and into the house. I kicked and twisted, tried to get away as he dragged me into the kitchen. Not again. Never fucking again.

Passing the kitchen and heading toward the basement, I froze, pure terror flowing through me. He wouldn't put me there, wouldn't make me a toy. He couldn't. As the door closed behind us, he hoisted me up against him and pressed his palm into my mouth, cutting off any sound. Then he took me past the first level of torture stations to the second floor, but he didn't let me all the way inside. Instead, he pushed my face against the slatted bars at the top of the door. And then I heard a whimper, a small whimper that took all the pain away, stole my breath, and broke my heart.

God, I loved the way she was perfectly blonde—so blonde her hair was almost white—with full lips, perky breasts, and a slim waist. She was a brilliant light in this place, and seeing her again sucker-punched me in the gut. Her body was perfection as she huddled on the bed in her cage, naked after being cleaned up. Her hair fell around her shoulders in wet clumps. Her lips were split—the corners were angry and red, a testament to what she had endured. A feature that made my heart go out to her. I was no stranger that pain. I knew what it was like to have the choice taken from me.

In that moment, I think I loved her a little. Perfect. Sweet. Stolen.

"Please," I whispered to my father. I wanted to see her closer. I wanted to touch her. Taste her. To tell her I was here and she wasn't alone. Her head whipped up, and I almost saw her eyes, but he jerked me away from the bars before I could.

"She will remain mine. Maybe one day I'll let you have one. After you prove to me you're a fucking man. After I know you won't choke and jerk your way to a nut like a boy who doesn't know pussy from air."

"I want her."

"You can't have her. But don't worry, son, she's got spunk and tightness. She wants to please even when her eyes snap in defiance. She's going to be here for a very long time. Maybe I'll let her suck you off one day."

I fought him as he dragged me away from her, separating me from the one thing I knew in my soul was my match. She was perfect for me. This action somehow ripped me to pieces more than anything else he'd ever done.

Because that toy, *that one*, wasn't a toy at all and should belong to me—should have from the start. My father had taken what had never belonged to him.

# Chapter Four

Alana

The embarrassment and shame lingered long after the bath. The whole humiliating experience played in my mind like a broken record from the moment that man forced himself on me.

After washing me, he proceeded to make sure every inch of me was shaved bare except for my long, blonde locks. I couldn't fight with blades so near my skin, so I held on and endured. Drying me off, he inspected me head to toe, making sure I lived up to the perfection he was trying to create. With a coat of polish on my nails and a swipe of gloss to my lips, he declared me ready to begin.

Now, standing bare in front of his gaze, I fought the urge to cover up. Squirming under his lust-filled eyes, I looked down to avoid making eye contact with him.

"You were so good, Alana, so good. I can tell you are going to be a favorite of mine." His words washed over me, making my stomach clench in disgust. "Now it's time for you to learn the rules."

Beginning to pace, the words came flowing from his mouth as if he had recited them a hundred times. From what Celia told me, this could have been true.

"Rule number one: you are mine. Every part of you is mine. When I tell you I want you, you will give yourself to me. Your body. That sweet nectar of yours. That delectable ass. All mine. Rule number two: you are never to disobey me. Disobeying me leads to consequences for you, and I don't think you'll like the punishments I dole out. Your first infraction, no matter what it may be, will call for twelve lashings. The more serious the infraction, the punishment is much more severe. If you make it to four infractions, you will not like what awaits you. Trust me on that, little girl. Rule number three: always address me as Master. I demand respect from you at all times. I am your Master, and you are nothing but a slave. Rule number four: when I walk into the room, you must drop to your knees, bow your head, and wait until you are spoken to. Lastly, rule number five: do not run. Do not *think* of running. Don't *try* to run. If you do, you will live to regret it … or maybe you won't live at all. Do you understand?"

Quivering in fear, I made a mental note to obey. The darkness in his eyes and the harshness of his voice scared me. I didn't want to obey because he was my Master, I wanted to follow the rules because he had the power to end my life. I needed to play along until I could find a way to get free of his prison.

"Well … Do you understand?"

"Yes, Master."

"Very well. You will be given meals twice a day. Breakfast and dinner. No complaints. You will eat what I feed you and be grateful for it. Every other day, you will be cleaned up. I expect you to follow all the rules and every directive I set out for you without you talking back. If I tell you to do something, you will do it."

"Yes, Master."

"Good girl."

Leading me back to my cage, he tossed me in and locked it behind him. With one last look at me, he headed back up the stairs. The room was silent until Celia's voice rang out.

"167."

"167? What's that?"

"The number of times I have been raped since I've been here."

"Why are you telling me this?"

"To prepare you. You had your first bath. That means he will be coming back tonight to make you his."

Trembling, I tried to block out what she was saying, but I knew she was telling the truth. After what happened earlier in the bathroom, I was already ashamed and scared for it to happen again. Now I had to think about the monster stealing yet another thing from me. The bastard had stolen me from my family and was now getting his rocks off treating me as if I were nothing, just something to bury himself inside. The fear and anger twisted inside me, and something come over me like never before. The pure rage inside my heart was telling me this man needed to pay. He needed to pay for his crimes against me, his crimes against Celia and those who came before and after. But *how?* How could I bring this monster to his knees and make him understand I wasn't like his other girls? Until I could figure that out, I had to live with what the villain would do to me.

Taking a deep breath, I prepared myself for the monster's special brand of torture by thinking of some of my happier moments. He may have been able to steal me from my family and take everything away from me, but he could never take my most cherished memories from me. He could stop me from thinking of my mom's smile as she tended her garden, or Dad's booming laughter every time I jumped on his back, or how my love for them swelled in my chest. Even Aaron with his ridiculous Cocoa Puff addiction made me smile. I knew I needed to live for them, to survive this no matter the cost. Surrounding myself in a veil of happier times, I prepared myself to be led into the darkness. He may get my body, he may think I belong to him … But these? These were all mine.

Jumping at the sound of the door clanging, Master appeared carrying our trays. Getting down on my knees, with my head bowed as he'd told me to, I willed myself to be strong.

"Good girl, Alana. See, you're getting it."

He handed me my dinner tray with a smirk. Steam rose from the spaghetti and meatballs and I swallowed my sudden hunger. Shocked, I had expected nothing more than toast or oatmeal.

"Don't look so surprised. I need to keep you healthy in order to do whatever I want to you."

*Of course, you stupid girl.* It was all about how it would benefit him.

"Hurry up and eat. I have plans for you. Oh, and unless you want more of what you had earlier, right here in front of your little friend so she can see what sort of whore you are, I suggest you eat it this time."

As the door closed behind him once more, I ate what little of the meal I could. I wouldn't let Celia see me like that. She wouldn't meet my eyes. She *knew* what I'd endured. My stomach was weak and trembling with fear, confusion, and anger, and I knew I wouldn't be able to keep much down. Nevertheless, I didn't want to be punished. Taking one last bite, I sat my tray to the side and tried to relax my breathing. Despite my earlier resolve, I was scared of what he had planned. Ryan was supposed to be the one taking my virginity. We'd planned it all out. The homecoming dance, the hotel room—it was going to be perfect. And now I was waiting for the monster to lead me to my rape.

"I know you don't want to hear it, Alana, but I am sorry."

"I know, Celia. Thank you for warning me."

"Don't fight him, or else it will be worse."

"I can't *not* fight him."

As I finished saying that, the man appeared once more, coming down the stairs. This time, all he wore was a pair of black jeans and a sadistic grin stretched across his face. He should have been a monster with a hideous face and covered in scars. Instead, he was rugged, with washboard abs and hair sprinkled over his chest and in a line over his abdomen. His body was worked into hard, angular lines, and if I'd seen him somewhere else, my friends and I would have drooled over his hotness.

Now, I was afraid that evil could be so beautiful.

By looking at him, I knew I was in trouble.

"Come now, little girl. It's time."

I approached him slowly, taking one last breath and letting it out. As soon as I stepped out of the cage, the man walked behind me with something in his hand. I didn't have to wait long to find out what it was when a collar, something a dog would wear, was wrapped around my throat and attached to a leash.

"Start walking, sweetheart."

Holding the leash in his hand, he led me to another room. I was met with a king-sized bed taking up the middle of the room and an array of instruments spread on a stand. On the right side of the room, a set of shackles was attached. On the left side were whips hung on a rack.

My body shook as Master led me to the right side. Unhooking the leash, he set it aside, only to turn me around so my back faced the wall. Shackling my wrists, he stood before me and looked down into my face.

"I need to see that you're ready for this, ready for me. Be a good girl, Alana, and it won't hurt a bit."

Still staring down at my eyes, he forced my thighs open and invaded my entrance with a blunt finger.

"Oh yes, you're a tight little one, aren't you? Maybe I was wrong about you being a slut. I'm going to have fun with you, girl."

Adding a second finger, he began thrusting harder as the tears welled in my eyes. I clenched my legs, attempting to lock him out. I couldn't do this. I couldn't stay docile. He forced his fingers deeper, twisting his wrists and scraping his nails against my insides.

"There is always a consequence. Now open up."

My thighs quivered as I did as he demanded.

"Do you like that? Answer me." He punctuated his question with another scrape of his nails.

"Y-Yes, Master."

I cringed as he pulled his fingers out of me and brought them to my mouth.

"Open up, little girl. Open that sweet mouth of yours and suck."

Afraid to tell him no, I did as he asked, shame filling every crevice of my soul as I tasted my own juices from his hand.

"So hot and wet. Good girl."

My muscles locked as he carried a candle closer to me. Smokeless fire wavered in the space between us, tilting oh so slowly, as wax slid over the edges. White-hot pain seared over my nerve endings. Fire, like that hateful flame, spread through my chest, chasing the dripping wax down over my quivering stomach. I couldn't catch my breath, couldn't think. Fear clouded my mind as it dripped further, twisting and burning across my flesh. I was fighting to hold back a scream. The tender lips of my sex swelled with blood, pounded with my heartbeat, pushing the pain higher as it rushed over me.

"Look at you. Look how vulnerable you are to me."

Putting the candle back in its place, it wasn't long before he touched me again. Grabbing my breasts, he pulled at my nipples, leaving me torn between pleasure and pain. How sick was I? Leaning over, he grabbed something. Curious but scared, I couldn't look away as he began to place clamps on my nipples. The initial rush of pain seared me, leaving me to cry out. Only after attaching both clamps did the monster unshackle my wrists and lead me over to the bed. Pushing me down, he unbuckled his pants as I closed my eyes as tightly as I could.

"Oh no, no. None of that, little girl. Open those eyes and watch. I want you to see my cock splitting you in two."

When I wouldn't comply with his wishes, he grabbed my hair, pulling hard and tight until my eyes flew open. Wincing in pain, tears filled my eyes and I cried out as an open palm flew toward my face. My head rocked to the left as the slap resonated. Cheek stinging, I rested my cool palm against it, trying to provide some relief from the white-hot pain. Every part of my body ached.

"What did I tell you about disobeying? What did I fucking tell you?"

"I-I'm sorry, Master," I managed to get out.

"Sorry isn't good enough."

Gripping my hips, he turned me around so my back was to him.

"On your knees. Ass up in the air."

Doing as he asked, scared my punishment would be worse if I didn't, I heard him pull his belt from the loops on his jeans and a second later, the leather seared my skin as the sound echoed through the room. Stifling a gasp, I bit down on my lip as he continued to whip me.

"Count them. Fucking count them, bitch."

"One … Two… Th-Three … Four … F-Fi-Five." The pain overcame me and I lost place with my count. All of a sudden, the whips came harder and more rapidly until I was a sobbing mess.

My ass burned, my eyes were swelling up from the tears, and the humiliation was unlike anything I had ever felt before. *Survive, Alana. Focus on surviving.*

After a few more minutes of being subjected to the monster's belt, he stopped and lifted me into the air.

"Look at those tears. Those beautiful eyes full of tears were what first caught my eyes. I had been scoping, waiting for weeks. I wanted the perfect girl. And then I saw you. Walking to school. You were beautiful. You didn't have a care in the world. I knew right then and there I had to have you. I had to break you. Make you weep for me."

He licked the tracks of my tears and made a path down my cheek. Throwing me on the bed, he forcefully spread my legs underneath his gaze. Stepping out of his pants, he stood there palming his manhood and looking like evil incarnate. I was in Hell and this man was the Devil. As soulless black eyes stared me down, his enjoyment of seeing me cry played over his features. My pain was his pleasure. My cries were the source of his completion.

Climbing on top of me, he pulled my legs to him. Without any hesitation, he thrust hard and deep inside of me, leaving me to wail at the intrusion. Thrusting harder, faster, the pain washed over my entire body. Every inch of me screamed in terror and agony. The sight of him between my legs, his hot breath panting in my ear, brought bile to my throat. Instead of throwing up, I swallowed, frightened beyond belief his punishment would be worse than what he was doing to me right now.

My virginity was gone, blood seeping down my thighs. Taken, stolen, by a sadistic asshole. As he slid in and out, I tried to escape the pain and draw up some of my happiest moments, but nothing, absolutely nothing came to mind. Over and over again, his hardness stabbed into me. There was no pleasure, only pain. I couldn't get wet and, without lubricant, he tore at me. The pain radiated through my body with mind-blowing pain, a hot poker slicing through my insides and scrambling them.

All I could think of was how one day this man, this monster, would destroy me. One day he would kill me. He would break me apart piece by piece, and when nothing remained but a few morsels of my soul, he would take me and kill me—without hesitation.

This thought propelled me into action, and I began beating my fists on his back and biting his shoulder.

*Fight, fight, fight,* my mind whispered to me. And so I did. I clawed at him, hit him with my tiny ineffectual fists. I knew I couldn't hurt him, not the way he could hurt me, but I had to try. I had to fight. I couldn't willingly give myself over to a monster and let him use me.

Celia's words rang in my head: *Don't fight him, or else it will be worse.*

It was too late.

With a mighty roar, he emptied himself into me. I cringed at his cum seeping out of me and down my thighs as he pulled out. Looking up at him, I knew Celia was right. I'd made a big mistake, and from the evil invading every pore of his body, I knew I was going to pay. Chills raced down my spine, and I cringed. There wasn't enough space, nowhere I could go, but I clawed at the mattress underneath me.

His fists flew, and I tried to turn my head away from the well-aimed strikes to my face, but they repeatedly landed. Hit after hit, the bones of my face groaned, and I feared he'd crush me. His rage soaked into my bones, leaving me terrified. My right eye tingled and then went numb, swelling shut after taking three consecutive punches. When I thought he was finished, he grabbed me by my hair and threw me off the bed.

Covered in cum, I was curled on my side, trying to hide from the kicks he was now aiming at my abdomen. A crack in my ribs shuddered through me when he kicked me repeatedly. I cried out in agony. My tears were coming faster. Unable to stop them, I let them fall, the monster's face lit up. The glee he exhibited at the sight of my tears sickened me. And then he was taking himself in his hand once more, jerking hard up and down. His gaze moved along my body, his release covering my thighs, bruises littering my stomach. Remnants of hot wax were dried across my abdomen, and my face was bruised and covered in wetness from my tears. With one last jerk of his wrist, his filthy seed was shooting toward my face and mixing with my tears.

*I fought, Momma. I didn't just let him hurt me. Please, save me.*

Looking down at his artwork, he examined me like a specimen instead of a human being he had defiled.

"Beautiful," he said.

Putting his clothes back on, he left me curled up on the floor, dirtiness invading every inch of my mind and soul. Something inside me shattered and darkness moved into my heart.

Grabbing the leash and attaching my collar to it once more, he ordered me to stand. When I could not, he began pulling me, dragging my limp body across the floor. I tried to get up, not wanting to be weak, but my legs gave out underneath me. Refusing to be humiliated any further, I gathered my remaining strength and stood once more. Walking behind him to the bed, where he left me, I made a promise to myself and to all the other girls he had done this to.

*I will kill this monster and take pride in seeing his blood on my hands.*

# Chapter Five

## Jacob

If I could have ripped my father apart with my bare hands, I would've. If I could have pulled his balls off with my teeth and left him to bleed out while I stood over his body and laughed, I would've. Anything but stand here, tied to the door, gagged so I couldn't make a single sound while I watched him take the girl who was meant to be mine. She was so amazing. With soft, pink nipples, her breasts were starting to fill out. Her waist was so small, I bet I could wrap my hands around it if I tried hard enough. She had long legs that went on forever. And her ass. Oh, it was so pretty and white, like the rest of her.

Until he messed her up.

Until he put his decrepit sex inside of her and marked her.

Now she was battered and bruised, filthy with his cum all over her. And she couldn't see me. She didn't know I was going through it all with her. That I knew so well what it was like to have him take what shouldn't have been his.

But she fought back.

With her tiny fists, she raged against him. Because she knew it too. She knew who she belonged to, and she hadn't wanted him inside her. I laughed maniacally in my head. We were both fighting to be together. I wanted to hate her for letting him inside so easily, for not fighting back. I didn't want her to be a perfect slave for him, only for me. But she gave in, sucked him and laid down to open her legs for him. Then she came alive, and I knew, I *knew* it was all a ploy to trick my father into believing she would be his. But she wasn't strong enough.

I would make her stronger.

I would find a way to give her the strength she didn't have. To survive his punishment and live only for me. I would reward her love and loyalty with my own, and she would never have to be afraid again. It was odd, really, finding her. She freed me. It was because of her that I even opened my eyes and understood the man my father was. The despicable being who took everything because he was meant to have nothing.

*Now* my name meant something. I understood it in a way he probably hadn't wanted me to. I truly was Jacob, the one who was prophesized to be blessed because it was *me* who was meant to rule. And my father was nothing but a pitiful Esau, an impersonator in sheep's clothing who wished he were me because I had more than he ever would. I was the one who was truly dark and twisted. The one who was meant to hold the power over life and death. *Her* life and death. He could have Celia and the fucking rest of them. I didn't give a shit about them. It was about finding the perfect toy. That endless supply of pleasure and knowing that at any time I could destroy her. Alana was perfect.

Always.

When my father crawled from the bed and left her there, I waited. Waited until he came back for me. I wiped the expression of anger and retribution as best I could from my features and mimicked awe. That he was so great. That he'd done so much to her, for her. When the door swung open, I didn't make a sound. I kept my eyes on her the whole time she was in the room, and that was all I saw as he closed the door once more and stood behind me. I memorized every bruise, every cut and break in her skin, and the way her lips trembled as she cried, even in sleep. Then he was taking me down from the door, leaving the ball gag in place, and pushing me up the stairs.

I didn't fight him. Instead, I nearly ran up to the kitchen where I sat in the seat, folding my hands in my lap, and waited for him. When he walked through the door from the dungeon, he was covered in muck, but my eyes adored him, envied him. I kept doing so until he finally looked at me and smiled that cruel smile I thought mirrored my own but was only a shadow of what I could be.

"You liked that, did you?"

I nodded my head vigorously.

My father frowned, looking at me. "I thought you'd be angry with me."

The look on his face didn't fool me. He wanted to see a crack, a fissure he could exploit. I would give him nothing ever again. I shook my head again and pointed to my mouth. Father stepped forward, unhitched the ball gag from the back of my head, and dropped it on the table.

Taking a few moments to rub the ache from the sides of my mouth, I gathered my thoughts. "Is that how training begins? For all of them?"

"That's how it's supposed to go. She's special. She's got fight in her. Most of them are scared. Been told by the television it's better not to fight back. To give in and rely on your captor's good side to let you go. That it's easier to heal from a trauma than be dead. She didn't care about that."

"But that made it better for you, right? She deserved to be punished, and we are made to punish women. To teach them their rightful place," I croaked.

"It's what I've been trying to teach you all along. They can cry and promise you the world. They will spread their legs for you and leave without a care. They say they love you, but they don't. They only love themselves. They only care about what they want."

"But her fighting means she's got a strong will. Good enough to pass to a boy, worthless on a woman."

My father sat across from me at the table, smiling again. "That's why I'm going to breed her. Every chance I get I'm going to fill that little bitch with seed until she gives me a son, and then, I'm going to get rid of her. Don't want her thinking she's special just because she pushed a child out of her cunt."

I forced myself not to grit my teeth at hearing that. Alana would *not* die. "I wouldn't have been able to control her. You were right. I wasn't ready, and it's because I didn't want to take those steps."

"Are you saying you are now?"

I had to be careful. I didn't want him to think I was feeding him the crock of shit that I was. I was going to take everything from my father. Bit by bit. Learn what I needed. Take on the darkness. And then I was going to kill him and save Alana. Make her mine. Make her more than the rest.

"No," I said. "I'm not ready because I am learning. There is so much I need to learn. I don't want to just *know* it, I see that now. I want to understand the ways of the world. I know you will have to punish me to teach me, and I'm ready for that."

I bowed my head, not quite hiding my eyes entirely—my father wouldn't believe that—but I could at least show some contrition. Holding my gaze up was the only reason I saw the hit coming, but I didn't try to dodge it. His fist connected with the side of my head, a throbbing pain spreading immediately through my skull as I fell to the floor. I got to my knees and kept my head down, balling my fists at my side.

"You think you can lie to me? You've got bitch in you. No fight. No power. Give up and die."

No. I wouldn't. I came up swinging. My dad wanted a fight? He wanted to see if I would roll over or if I had that killer instinct? I'd show him. I'd fucking show him. My first two hits were wild and missed, but he backed away from me. That was enough room for me to run back to the other side of the table and push it forward. I rammed it into his gut, knocking him into the counter behind him. Glasses fell from the dish rack and smashed into the ground. I didn't care if everything broke apart. I pulled the table back and went to hit him with it again, but he got his hands behind it. He was stronger than me, so much stronger, and flipped the table. I fell back, wrapping my arms around my skull to protect it as I hit the ground. My father gave me no mercy, and he was there, kicking at me under the table. I grabbed one of his feet and held on for dear life.

"Get off!"

He yelled at me and tried to shake me, but I didn't let go. I used my free fist to punch his shins. Something crunched, but I didn't stop swinging, not until he went down to the floor. I scrambled from under the table to get on top of him. I punched his chest and stomach, his face, anywhere I could get my hands, until he reached back and swung. One hit from his meaty fist sent me sprawling, but he was laughing as he sat up.

"You scrappy bastard, I did fucking help make you." It was the first thing Father had ever said to me that was kind.

"You taught me to be." I still hated him, but I knew I needed to dance with the devil to overthrow him.

"I'll teach you so much more. But that toy down there? Alana? She's mine. You lost your chance at having her and will have to wait your turn again."

"I know." I let some of the disappointment and jealousy cover my voice. It wouldn't do good to have him thinking I was completely where I needed to be. And I didn't know if I would have been able to swallow all the agitation over him touching her in the first place. Thinking about it made me sick to my stomach. Father got to his feet with a groan before helping me off the floor.

"Go get that Celia bitch to clean all this up. I've got to take care of Alana for a bit, after I have her again."

"Yes, Father."

My heart stuttered when I walked down the stairs to the basement. I could hear her crying. My love. My girl. She was crying, and I couldn't go to her. I couldn't lick the tears away and teach her how beautiful she was in pain because it made me love her. Made me crave her pain and her sweetness. Her blood and her heartbeat. But I walked by her, ignoring her, and kept heading down the stairs to the dark-haired toy I didn't give a shit about, to make her clean up a mess that was fucking stupid, all so I could convince my dad I wasn't going to betray him.

Maybe he should have named me Judas instead.

I slipped into the basement holding area quietly while my father snored away in his bedroom. My heart pounded so loudly I feared it would wake him, but I had to check on her, to make sure she hadn't lost her will to fight. My shoulders ached, and I held my arms across my stomach to support them. But it didn't matter; battered and bloody, she still needed to see me. To know I was going through hell too. That she wasn't alone. That we were together in this. At the bottom of the stairs, Celia jerked in her cage, her eyes wide with fear.

"I'm not him," I whispered.

"Jacob? What happened?"

"Dad's punishment."

"You want to hurt her too?"

"Never," I said in a harsh whisper. But maybe I did. I wasn't sure. She confused me. Right now, I wanted to pull her into my arms and run my fingers through her hair to soothe her. I wanted to kiss her and rock her to sleep. I wanted her protected. But I wanted to be inside her. With me inside her, my father's touch would be replaced. I'd erase him from her psyche the only way I knew how. But I wanted to stretch her over my knee and beat her ass blue for letting him in, for not fighting hard enough.

"You want to do to her what your father does, Jacob. What do you think that means?"

"I'm not my father, but I don't know anything else."

Celia pulled back in her cage, dragging her knees under her chin in the faded light. Only a singular bulb lit my way to Alana. I had no way to open the cage. My father never let the key be away from him, and breaking the lock would let him know I was here, or get her hurt before I was strong enough to get her out of here.

"Alana?"

She tensed but didn't turn around.

"Please, Alana. Let me see your face," I begged.

Slowly, gingerly, she rolled over, and I sucked in a pained and angered breath, resting my head against her cage. Her face was puffy and red, bruising already turning blue around her mouth and right eye. Tears streaked down her cheeks, leaving dirty trails in their wake, and her hair stuck to the grime on her skin. He'd pounded her, leaving bites and scratches down her bare back. She hadn't earned the right to wear clothing yet, and she covered her breasts with bruised arms and hiked up her knees to her chest.

"Talk to me," I said.

She looked at me, her gaze scanning over my swollen face, split lip, and mussed hair.

"Yeah, he hurt me too," I whispered. "Are you okay?" I sighed roughly. "That's stupid, of course you aren't okay. I don't know how to do this. Help me."

I closed my eyes, pressing harder against her bars, wishing I could get to her.

"Does it hurt?" she croaked.

"No." I didn't hurt like she did; there was no comparison.

"It's agony," she said. Her eyes were hollow pits.

"I wish I could hug you."

*Stupid. Stupid. Stupid.*

"I'm sorry, I don't have to touch you. I …"

She bit her lip. "Can you hold my hand?"

"Yeah. I can do that."

I stretched my arm, pain and all, as far as I could through the bars, ignoring the screaming rush of fire spreading down my back. I didn't care that holding my arm at that angle made tears clog my throat. I didn't give a shit about any of it. I turned myself sideways and forced my body partially into her cage until all she had to do was reach out and I was there. She didn't even have to get off the mattress. I bore the brunt of the pain, and it didn't matter. Her cold, slender fingers wrapped around mine, barely a grasp, but enough, and I held her. I let her close her eyes and slip into restless sleep. And when Celia tried to call me away from her, I ignored her. Alana needed me, and I was here. I could do this at least.

"A little longer, then I'll leave."

I don't know who I was trying to convince, Celia or me, but I still held on. My heart jerked with the way she gripped me, and it felt different to be an anchor. Without pain or violence, just touch. My father had never shown me this, and a flash of my mother warmed me—a moment of her arms around me, her kissing my skinned knee.

*"There, all better."*

"There, all better," I whispered to Alana and released her.

It took everything inside me to leave her behind and find my way back to my bedroom. Right then, I would have gladly switched places with a toy, and it terrified me.

"That fucking bastard. That insignificant, piece-of-shit bastard!" I raged in my shower because it was safe.

The water made noise as it pelted my body and the walls, keeping my voice muffled even though I faced the door. I didn't close my curtain so I could see if my father was trying to sneak in. He took Alana, not once but twice, while Celia cleaned up the mess we'd made in the kitchen before I dragged her back to her cage. And then the fucker had her too. He made sure I couldn't see Alana when he cleaned her up and was far enough away after he was finished that it wouldn't have made any sense to go back downstairs. He may like the way I was changing, but he didn't trust me yet.

Not that I would have expected him to, but it didn't make the situation any better. I hated that he touched her, that he knew her taste. That she had to accept him or he would kill her. That he knew I hated it only made him enjoy it more.

"I'm going to kill him, Alana, I swear. One day, I'm going to lay him at your feet, cut open from neck to gut, and it's going to be my gift. I promise you."

# Chapter Six

## Alana

### Four Months Later

"**A**lana! Alana, wake up," Celia whispered into the darkness. "Alana!"

Caught in the midst of a nightmare, it took me a moment to realize the screaming I heard was coming from me. The nightmares had become more frequent ever since I'd put the pieces together: my period was late, my breasts were tender, and the nausea could no longer be kept at bay. I worried I may be pregnant. I hadn't shared my suspicions with Celia yet, too afraid to admit the truth aloud. I didn't want to be the pregnant eighteen-year-old. And I sure as hell did not want to be pregnant with my kidnapper's baby.

"I'm sorry I woke you, Cel. Another nightmare."

"I know. I get them too. But you're having them a lot more lately. What's up?"

Knowing I needed someone to talk to and confide in, I opened my mouth. The words came tumbling out in a rush, finally free.

"I'm pregnant. I just know it. I haven't gotten a period and I'm always on time. I can barely touch my breasts because they are so tender, and everything is making me sick. Oh God, what am I supposed to do? I can't be pregnant. I can't. I can't have the monster's kid. Cel, what if it is like him?"

I couldn't catch my breath. I sucked harshly, forcing air into my lungs, but it wasn't enough. Too much weight crushed me, and my vision winked out. Dizzy, I closed my eyes to keep from throwing up.

"Shhh, Alana. Take a deep breath. You're hyperventilating."

Doing as she said, I calmed down, sucking in deep breaths and releasing them slowly.

"There you go, hon, there you go. That's it. Just breathe. Now here's what we're going to do. You don't want this baby, right?"

"I can't have it. I can't."

"Don't tell him you're pregnant. When I'm on kitchen duty, I'll steal the cinnamon when no one is looking. We learned in health class last year that some herbs and spices can cause miscarriage. I'll try to get my hands on them and then you'll take them. Hopefully, that will work."

Celia got to clean the house and work outside of the cage sometimes. She could easily sneak it away in her pockets as long as she was careful enough.

"What if it doesn't work?"

"If it doesn't work, as painful as it might be, you may have to get him to give you a beating. If you can put yourself in a position where he's directing his blows to your stomach, you are sure to lose the baby."

Baby. There was that word. I was pregnant with a *baby*. A kicking, fussing, crying baby, who would someday grow up to be a man. To be a monster like his father if that man got his hands on him. As painful as it was, as much as it clenched at my heart and radiated pain from every inch of my being, I knew it was best. If I gave birth, that monster would steal him from me like he had stolen everything else. And once the monster had his hands on my precious child, he would mold *him* into his image, or raise *her* to be a toy like me.

I couldn't stomach either possibility. But it was easier, somehow, to imagine my little one as a boy, a child who may have the chance to fight back. But then, I wouldn't be having *him* at all. We were discussing how much I'd have to take and how to get it down my throat when the door to the basement opened. We shuffled to our knees, heads down, for Master.

"It's me."

I lifted my head and gripped the bars of my cage. Jacob had become our friend. The Master's son, who was tossed back and forth like us. Even Celia had warmed to him during her time cleaning upstairs. She said she had to clean the kitchen a few times after Jacob had run-ins with his father, and he suffered things we had to. It softened my heart toward him. He was more than a way to get away; he'd morphed into a friend.

And maybe something more, if the time had been different.

He knelt in front of my cage and wrapped his hands around mine, his warmth seeping into my skin. "How are you today?"

I glanced at Celia, and she shook her head, but I took a chance. "I've been sick."

Jacob frowned. "Do you need medicine? I can try to sneak some down here."

"No. Jacob, I'm pregnant."

His fingers tightened on mine, and I winced. "He knocked you up."

I nodded.

Jacob reached through the bars and placed his palm on my belly. It did funny things to me, his hand covering the child I refused to have. What would it have been like if I'd met him in a different place? His fingers were soft against my skin, and he didn't stray up toward my bare breasts, or down. I'd become accustomed to being naked in front of him, and his gaze always stayed on mine when he looked a time. But now, he looked at my stomach with a clenched jaw and tears in his eyes.

"This should have been mine, and he will …" Jacob let the rest of his words fade away. "You can't have his kid, Alana."

"I know. I don't want my child to grow up—"

"Like me or you," he finished for me.

"Celia has an idea, but she has to be able to sneak some things down here."

"I'll help her, and there's also some medicine my father keeps on hand for certain situations. Alana, it's going to hurt. So bad."

I swallowed but nodded. "It's the right thing to do."

"Do you want me to be there?"

"Yes, if you can find a way."

He lifted his hand off my stomach and thumbed my cheek. "For you, anything."

He was my hero when he said things like that. We were doomed, of course, but I could imagine different things. Imagine he was a normal boy, who liked this normal girl, and we could have a date at the theater. But he wasn't normal, and I was slated to die. We were impossible. Even if he helped me escape, he was too broken to have any sort of relationship.

"Thank you."

"Celia, I'll get the medicine to you and help you get it down here after you have kitchen duty tonight. You'll be stripped when you get here, so you'll have to put it in a cavity."

"I know," she whispered.

"I'll wrap everything for you, don't worry. We'll get through this."

He left, and a few hours later, Celia was taken upstairs to clean and be used. She always came down lackluster and withdrawn, but once Master left, she went to the edge of her cage and pulled something from her body. The tightly wrapped bundle was the solution to my problems, and she unwrapped it carefully before handing me the contents.

"Jacob added a packet of jelly in there. Blueberry, since you like that flavor. He couldn't get much more in there, but he said it will help get the herbs and pill down since you have nothing to drink."

I mixed the herbs, pill, and jelly in the palm of my hand before forcing it all down and waiting for things to start. Celia was right. The right combination of herbs and spices, and the pill Jacob added, started me on my way to miscarriage. And with a few well-aimed blows to my own abdomen, the process sped up until I was cringing in agony, tears streaming down my face as blood ran down my thighs. My insides clenching and unclenching was nothing compared to the emotional pain of my first child slipping away and knowing their death was on my hands. I was a murderer. A murderer of an unborn baby who, under any other circumstance, I would've loved. I *did* love. I had to keep reminding myself I did this to protect my child so he would not have to live under the thumb of such an evil monster.

But Jacob was missing. I needed him here, wanted him close to hold my hand like he always did when the pain was too much. I looked at the basement door, willing him to appear, but he never did.

"Jacob," I moaned.

"He's probably been held up. You know he'd get here if it could."

"He promised," I said.

Jacob telling me he'd do something was a promise. We didn't need the stupid extra words, and I didn't realize how I'd come to rely on that from him.

"He'll get to you," Celia said.

As the pain became unbearable, I screamed. Hearing my screams and my pitiful wails, Master came running only to find me curled up losing my child, his child. Sweeping me up in his arms, he ran with me until we reached a bedroom on the main floor. Placing me on the bed, he went through the doorway to the side of the room, only to return with towels and hot water. After pulling an oversized t-shirt over my head and forcing my arms into the sleeves, he settled me in. Placing the towels underneath me and a cold compress to my head, the monster showed me the most compassion he ever had. Walking out of the room, I could hear him speaking. He must've been calling for help. Maybe, just maybe, something good could come from this nightmare. Maybe he was calling an ambulance. Maybe a paramedic would recognize me and save me from this hell hole. It was too late to save my baby, but maybe it wasn't too late to save Celia and myself.

With every cramp that ravished my insides, with every wince of pain, more tears streamed down my face. Body trembling, snot poured down my face, and I couldn't stop screaming. Screaming for the loss of my child, the loss of my innocence, my family, my friends, my life. Lost, lost, lost. Everything was fucking lost. *I* was lost. My mind raged against the injustice of it all. How could this be? My biggest worries used to be homework and girl drama. Now I was trapped in this prison, within my mind, and now I was losing a piece of me, my own flesh and blood.

An eternity later, the monster led a man with a medical bag inside. He set his bag on the bed and paid little to no attention to who I was. Never shifting his attention to my face, he spread out an array of tools and hooked me to an IV bag. The prick of the catheter sliding into my hand was nothing compared to the streaking pain in my groin. Blood, warm and sticky, pooled between my legs as cramps stole my breath. I was broken. I didn't want to have Master's son or daughter, but I was losing *my* little one too.

*I'm sorry. I'm so sorry.*

The monster sat in the corner, elbows on his knees and face in his hands. He glared at me, his eyebrows lowered over his eyes and a muscle ticking in his jaw in rapid-fire clenches as all the pieces started to come together. *Where was Jacob?* Directing a quick glance my way, the doctor began to speak.

"Miss, you're having a miscarriage. I've added something to your IV that will help you begin dilating, and when you're ready to push, I will deliver the fetus and dispose of it. After that, I'll clean out your womb."

He spoke so clinically, so detached. I didn't matter, not the pain. It was just a system of motions. I couldn't even gather enough strength to scream. There was nothing as my body contracted and deep pressure swelled through me. The pain was indescribable. My hips burned, and my insides clenched so hard I bit the back of my tongue to keep from screaming. My hopes that this could lead to freedom were squashed. And never once did he wonder who I could be, or what relationship I had with my captor. The doctor knew the monster. He helped him. How many girls before me had been treated for miscarriages or beatings?

I was on fire, being ripped in two. I'd heard stories of childbirth, but the contractions, the spasms rippling through my body, were absolute torture. And for nothing. There was no happy ending for me. I would push out a corpse instead of an infant. I wouldn't know the joy of holding my child at the end of a grueling labor. I would never hear him cry. I would never smell his sweet skin or kiss his rosy cheek. I would forever be a murderer. My victim, innocent blood on my hands.

And then the vacuuming started. The horrible, gurgling sucking as he scraped something against my insides. The spectrum holding me open pinched, and I was more exposed than I ever had been. Rubbed raw, every trace of what Master had put inside me was gone. But it was better this way. If I'd had the baby, Master would have taken it, and then I'd have to watch my child become a monster like him.

Leaving me to my misery, Master and the doctor left the room to speak in harsh whispers in the hallway. Curling myself into a ball, I kept crying harder and harder until I was gasping for breath. Master threw a glare my way before leading the doctor far away from my room.

The pain, the loss, shot through me like I was taking a bullet to the heart. How could I have done this? How could I put my precious little one through something this awful? I was as bad as Master. I was a monster like him. Crying harder at my thoughts, my eyes caught on the doorway in time to see someone peeking in. My body relaxed in one great *whoosh*. Jacob was here. He slipped into the room and crept into the bed with me. Ignoring the blood and filth on the towels, for the first time, Jacob took me into his arms. I curled into his chest, inhaling his clean, crisp scent through the tears.

"I'm sorry, Alana. I couldn't get here sooner, and I can't stay here long. He'll come back soon."

It didn't matter. He was here now, and I clung to him, curling my fingers into his shirt and holding on desperately. In his arms, the pain dulled, and I could handle it. I could cry into his chest and be held. I could be fragile, and he'd catch the broken pieces. His lips trailed up the side of my neck, soft kisses that pushed away the agony and warmed me.

"You can do it. You're strong enough. Hold on a little longer," he whispered into my skin. I believed it because he did too.

So I lifted my face so his lips could touch mine.

Soft and warm, his mouth was different. He slipped over the scars of my abuse and filled in the cervices left behind. Maybe it was the medicine making me fanciful, but I thought I could ask for this. That maybe I would ask him to take me. That I'd like to have him. But then, he was pulling away.

"I have to go. I'll be with you later. Look for me."

And as fast as he'd come, he was gone, but the pain was behind a wall, one he'd built high. He gave me strength, and I would use it to survive. I'd done the right thing, as horrible as it was, and I knew he didn't judge me for it. We'd done this together, and it made the load easier to bear. Master stomped his way back into the room, face scarlet and chest heaving like a locomotive. I wanted to cringe at his bald fists, but I couldn't move. I was too tired, or too resigned maybe, to care.

"You killed it, didn't you?"

"No, Master." I couldn't tell him the truth, I knew it. That would have only caused issues for Celia and Jacob.

"Don't fucking lie to me, bitch."

This time, I *did* flinch. I was always his little girl or sweetheart, but when he was angry, I was a whore, cunt, or bitch. He was on the edge, and a bit more would push him to finally killing me. *Did I want to survive? Or would I choose to die?*

"I didn't kill him, Master. I couldn't hold it."

"You're lying, and I'm going to find out how. And I will make you pay. I promise you that."

I trembled because I knew he told the truth.

A month passed, and I finally emerged from the darkness surrounding me after losing my child. Five months. 152 days. 3,650 hours. That was how long I had been kept captive by the monster who'd destroyed me. I counted the days by my meals. Twice a day he would bring us sustenance. 304 meals consisting of breakfast and dinner. Nothing fancy. Usually oatmeal, fruit, or pasta—everyday staples. My will to survive had all but diminished, my happiness lost. What little fight I had was mercilessly beaten out of me day after day.

And then there was 152 again—the times I'd seen Jacob. How he gave me a reason to move on. Promised that we were both getting stronger, and soon he'd have a way to get us all out of here. We had to hold on a little longer. As I thought about the past, the girl I used to be, I shuddered at the pure joy she exuded. Now, I was a slave to a Master who mocked me with his words, taunted me with his fists, and brutally raped me. My spirit had been broken, and I was all but ready to give up, but Jacob would never allow that to happen. So I allowed the Master to taunt me. Let him tell me that when I died, it would be at his hands, by his design. When he took me five months ago, he made sure I was nothing. I no longer belonged to myself, but to him. Only when he deemed it time for me to perish, would it be so. A monster in my eyes and in Celia's. He played our strings as if we were his puppets, as if he was our god. We were toys to him. Expected to play our roles silently without a fight.

I tried not to think of my parents too often. The pain was too much to bear. Were my parents still searching for me? Was Aaron missing his older sister? In the beginning, I waited, hoping for my Prince Charming to come riding in on his white horse and sweep me away from this nightmare. But life was no fairy tale. It was cruel, painful, and merciless. Once a firm believer in happily ever after, I no longer believed in those fairy tales. I no longer believed in tomorrow. Instead, darkness cast its veil over me.

Each day I was kept captive, my heart shattered a bit more as the darkness seeped in. I was no longer the golden girl. I was tarnished. I had an angel on one shoulder trying, and failing, to bring me back into the light. On the other shoulder, a devil whispered it was either time to let go or find the strength to fight. In the end, I didn't know which would be my voice of reason. It was a waiting game to see if the darkness would drive me to the brink of insanity, or if the hope would come once more.

Jacob was the only light, but even he couldn't save me from my eventual slide. My body understood the darkness, not the light. It didn't trust the sweet, and I needed the dark. I came with Master inside of me. I liked the rush of being held down. It was sick, and I kept it inside, but I think Jacob knew. Something in his eyes heated when he looked at me, and my body answered. I couldn't hide the response. Maybe I was no better than a fuck toy and men would always look for a chance to have me. But I kept it all at bay as best I could, and Jacob never touched me when I didn't ask to be touched.

Celia got progressively worse as time went by. Where once there was a bit of spark left in her, it was all but gone. Nothing but skin, bones, and a white pallor, she was like a ghost. Nothing was left to her. No fight, no words. Spending most of her days curled up on her mattress staring out into the nothingness, Celia was lost. The monster had finally broken her once and for all.

She became my confidant in this hell. The only one I could speak to, confess my fears to. In turn, she taught me how to survive in this prison under the unrelenting bastard who'd stolen us away. As she began opening up to me about herself, about her family life, our captor tore her to shreds. Where he'd lied about killing her mother before, this time it was true.

And it was all my fault.

She'd helped me to end my pregnancy, and she received punishment.

Now, a month later, I suffered daily with the blood of my child on my hands. Sweet, sweet Noel, an innocent child who'd died at my hands so I would not have to hand him over to a monster and see him corrupted. Even knowing this, the pain was great. Each day, it took a bit more of my soul. Hatred for this place, that monster, and for myself gnawed at me until I wanted to rip my hair out, scream, rage. But I remained docile. The perfect toy, the porcelain doll.

While I was wracked with pain on soiled sheets, screaming at the world and losing my child, the monster had gone into Purgatory. Searching, pulling my cage apart, he found what he was looking for. The stolen goods from the kitchen could only be from one person: Celia. And Celia paid for her betrayal. So did her mother.

Like a bat out of hell, the monster went on a rampage destroying everything he came across. When it still wasn't enough, he tormented Celia with the most damaging thing. He made good on his word. A hit and run, the news claimed, but Celia and I both knew better. The monster killed her mother, running her over as she walked across the street. She never had time to get away. The day after, as I laid on my mattress—overcome with guilt, pain, and tears—Master came down and threw a newspaper at Celia. As soon as she saw the front page, her world crumbled out from underneath her, and she was left with no hope.

## MOTHER OF MISSING DAUGHTER KILLED IN HIT AND RUN

Right there, in black and white, was Master's crime laid out for us to see and fear. Celia broke; I became docile. If he could do this to Celia's mother, what could he do to my family? I'd lost enough. I couldn't bear the agony it would bring me if something happened to my family, especially if I were the cause.

Stroking the wicked-looking zigzag wound that ran down the length of my ribs—my punishment for killing Master's child—I tried to recall some of my happiest times. But lately, the happiness was too much to bear. I was lost. Completely lost and utterly mad. The happiness drove me toward insanity, but I didn't want to forget. I didn't want to forget being Daddy's "Lani Girl" or the apple pies and kisses on the cheek from Mom. I didn't want to forget being Aaron's sister despite how crazy he sometimes drove me. It hurt to remember, but I couldn't forget. Even though I'd lost my fight, my family left a small spark of hope.

"Alana … Alana," Celia's weak voice called out.

It had been weeks since I'd last heard her speak. No matter how many times I tried to draw her out, it hadn't worked. Celia lost her hope, her strength. Hearing her now, her vulnerability and pain stirred something inside me.

"Celia. Oh, Celia."

"Alana, listen to me. Please."

"I'm listening. Tell me."

"If I don't make it … please, Alana, please tell my dad I loved him so much. That I thought of him and Mom every day. Please, Alana. I need you to promise me. He needs to know."

"Don't talk that way!"

"It's true, Alana. Master cut off my food and water days ago. I was slipping. There's nothing left for me, but your family is still out there. You have a chance to survive. If you make it out of here, *when* you make it out, please find my dad and tell him. Promise me."

"I promise. I promise. I'm so sorry."

"Don't be. I knew what I was doing. We did what was right. I don't regret it."

"Thank you, Celia. Thank you for being my friend. For saving me in your own way."

"You're welcome, Alana."

A few moments later, she fell back into a restless sleep. Tossing and turning, the nightmares were affecting her more lately. Hearing her cry out once again, I wished I could go to her. Hold her. Be the friend she truly needed.

Hours later, the man's heavy boots stomped down the stairs and headed in the direction of Celia's cage. He stood looking down at her. I wondered if he saw what I did: the paleness, the prominent skin and bones from her starvation, the brokenness.

He stood, silent, and I thought he would never speak. His booming voice took over the room, putting a chill in the air and making the hair on my neck stand on end.

"She deserves to suffer. She dared take my son from me? She dared to take my flesh and blood and think I would never find out. This is what she deserves."

Turning his head to stare me down, his evil eyes caught mine.

"This is what you deserve. You deserve this, too, you bitch. To die at my hands. But don't worry, you'll get what you deserve in due time. But tonight, I want to you to watch and know this is all your fault. *You* did this to her."

Opening the cage, Master dragged Celia out by her hair. Barely conscious because she was so dehydrated, she only whimpered weakly. She had no fight left in her, no fire.

Once he had her out in the open for me to see, he pushed her down to her knees. Eyelashes fluttering, her eyes finally popped open and stared into mine as her mouth moved to form words.

*This is not your fault.*

But it was. I was the one who couldn't carry a monster's baby.

Who needed it gone because I wouldn't have been able to protect it. This was my fault. I was to blame. And now Celia was facing the consequences for my decision.

Stepping behind her, he drew her head up by her hair once more only to put a knife, one I was intimately familiar with, to her throat.

"Don't … please. No. Don't kill her. Please. Please, Master." My tears flowed, and my words were barely coherent as they came rushing out in a torrent of screams. My words rained down on him, pleas for Celia's life, promises to be good, to bear him a child. It all escaped my mouth in a rush. "Please, Master. It's not her fault! It's mine. Please don't do this."

But with one look into his eyes, I knew my words weren't good enough. They weren't enough and never would be.

"I'm sorry, Celia. I'm so sorry. I'm so, so sorry."

*I promise, Celia. I promise to tell your dad.*

With a nod to me, Celia closed her eyes and became limp as she gave up. With one quick, deep cut from left to right, Celia's throat was sliced open. The blood poured, streaming down her neck and onto her naked body. As if she were a puppet held up on strings, her body folded into itself, and I was marking an eternity of time as her blood seeped onto the floor into a puddle. The life sucked out of her, Celia Jane Whittaker took her final breath succumbing to the fucking monster's hands. I hated him. With a fiery passion, I hated him. Every single thing about him.

Walking over to my cage, Master put his face right in mine.

"Remember this. This was all your fault. Every time you close your eyes, remember her death is on you. Remember her red blood pooling around her. You're next, little girl. You're next."

Leaving her body there to taunt me, Master stalked out of the room. All I could do was collapse onto the cold floor and cry. Cry for everything that was lost and cry for poor, sweet Celia. As the sobs wracked me and guilt filled me, I passed out on the hard floor. I woke the next morning to find Celia's body gone.

But the bloodstain was left behind to remind me.

# *Chapter Seven*

## Jacob

It was horribly cold outside, like Mother fucking Nature was pissed at me for letting my father once more hurt my girl. With each step, leaves crunched under my feet, and I wondered where summer had gone so quickly. But then Father was yanking the frail body forward, and I stumbled to keep up.

Dead weight was heavy, no matter how slim the form.

Celia was quiet now, her blood drained out of her on the floor in front of Alana's cage. Now, she was a skeleton wrapped in alabaster skin so fine I could see bruising from weeks ago still bright and tracing a path of her abuse. Her dark-brown hair was caked with congealed blood, and it almost looked like rust in places. Her eyes, though, they were the sickest part. They were wide open and guileless, as if in death she finally got the release she'd been searching for.

My father hadn't owned her soul as much as he believed.

Her death fucked with me. Somehow, she'd become my friend. My confidant who knew my how I loved Alana. Alana didn't stop screaming until she passed out, and I was helpless as I watched the way she tried to hold her body away from the ever-increasing pool of blood in her sleep as it seeped against her body.

"Move it, boy, or we'll be out here all night!"

I shuffled faster with my package, gripping the grainy cover tighter in my fists to haul her to the other side of the barn. The closest neighbor was over three miles away, so we had plenty of land to get rid of the body. Father had a pit where he kept lye in large quantities to decompose the bodies quicker and keep the smell down.

"I'll have to scope out another girl, but it's been too soon since Alana was taken and since I killed that bitch's mother."

"Keeping the snatches from eight months to a year and a half between them has kept the cops away from our door. Atlanta is big with the big press too. Macon, Georgia is already uncomfortable with the sequence of events of missing girls."

He stopped, looking at me over his shoulder. "You've been paying attention."

"I told you I would. Willacoochee has enough farmland to keep us hidden, and the money in the family keeps us operating, but touching Atlanta or Macon again could be risky. Athens might not be too bad, or even Savannah, the direction is different. Might take a minute before they even connect one missing girl to the others."

He scrubbed his chin for a moment, eyeing me approvingly. "I like the idea of Savannah."

A new toy coming in wouldn't bode well for my girl, though, and I'd have another one to save. He was already angry she'd lost his kid. That she was strong enough to kill it and defy him. If she were mine, she wouldn't have done it. She would have been happy to have my child. Would have loved it. I didn't want him to bring a new one in too soon and risk getting rid of Alana. I wasn't ready to get rid of him yet. Didn't know his business, how he ran the money or kept things moving. Without that knowledge, I wouldn't be able to keep Alana safe, and that was what mattered.

"Still, it's too soon after everything. And you still can get good use out of Alana. She hasn't learned her lesson yet and isn't broken. The bitch killed my little brother and she needs to pay. Dying quick and easy is too good for her."

Father picked Celia back up and kept trudging forward toward the gravesite. We'd shoveled out the deep top layer the day before, exposing the sixteen other bodies I could still faintly make out. But I knew there were more down there. That my mother's body rotted in the grave too. She was probably nothing but bones now.

"She is going to pay. Long and hard. She wants to die, I know that. I'm going to keep her alive until she's so broken she only wants what I need. Until I've got her fat and pregnant again. Then, when it's time, I'm going to rip it right from her stomach, let her feel every moment of it. Watch her bleed the fuck out. Doc will make sure it's a boy. Anything else will be terminated before she can have it."

Time. Death and time. That's all I could give her—I could provide—but it would have to be enough, for both of us. Right? I dumped Celia over the foul corpses, struggling not to puke while I thought about death and time.

The death of my mother came long after it should have because my life had bought her time. Celia's throat was cut because she'd stolen time from my father. Time to raise the perfect son. To gain a true heir the way he hadn't with me. And then I thought of my father's death at my hands. I would bury him along with his prized bodies. I'd cut him into pieces and place a part of him in each of their mouths so they could taste his death. He'd be part of them instead of the other way around, and I'd have all the power.

My cock stiffened as I shoveled dirt over Celia. It pounded, sending sharp darts of pleasure and desire as I imagined Alana on her knees, sucking it down, deep in her throat. It burned me up as I imagined her bloody and tied up, waiting for me to take her, hurt her, fucking degrade her with my seed spurting all over her wounds. I'd make sure we were combined that way.

Maybe I'd even make her drink my blood too. She'd started to like the fucked-up shit my dad did to her, that *I'd* one day do to her.

"You like dead things? You're damn near humping the fucking shovel. Is that what gets you off? When they're already dead? When their snatch is dry and splitting, bloodless, because their heart isn't pounding?"

I blinked and saw my dad was standing next to me, staring down at my pants. I shook my head, not sure how to answer. Telling the truth was out of the question. If he knew I still wanted Alana, everything I worked for would be lost. If I said I wanted the dead Celia, I knew exactly what he'd expect me to do. As perverted as I knew my wants were, something dead was not one of them.

But I could give him *some* truth.

"No. I was thinking about a toy. Training one. I like what I did to that one before, but I want to do more. Cut it and feel the blood on my skin while I fuck it. You like to beat them; I like the blood."

"Every man has his desires. But bleeding a toy out will only make it so you can't play as often. They can't submit if they don't have enough blood to function," he lectured.

Making sure to check my tone, I turned toward him. "Is it any different than beating them until they can't stand?"

"It can be, but then that's the fun in it. It hurts all the more when you fuck them that way. They are there, in pain, awake, feeling every part of it. Not like when they are low on blood. Their bodies shut down on them. A shot of adrenaline can keep most people wide awake for whatever you want to do to them. Blood loss though? Too hard to fight the body's natural reaction."

"Then I'll learn to cut shallow and painfully. Maybe skin a few pieces."

My words caused my father to burst into a fit of laughter. It transformed his face. Made it lighter, kinder. I'd never seen him that way. I wondered if that was the face my mother fell in love with.

"You are a sick fuck. I'm glad to see it. You remember who runs the show around here. You will have your chance, but it'll be when, and if, I say so. You can practice your cutting on a hog. I'll get you one. Do it wrong on a toy and you can fuck up a year of good planning if she dies too quickly."

"How about a deal?"

"What sort of deal?" My father stopped shoveling and wiped his head with a rag before leaning on the top of his shovel.

"I learn to cut right. Skin a dead hog until I get the mechanics right. And then start on a live one, practicing until I can keep one alive but completely skinned. When I can do that, then we get that toy from Savannah and I train her."

Taking the time to hone my skill would keep him from going after another girl and keep Alana alive. I'd learn to cut so I could do it to him. Strap him to the slab in the Punishment Room and have Alana there. I'd give her the gift of his pain. Cut him up while he screamed and begged for mercy. Keep him alive and healing, only to do it again. And then, after he's so broken he can't do anything but close his eyes when I come, I'd cut him up in big fat chunks and do with them what I thought of before.

"That could take some time, son."

Son. That was the first time he'd called me such with that tone of emotion. Like I actually meant something to him. As if he hadn't raped me, hadn't beaten me. As if it would change the hands of time and I wouldn't want to kill my father any longer. Nothing had changed, except now, I was winning the game.

"We have to wait for the media to cool a bit anyway. Then we have to scout our girl and follow her. You and I both know you don't pick the first girl you see, and you've got to plan the escape route, time, and everything."

He chuckled. "That's right. I like that idea since it doesn't really go against what I would have to do anyway. You have a deal. When you can skin a live pig and it doesn't die, you get to help me scope the next toy and train her. No new toys until then, unless you can't do it. Then I get a toy on my own, and you go into this ground with the other worthless trash."

He held out his hand, with that fucking smile, that asinine grin that should only belong to me. I shook his hand, my smile— darker, more real, and crueler—sliding into place.

*Signing your fucking death warrant for touching her. Hurting her. When I love her. When she belongs to me. And she can't know it, won't understand it, because you've hurt her.*

"Deal."

Releasing that darkness from my soul and letting it flow through my bloodstream and swell in my heart was powerful. I was finally the monster my father had always wanted me to be. All because of a girl. Because of her. Alana. My baby. My obsession. And he'd die knowing what he'd lost, and the care he should have taken with me. He should have fucking bowed down at my feet, but he didn't, and now it was too late.

I shoveled the last bit of dirt over Celia, wiping away her all-seeing eyes.

*It's okay, Celia. She'll be okay. She'll survive. And then I'll have her.*

A cold breeze swept up, ruffling the leaves and dancing on the back of my neck. As a chill raced down my spine, I wondered if it was Celia's nails, denying my promise. Telling me that Alana deserved to be free, not owned by a monster like me.

*Fuck you, Celia. She's mine.*

# Chapter Eight

## Jacob

The pig's skin was the closest thing to human flesh. It's why I chose one to practice on. My father didn't ask too many questions when we purchased one. Of course, we used cash and an alias while getting it a state away so nothing could lead back to us. I laid it out on a slab in the Punishment Room, dead, as silver glinted off the knife in my hand.

"You want to make this your signature?" He humphed at me, crossing his arms.

"I'm not you, and I know that. I don't want to taint your work with my mishaps. If I do a new punishment, it's all on me."

I lied. I would be better than my father. But that wasn't something I could dare tell him. His gaze followed me like a hawk, waiting for me to mess up, to show him I was nothing more than a tool for him to work out his hell on. I played my part.

"Any pointers?"

My father rubbed his jaw thoughtfully, looking over the pig. "Soft tissue will hurt the most. Breasts, ass, under the arms, inside of the thighs. If you can find a way to keep them awake longer, start with the back to work them into a frenzy, then move forward. If you don't want them kicking too long, go for those places first."

"I wonder if I can use some sort of adrenaline to keep them aware, like when they go into the Witch's Redemption," I mused.

I. Hated. Him.

He nodded. "Would be worth a shot. A live pig would have been better to try that out on."

"Next time, then. Might as well get the practice in now."

I thumbed the edge of my honed blade. The back would be my starting point, for now. Pigs didn't have breasts and pussies like my father would like to see, so it didn't matter. I went around the slab to face the back of the pig and my father and placed the knife to the pig's skin. It was supple but a bit stiff from death. The first scrape only took an ugly shaving of misshapen skin.

"Too soft. It takes more work to pierce human skin. That'll hurt, but not the way you want. Even the sharpest edge needs pressure to get in."

"Okay."

I tried again, this time pressing hard on the blunted side. A chuck of pink and white hung open over a bloodless wound.

"Too much, and you ruin your toy."

I wanted to throw my knife at him, but he was right. I needed to learn this, to master the skills. The only way I could hope to save Alana and myself was to learn everything I could. I took a deep breath to let go of my impatience and tried again.

Each cut was better than the last as I learned how precisely to move. I was covered in sweat and pig, my muscles shaking with exertion, but I kept at it. My father never left, paying attention as I practiced. But then, he got off the wall he'd leaned on and approached me. I went still, flipping between wanting to sink my blade into his neck right now, or waiting to see what he'd do.

His steps were loud in my ears, the thuds from his boots marking time with my heartbeats. What was he doing? What torture would he use next? *Stop it. It won't change a thing. You'll end him eventually.* But thinking that didn't stop my mouth from going dry and my eyes going wide as he put a hand on my shoulder.

"Go clean and sterilize the blade."

I swallowed and went to the bathroom area to do as he said. I thoroughly washed my weapon, then doused it with a sterile solution. If he was going to use this on me, I'd rather not catch something from a dead fucking pig. Hiding my fear, I walked back to him with my head held high and a false questioning gaze.

"What next?"

"Come closer."

I did, keeping my back straight as I stepped next to him at the slab, the knife between us.

"Real skinning, when done right, can take time for the bleeding to actually start, but you need something razor-sharp. A scalpel or something like that. But the work you've done on the pig tells me you've got this one pretty sharp. Let's see if we can make it better."

My father lifted his right hand and showed me a blade sharpener. He must have gotten it while I cleaned the knife. He handed it to me, staring pointedly until I used it.

"Keep going. Wouldn't want any mistakes, now, would we?"

"No, sir."

*What was he planning?* My heart thudded, and my head swam, trapped in a fog. Each metal slide rang loud in the quiet room. It was a mark of what was to come, but I didn't know where my father would strike at me. I never knew with him, and it kept me on my toes.

"That's good. Now, I'm going to let you skin a space on my arm. Get it thin enough, you won't get the same."

Everything went still. Here it was—an opportunity. One I knew I'd have to let pass because my father would be ready for me to hurt him. I forced myself not to look for another weapon my father had tucked somewhere. No way he'd let me hurt him without some way to protect himself. He was in control right now.

"I don't want to hurt you," I said.

"But I want to hurt you. Gamblers say you can't learn how to play without having your money on the table. I bet you'll learn better trying to skin me one perfect time to save your hide than you have cutting up that pig."

I didn't have any other choice. There was no way I could hope to not mess up. My mind whirled as he extended his left arm, placing his hand flat on the table.

"Right here," he said. He pointed to a small expanse on his forearm, halfway down under the bend of his arm. It wouldn't hurt him permanently if I messed up. And if I tried to cut too deep, he'd stop me, and it would be all over. *Do what you have to.* I forced my hands to stop shaking as I wrapped my free hand around his arm, above where I'd cut, and pulled the skin taut. My breath was loud between us, and I tried to silence it. But when I lifted my knife hand, I saw it. My father had a scalpel in his pocket—a threat, a promise. He'd take that thing to me if I didn't do this right.

*Thin. Be razor-thin.*

I stopped thinking and let my hands follow the body memory I'd created over the hours of working the pig. I peeled back a layer, pinpricks of bright-red blood dotting the meat under his epidermis, the thin, onion-like slip of skin curling wetly over my fingers. I was skinning my father, and he never made a sound. His gaze burned into the top of my head, and he never fucking moved.

"Good, son. You've done well."

I released a pent-up breath and looked up at him. "Let me get something to clean that up."

"No need. My favorite toy can take care of it. But first things first."

I gasped as he gripped my neck and slammed me face first into the pig. "I did it right!" I yelled.

"Yeah, but I told you I wanted to hurt you. Don't scream and it'll stop quick. Take it like a man, like I did."

I didn't fight as he lifted my shirt. It was hell to keep my muscles relaxed as his fingers slipped over my skin and down over the flesh of my hip. Then the cold metal of the scalpel traced the same path.

"Stomach is soft tissue too. It spans to the obliques and a bit of this above your ass."

I didn't take in what he said before the blade sliced. I bit my lip until it bled, holding in my cry. Sweat dotted my brow, but the pain was paralyzing. I couldn't move, couldn't think. Everything I had was focused on not screaming. Warm blood trickled down my side, pooling under me, but my father didn't stop. Light-headed, and clenching my fingers around the edge of the slab until my bones grinded, I counted the seconds. Nerves screamed, pain radiated, and my blood wept. But it didn't end. One long strip—

from the center of my back on the right side, down to where my jeans began—became a mile-long live wire my father played with. But I made it. I never screamed.

"I'll make a man of you yet," my father said, pulling the scalpel away finally.

*Yeah, the day I kill you, old man.*

# Chapter Nine

## Jacob

"**W**hat's it like, going to school?"

Alana shrugged, and the glide of her hair over her shoulder caught my attention. She was so beautiful. My father kept her cleaned and fed well between uses. I knew he did it because it made sense to keep her healthy to use her. The minute he took worse care of her meant he'd be moving to a new toy. He would let her slowly fade, much like he'd done with Celia when he'd gotten bored with her. But, to me, it was because even he knew Alana was special. She wasn't like the other toys that had come before.

"It's school, I don't know. You've never been?"

I shook my head. "Dad homeschools me."

There'd never been a reason for me to be like other children. My place was by his side, learning how to handle toys correctly once I was old enough to understand. I cut my teeth on screams and blood, learned to not be sickened by it, and how to go to sleep lulled by lullabies of dying women.

"Ah, ok. Well, it can be pretty boring during the day but loud and chaotic before class or between the bells."

"Bells?" Is someone standing in the halls ringing bells? What the hell for?

"Yeah. They have these metal bells mounted on the walls that ring at the beginning of the day to tell you when to get to class, and then at the end of class and start of each class too. You have a few minutes to get to your locker and change your books out for the class you're going to next. Most of the time I almost missed the bell."

"That sounds confusing," I said. I'd never really been around a lot of people, except my father. He never took me out on his runs to get toys, and I rarely left the property. Homeschooling was mandatory by the state but didn't have the same rules regular kids going to school had to deal with. I understood controlled environments, not chaos.

"Not really. You get used to it fast, and new students have guides to help them get to new places when they don't know where they are going. And most of the time, your classes are on the same side of the campus with your grade."

"Do you miss it?"

She sat cross-legged on her mattress, hands between her legs and her hair covering her breasts, but I could still make out the dusty-rose of her nipples. The strands had grown longer in her captivity, and my father didn't allow any toys to have it short. She looked comfortable, and while I liked that she could sit with me like this so easily, it also bothered me that she'd grown accustomed to this way. I sat across from her, on the other side of the bars, fully clothed, and kept an eye on the time while my dad went to the store for supplies. Times like these were the only chances we had to have longer conversations.

"I do. I miss my friends and … well …"

I leaned in to hear more. "What?"

"Ryan," she said and ducked her head, her hair shielding her face.

"Were you his toy?"

"Jacob, the toy thing is messed up, you know that, right? Ryan was my boyfriend. He asked me if I'd go out with him after we became friends, and we went on dates and stuff."

"Is that different than me asking you to be my toy?" I cocked my head to the side. I didn't understand. And I didn't like this Ryan guy.

"Very different. When he asked me to be his girlfriend, he didn't think we'd have sex anytime soon and didn't think to have me locked up."

It's good he didn't think they'd have sex. I would have found him and showed him what happened to people who touched what was mine. This Ryan kid wouldn't be nearly as strong as my father, so I could take him. But I was interested in how she allowed herself to be taken by him but didn't like the idea of being my toy.

"Then how did he make sure you loved him and followed his rules?"

"There weren't any rules. We liked each other, and we wanted to see where it would go. He had to do things I liked that he learned about me over time, and I had to do the same for him. We respected each other, and I wasn't his property," she argued. She glared at me, her cheeks red, and I lifted my hands to placate her.

"I'm sorry. I didn't mean to upset you. I don't get it."

A toy was a toy. That's what men kept when they had women. They used them to fuck and enjoy or get children from when the time came. They had no other uses and spent their time in the cage. School and going home didn't add into that, but Ryan allowed Alana to do both. He wasn't very strong at all.

She sighed roughly. "Look, if we met out there, and you liked me, you'd try to talk to me to get to know me. If we liked how it went, then we would start to date. Maybe one day we'd think about getting married or having a family, but to start we'd be together."

"Are you my girlfriend?" She and I talked, and we were learning about each other. "I know you like Blueberry Pop-Tarts and jelly. That you don't like when your hair gets in your face, unless you are nervous, then you hide behind your hair. I know you blush down your chest, and you like to be held when you cry. You don't like being in the dark, and bugs freak you out. And, I like you. I think you like me too. Isn't that a boyfriend?"

Her quizzical gaze met mine. "Is that what you want, Jacob? To be my boyfriend and see where it goes?"

"It'll go to you being my toy and free. You won't ever have to worry about my father again, and you'll like the things we do together. I won't hurt you just to hurt you. Only to make you understand what we are to each other."

She shook her head, and my stomach bottomed out. "That's not what we should hope to be though. What about dates, or having a life? Will I go to college, or see my family again? What about life, Jacob?"

I frowned. "But you'd leave me if you went back home. And your family would get in the way of us being happy. They would want your time, and you're mine."

"I have the right to leave. You'd trust that I want to be with you enough that even though we aren't physically together, I'm still your girlfriend."

I wanted that with her, something normal, but I didn't see how it was different. But, for some reason, I wanted to be acceptable in her eyes, to be different than my father. I wanted more with her, and maybe I didn't know what *more* was. Was it family? Or the choice to come and go, even when you didn't want to leave? Why have the choice then? If you'd stay anyway, it made more sense to follow the rules and live in that life. A perfect submissive to the Master's Dominance. But Alana didn't see it that way, and I wanted what she wanted.

"Would you be my girlfriend if I agreed to learn?"

My palms were sweaty, and I sucked in a breath, waiting for her answer. Why was this so important? I rubbed my hands on my thighs, not able to look at her, and flames raced up my neck.

"Look at me," she said.

I forced my gaze to hers and took in her smile. I'd never seen her look like that, carefree and blindingly light. She was an angel, stuck in Hell, and I was the spawn of Satan hoping I could touch her golden halo. But I craved it. Even knowing I'd dirty her up and she wouldn't be pristine, I wanted a chance to know something good. I didn't deserve it, but I wanted to be saved. I never realized she was saving me as much as I was saving her.

"You really aren't your father," she whispered.

"I don't know how to be anything *but* like him, but you can show me how to be better. I want to be what you need."

I swallowed. That didn't sound right, but I'd said it, and I couldn't take it back.

"I think I'd like that."

"Like what?"

"Being your girlfriend. But I won't be your toy, Jacob. I never could be. Do you understand?"

"What if I lose you?"

"Then find a way to get me back, but you can't own me."

I nodded, not quite understanding, but if I could get her back, and she gave me permission to, I'd find a way. She'd always be mine.

"So you're my girlfriend now?"

"Yeah."

Her voice was small, but her shy smile only made happiness swell within me. This was mine, and my father had nothing to do with it. No matter what happened, Alana chose me, and that's all that mattered.

"Awesome."

She giggled, and it was like bells ringing in the wind. I liked the sound, and I'd have to do it to her again. But for now, I needed to leave. My dad would be home soon, and if he found me with her, we'd both have to pay the price.

"I have to go."

She tucked her hair behind her ears. "Oh, okay. Will you come see me again tonight?"

"I'll try. Sometimes Dad has me practicing."

"Practicing?"

"We made a deal. He won't go look for a new toy until I can do some stuff first. It's the only way I could hold him off from doing some worse stuff to you. You're as safe as I can make you, for now."

"Okay."

I got up, light on my feet.

"Jacob?"

"Yeah?"

"Thank you."

"For what?"

"Being you, even though your dad tried to change you. You've already beaten him. And for getting us out of here. I know you will."

"For you, anything," I whispered.

I liked that phrase becoming something that linked us, my own promise to her. Because I would do anything for Alana Masters. No matter how much it hurt or how fucking ruthless I had to be, she could ask anything and I'd move heaven and earth to give it to her. I wondered if this was that weak emotion my father called love. If it was, then he'd lied about it. Love didn't make you weak; it gave you hope and strength when you thought you'd lost everything.

# Chapter Ten

## Alana

### 1 year, 6 months later

"I am Alana Ann Masters. I am twenty years old. I have parents who love me. I have a younger brother named Aaron. My name is Alana Ann Masters, and two years ago, I was kidnapped."

Losing my mind, driven to the brink of insanity, I had to remind myself time and time again who I was. That I was Alana Masters. That before I was a slave, I was a person. A girl who was loved. It became a routine to me, a game I played to keep myself occupied while waiting for the agony to come each day.

"My name is Alana Masters, and I miss the sun on my face. I miss the taste of chocolate milkshakes, the coldness hitting my throat as it slides down smoothly. I miss my family, my friends. I miss cheerleading. I wonder if Ryan has found another girlfriend yet. I wonder how to tell him I've found someone else too."

Taken prisoner and held captive, I was forced away from everything I loved and made to live in a cold, dark basement as a ghost of my former self. Once a beautiful girl of blonde curls, emerald-green eyes, and skin as smooth as silk, I was now a toy used only for a sick bastard's pleasure and torment. My skin was now littered with an array of sickening bruises, cuts, and scars. The most prominent scar, a jagged knife wound running up and down the entirety of my rib cage. The scars weren't solely physical. They went beyond skin and looks and cut deeper into my mind and soul. My hair, dirty and tangled, had lost its shine and hung dully to my waist. My eyes had lost their sparkle. Too many tears cried at the hands of Master left my eyes almost swollen shut. In nothing but a filthy white t-shirt and navy-blue, threadbare panties that Master finally gave me permission to wear after he thought I'd earned them, I sat huddled in the corner trying to escape the chill.

Where once I was delicate and innocent, my body and mind had taken the brunt of the monster's punishments. I was no longer the naïve girl who gossiped about boys and fought with my brother about whose turn it was to do the dishes. I had been the subject of abuse—pummeled with fists, taunted with brutal, hateful words, and tortured in ways a human being could not even begin to comprehend. After what I had seen, what I had been forced to do since he'd taken me captive, it was no wonder I was at my breaking point. My psyche was fragile, and in no time, I would be completely shattered, exactly what the monster was waiting for.

In the beginning, I screamed for help while trying to fight off the monster as he laid on top of me. My fighting spirit only spurred him on more. The more I fought back, the more aroused he became and the more pain he inflicted. The pain, the terror in my eyes, it got him off. He was tall with a sturdy build, but he wasn't a man who would easily capture a woman's eye, something that had changed during my time with him. Losing Noel twisted him up, too, and he lost the brutal, edgy looks he'd once had. His black hair was thinning, and on nights when he forced me to be on top, I could easily see the bald spot that was becoming more prominent as time went by. I made it a point to avoid looking at his face as much as I possibly could, but his smug expression and those jet-black, ice-cold eyes lingered in my mind at night.

Only Jacob gave me anything to hold on to, but he frightened me too. As we got older, the darkness burning in his gaze grew. One day, he'd want the things his father had taught him to crave, and I'd want to give them to him. I knew doing so would only cement my abuse and leave me shattered. I had no strength, no choice, and I'd wilt under that weight. But losing Jacob left a bitter taste in my mouth. How do you leave love behind, even when it's twisted and barbed, stuck so deep in your skin your scars have grown over it? I wasn't sure what the answer was but knew I'd eventually have to escape Jacob and use the love he had for me to do it. It made me sick to my stomach, but I wanted to live, to be free, and Jacob, no matter how much I tried to teach him, didn't understand the real essence of choice.

He'd never had the chance to choose either, and maybe that's why it was so hard.

This morning, the stench of urine filled the air, reminding me Master hadn't cleaned my cage in three days. The smell was overwhelming, making me sick to my stomach. Usually, the man paid four visits to Purgatory each day—twice to deliver meals, once to clean the cage and at night when he needed a body to use or a hot mouth to fuck. To him, I was a ragdoll to be used and discarded, and he made sure I knew it every time he grabbed my hips and sank into me. Lately, though, something was different. Fewer visits, less food. Whereas he had little to no regard for me before, now he was completely indifferent. He still used me to get off, but other than that, there was little to no contact. And now I was stuck in my cage as the smell of piss wafted up my nostrils. Between that and my own stench, my nose curled in disgust.

The door to the basement opened, and I dropped to my knees and bowed my head as I'd been taught, waiting for my next demand to follow. Instead, Jacob reached through the bars of my cage and tipped my chin up to capture my gaze with his.

"Have you been eating the last couple of weeks like I told you? Hoarding food when you could?"

I warmed, afraid to ask if this was it. If, finally, all his promises would come to pass. "Yes. I've felt stronger lately but haven't let on with your father."

"Good girl. He's been talking about a new girl and going out to scout. I finally finished the training he had me on, and you've done so good keeping his attention."

"But if he's getting a new girl, that means my time is up," I whispered.

"It doesn't happen overnight, and you won't have to worry about that. Just trust me, and when the time is right, we'll act."

"What if we make a mistake?"

"I'm going to make things right, Alana. I swear it."

"That's a nice thought, Jacob, but your father is an evil bastard. He'll only hurt us if we try anything."

"He won't have the chance. Stand up, baby. I've got something to tell you."

Bringing his face closer to where I stood, he filled me in on his plan.

The next night, Jacob came back. It was a brief moment, but I needed it for the plan to take place. Loosening the cage's lock, he prepared me for what was to come. I took a calming breath and nodded to let him know I was ready. When he headed back upstairs, I sat back and got ready for my part to play. I stuck my hand underneath my mattress to make sure my tool was still there.

A few hours later, I heard the clomping of the man's boots heading for me. My eyes popped open, and I grabbed hold of my hidden object. As soon as Master came into view, I made a run for it. Swinging my cage door open, I went flying at him, a tiny ball of fury, knife drawn and aimed right at his stomach. He stalled from the shock as I flew at him from my opened cage. All the pain and anger, the hopelessness of my captivity, gave me the strength I needed to thrust the knife into his gut and twist. Repeatedly, I turned the knife into his stomach, wishing and hoping he could experience a fraction of the pain he'd inflicted on me. Coming up behind him, Jacob got a grip around his neck.

Drawing closer to his father, I heard him whisper "Surprise" into the bastard's ear.

Letting out a grunt, Master struggled to fight both of us off, his fists and legs flailing. Separately, we never would have been able to take the son of a bitch down, but together we worked as a well-oiled machine. Coiling rope around his father's wrists, Jacob made sure he couldn't get free.

Drawing the knife from his lower abdomen, I found myself entranced by the blood. Unlike the horror of witnessing Celia bleed out, I found a sick satisfaction watching Master's blood drip all over the floor.

Drip, drop. Drip, drop. Blood everywhere. Licking my lips, I found myself ready to begin. Jacob, taking him into the Punishment Room, paused to look back at me.

"Alana?"

Shaking myself out of the trance, I held my head high, chest puffed out, and marched through the door like an avenging angel. Master had tortured me long enough. It was time for the tables to be turned and revenge to be enacted. Long ago, I'd promised myself this bastard would die at my hands. Tonight, that promise would come true. I would make him pay. For my family, for Celia, for Jacob, and for me. I would make him bleed and take glee in it. A malicious laugh filled the room and it took me a second to realize it was coming from me.

Before I could lose my nerve, I had one last thing to do. Positioning myself in front of Master, holding the blade to make sure he didn't try anything, I grabbed Jacob's head with my free hand. I pulled his head over his father's shoulder and kissed him. Thrusting my tongue deeply between his lips, I kissed him with everything I had left in me.

"Thank you."

A stunned expression on his face, Jacob dragged his father to the medical table that had been used countless times to tie me down and punish me. Even with his hands tied behind his back and no way to fight back, knowing this would be the end of him, Master's tongue was merciless, taunting.

"I'm going to fucking kill you brats. How dare you fucking betray me, boy? How fucking *dare* you? I *made* you! I made you who you are. How dare you fucking defy me? And you, missy! You're nothing. No one. A cum bucket."

"Enough! Gag him, Jacob."

Bound and gagged, he could do no more but struggle against his bonds and glare ineffectively at us.

Surveying the tools, the very ones he'd used on me countless times, a plan formed in my head. Walking over to him, I had no fear. My life was no longer in his hands. Instead, his was in mine. I opened his pants, letting them drop to his ankles as I pulled down his boxers, so he was left standing there in his impeccable white t-shirt, staring down at me as I got to my knees.

"Did this make you feel like a man? Every time you put me on my knees. Every time you forced your disgusting cock into my mouth and fucked my face? Did it make you feel like a man to *rape* me?"

With knife in hand, I began making shallow cuts down both thighs, watching the blood trickle from the wounds. Seeing his blood run at my hands gave me control of myself for the first time since he'd taken me. The darkness in me cackled in glee.

Jacob came up behind his father once more, and in the seconds it took me to understand what was going on, his father was screaming in agony from behind the gag. Mercilessly thrusting something into his father's ass, Jacob's face was washed with sadistic pleasure. He enjoyed watching his father get his just desserts. I sat back and watched, realizing this was the pain Jacob had experienced. His father doubled over the table, unable to fight back while gagged and bound.

With one last thrust, Jacob deemed the act done.

Bringing my knife to his neck from behind, I pulled the gag from his mouth.

"Tell me why I shouldn't kill you like you killed Celia." My demand was met with stubborn silence, and I dug my knife into his neck. "Tell me!"

Jacob's stare touched my skin. I caught his eye as he told me to help him get his father on the table. After doing so, both of us worked to strap him down. If he was going to be a sick, stubborn bastard even now, at the mercy of his son and prisoner, I wasn't going to make things easy for him. And neither was Jacob.

The gaping wound on Master's abdomen was still gushing blood, and it was doing funny things to me. While I should be sickened by this whole thing, I was taking pleasure in it.

"Let me tell you a story. Celia Jane Whittaker was sixteen when you took her from everything she knew. She loved to play the piano, she was a fan of One Direction. Her favorite food was peanut butter pie, and she had parents who loved her. She had two little siblings. You took her from her family. For your own sick pleasure. For your games. And then you killed her mother because Celia helped me. You killing her mom was what actually killed Celia. All your actions did was put her out of her misery."

Seeing no remorse in his eyes, I continued, all the while dragging my knife around his body. Following it with his eyes, he waited for me to strike.

"I am Alana Ann Masters. I was a cheerleader. I have parents who love me, *truly* love me. I have a brother who was an ass but will do anything for me. I loved to dance and act. I had friends. I had a future. And then you stole it all from me. I would've had a child, but I couldn't risk it. I forced a miscarriage on myself so I could protect him from you. This is for Celia." Thrusting the knife into his right thigh, I pulled it down, cutting through tendons and nerves, making sure he felt the pain.

"This is for her family." This time, I stuck his left thigh, repeating the process.

"This is for my family." Landing another thrust to his abdomen, blood pooled around the knife. As it ran down his stomach, around his belly button and lower, the darkness in me let out another malicious laugh.

"Your turn." I handed Jacob the knife

Taking the blade, he looked his father up and down, and I wondered what he was thinking seeing such a strong, evil man reduced to such pitifulness. As Jacob's gaze hit lower, the rage entered his face and his eyes narrowed.

"This is for me, Father."

With those five words, the knife arced through the air and his father wailed.

Master was a man no more.

"And this. This is for Noel and me."

One final thrust of the knife, directly into the heart, and we were free from the monster's thumb. Noel and Celia were avenged. Looking down at the warm, red blood on my hands, my darkness rose up and smiled.

Looking at Jacob, I knew I couldn't stay, even though it pained me to leave him behind after what he'd done for me. Despite what he'd said about not forcing me, I knew he was his father's son and all he wanted was for me to be his toy. I loved him, and he loved me, but this sort of love was wrong. I refused to be put in that position again. Even if the darkness in me craved him, I was terrified Jacob would end up like his father.

"Can I wash up? Please?"

"Yeah. Yeah, of course. I'll show you to the upstairs bathroom and then dispose of his body," Jacob said with a sneer in his father's direction.

Leading me upstairs to the main floor, I was amazed by the sheer size of the place. For years I was kept in a dark, damp basement thinking I was in some run-down house. Instead, I was in a mansion. Crystal chandeliers hung from the ceilings, white marble tile lined the floors. Walking me through the house, Jacob seemed unsure what to say to me now that the deed was done. Honestly, I didn't know what to say to him either, especially knowing I was planning to run once his back was turned. Only two words came to mind, and I wanted him to know how much I truly meant it. Turning to face him, I looked right into his eyes as I spoke.

"Thank you."

A smile filled his face; it was perfect. It was carefree, bright, and beautiful. In another life, this boy would be the perfect man for me. But in this life, he was damaged, abused and traumatized by the same man who'd subjected me to torture. The only difference between us was the monster was his father. We were both his prisoners, just in different ways.

Opening a door, Jacob turned on a light. The brightness bothered me after having become so accustomed to the dark. I looked around the room and spotted a walk-in shower that could hold at least four people. His toilet was in one corner across from the sink, and a huge, porcelain tub was on the opposite wall. The bathroom was decorated in all whites and gold—a bathroom fit for a princess, not a girl with blood dripping down her hands. A drop of blood fell onto the spotless floor, and I took pleasure in seeing Master's sparkling white floors tarnished with his own blood.

"I'll let you clean up and head back downstairs. Call me if you need me."

Jacob walked away, and I headed to the sink to begin washing my hands. Once I was finished, I gave one more glance around the room. And then I did what I had been dreaming of since the very moment I woke up in that cage.

*I ran.*

Three miles, in borrowed clothes from the house and shoes that belonged to some girl before I'd come along. Tree branches snapped at my face, splitting my skin, but I kept running. My lungs labored, but it was nothing compared to the pain Master had trained me to endure. Despite being tired, haggard, and weakened, I could function.

*The bastard was good for something.*

Owls hooted and night insects sang as I pounded through the darkened woods. I didn't know which way I was going, but I had to be close to something. Mail in the house near the front door told me I was still in Georgia, and I could make it somewhere. I didn't have a map, but I'd find a way. Lights on the edge of the darkness grabbed my attention. I sped toward them, pushing myself faster. Life, it *had* to be life.

I'd left Jacob behind. After everything, I ran because I couldn't face loving a man like that. He was Master's son, and what he wanted from me would be no different. It didn't matter the odd connection we shared or the fact we'd shared killing his father. He would want to harm me. But he was messed up, and he needed help. Just not from me. I kept telling myself that as I ran to keep from going back. The lights grew bigger, and I could make out the edge of a house. Relief and hope filled me.

*Almost there.*

The small brick home only had a porch light with a single window illuminated. I pounded on the door, afraid this would be my only chance.

"Please, help me. Please!"

"What the hell?" a gruff voice answered, and I froze when he opened the door. What if he would hurt me? Take me and rape me? I jerked back from the door, poised to run away.

"Who are you?"

"Please ... don't ..." I couldn't get it out. Nothing.

"Whitney, come here, quick. I think it's that girl from the news."

"What?"

A petite woman with wild, blonde hair came into view, pushing the bear of a man back from the door. "Oh, sweetheart. You're Alana Masters, right?"

I crumbled. My name. She knew my name. My family hadn't stopped looking for me.

"Tommy, call the police. We have to get her home."

Tommy ran back into the house, and Whitney came outside with slow steps. "It's okay. You're safe. I promise."

"Can I ... have a hug?"

I don't know where the request came from. But once I'd voiced it, I didn't want to take it back.

"Come here, baby."

I fell into her arms, clinging tightly as I sobbed. She rocked me, rubbing my hair, like my mother would do, and whispered things that soothed me. She stayed with me, even as sirens and flashing lights filled the air.

It was in her arms—when I finally knew I'd escaped—that I made the decision to not send Jacob to prison. He'd helped save me, and maybe they could get him into a hospital. The only man who deserved to be punished for it all was his father.

# Chapter Eleven

## Jacob

I was the happiest I'd been in a long time. Sharing the murder of my father with Alana was better than any gift I'd ever planned to give her. She was magnificent, amazing. Beautiful. An avenging angel. I wondered how proud of her Noel would be if he could have seen what his mother had done for him.

She was so fucking perfect. She took pleasure in the pain my father went through and joined with me in blood and hell. And that kiss—the taste of her mouth still lingered on my lips. It was her I smelled over the musk of her ill-washed body She smelled sweet, like lily mixed with the blueberry Pop-Tart. If I sucked hard enough, my saliva still held spots of her, but I didn't want to waste it. I would be back with her once I had my father cleaned up and out of here. She wouldn't need to be in the cage anymore. Instead, she'd be in my bed, and we'd only come down here when she needed to be punished. When she had to be reminded of who was in control.

"But that is later, much later," I said aloud. I whistled as I walked into the Punishment Room. Blood was all over the floor, coating the already dirty, stained concrete bright-red.

"So much work to do. I shouldn't be wasting my time with you while my girl is getting ready upstairs, but I don't want you around her anymore. And we've got work to do, don't we? I made a promise."

It took time, but I did it. I painstakingly cut him up, using a hacksaw for the larger parts and a miter saw to cut to better sizes. I dumped his insides into a refuse bucket. I was covered in fleshy bits and blood by the time I dragged the tarp to the grave I'd exposed, but it was done. Enough time had passed for Alana to be finished with her bath and maybe getting some good rest in my bed.

I was eager to get back to her, so I wouldn't take the time to cover the grave. That would be hours I'd have to spend away from her, and it had already been long enough. We could come back out tomorrow and do it. I spread the lye heavily, so the smell wouldn't attract any wild animals, and headed back to the house.

But something was wrong. The moon was rising in the sky. Daylight had come and gone. I had worked longer than I thought, and flashing blue and red lights twinkled near my home.

"Alana!"

I didn't think, didn't care. I had to get to her. They couldn't take her from me. Not after all we'd been through. Not after what we'd done. They'd think she had something to do with it, and she'd get in trouble for killing my father. I knew it. I fucking knew it. I'd stop them. I had to. I pumped my legs hard, reaching the house in minutes, only to stop when a spotlight swung my way.

"Alana!" I screamed again. "Where are you?"

"Son, we want you to lie on the ground, legs spread, and put your hands on your head."

"Where is she? Please tell me where she is. She can't be out here alone. You can't take her. Please."

"I won't tell you again. Get down on the ground, legs spread, with your hands on your head. If you do not comply, we *will* shoot."

"You aren't supposed to be here," I said. I knew she was gone. They took her. She was somewhere, in another cage, crying for me. Trying to get back. And they had me.

I cried into the dirt. We'd been free. Those precious few hours I'd spent cutting him up and cleaning were too long. I should have stayed with her.

Feet pounded the ground next to me and hands gripped me. I didn't struggle as they handcuffed me, the cold metal biting into my wrists.

"We'll take him from here. Based on the witness report, he's got a lot of questions he can answer." The man who spoke wore a navy-blue jacket with large, yellow letters reading FBI.

"This is our town. He's going to the sheriff's department here and then, after he's questioned, he can be moved. Macon and Atlanta want to speak with him as well."

"You had our behavioral unit called in and we came to help. He's been traumatized as much as the girl. We were told that. If you want him to talk, then he talks to us."

"He's that sick fuck's son, and he's covered in fucking blood. He was part of it, not a prisoner." I recognized the country visage of Willacoochee's Sheriff Green. He watched me with cold, blue eyes. I wished they were green. That they were Alana's and she would kiss me again.

"Now who's jumping to conclusions and ignoring the information we've received? This could potentially be the break for twenty years of missing persons all over the state of Georgia. You want to be the ones to mess this up, or get it right?" The FBI agent held me firmly in hand as he waited for a response from the sheriff. I didn't care either way.

"Take him and get the information we need," Green said.

"He goes to the hospital first, and we go from there. Load up."

There was nothing to say or attempt to do as they lifted me to my feet and walked me to a squad car. All I could do was stare at the house—our house, our sanctuary—as they put me inside the car. I kept my eyes on the house, remembering and praying as we drove away until I couldn't see it anymore.

Then, the world changed. My father hadn't let me out of the house much except to help him on the property, so the most of what I'd seen of the world had been on TV. Homeschooled, my father was my entire existence, except on those nights I could sneak away and look at cable channels to look at how other people lived. The only approved shows for me were news channels so I could keep an eye on what was happening in the areas my father took his toys. Now, things were *real*.

I hated the hospital. They handcuffed me to the bed and made sure I was treated, but it smelled funny inside the building. My clothes were cut from my body and I was provided a gown that opened in the back. They took blood, did X-rays and so many tests that I couldn't keep them all in my head. Then they put me on IVs and fed me. They'd said something about me being dehydrated and malnourished. I ate. I always did. But like father's toys in the basement, I was allowed two meals a day and nothing extravagant. Eating large meals was wasteful. Then the FBI agent came back.

His dark-blond hair was cut short but left a little longer on the top, and he had green eyes. Like my Alana. My love. My girl. Where was she? Was she afraid? Looking for me? Were they doing horrible things to her in a fucking cage somewhere? Things only I had the right to do? I wanted her back. I wanted to hold her. Kiss her. Fuck her. Love her.

"I'm Supervisory Special Agent Amery, from the Behavioral Analysis Unit of the FBI. I want to understand what happened to you and the women who disappeared in that house, Jacob."

He knew my name. And he looked like her. Reminded me of my toy. "Where's Alana?"

"I know you're worried about her. She's okay. And as long as you talk to me, you will be okay too."

"Are they hurting her?"

"What do you mean?"

"Hurting her like he did."

"Like your father?"

"Yeah. I don't want them hurting her like that," I said. I knew well enough to not tell him I wanted to hurt her like that. It wasn't his business. That was between Alana and me.

"How did he hurt her?"

"He's dead. He can't hurt anyone anymore."

"The blood on you belonged to your father, didn't it? She was telling the truth that you killed him to get away."

"You've talked to her? Let me see her. Please. Just once, so I know she's okay."

"She's in the hospital, Jacob. She's been through so much, and her body is shutting down. You want her safe, right? Don't want her to go to jail? Put back in a cage? Then you have to talk to me. I'm the difference between her falling on the wrong side of the law or walking away."

For her, my Alana, I'd do anything.

"My father has been killing women longer than I have been alive. The first one I remember was my mother. Josephine Mettlebrook. She was from Athens, Georgia, and he had her for three years before she got pregnant with me. He killed her when I was five. I remember what her blood tasted like if I think back. She held me in her arms when he shot her in the arm for punishment one time. He learned guns caused injuries that put toys out of commission for too long."

"Toys?"

"That's what he called them all, his toys. Women who were whores and needed training. When he tired of them, or when they got pregnant with girls, he got rid of them."

"How did he know they were pregnant with girls before they delivered?"

"Because the same doctor who delivered me treated all the toys. Treated Alana when she lost our Noel."

"Our? Were you the father?"

"No. He would have been my brother. But … it's nicer to think he was mine because I would have loved him."

"I'm going to say the names of ten girls from the last ten years. I want you to say yes if your father was responsible. Can you do that for me?"

For Alana. This was for Alana. If I gave them the truth, they would understand we had to kill him. Had to be free of him. They never had to know how far we went. That was our secret.

So I answered the only way I could. "Yes."

"Maria Vargas."

"Yes."

"Tammy Pullock."

"Yes."

"Sarah Weissman."

"Yes."

"Tasha Byrne."

"Yes."

"Teresa Cole."

"Yes."

"Katherine Yates."

"Yes."

"Celia Whittaker."

"Yes."

"Alana Masters."

I closed my eyes as I whispered, "Yes."

"And did you kill your father, Jacob? With Alana's help, did you cut his throat and dump him into a lye grave?"

That was the story Alana had given. She'd kept our secret too. I was proud of her. So fucking perfect. Always perfect. "Not exactly. After the grave, I sent Alana in to get some rest and cleaned up. Then I cut him to pieces."

They would find the grave and see he was chopped up. There hadn't been enough time for him to decompose. I wouldn't want them to say we lied and then bring charges on us, so I had to take the blame for the rest. Then they'd give Alana back to me.

"Why did you cut your father up, Jacob?"

"Because he held me there. Beat me. Controlled everything. He ripped my soul out on the kitchen table when he took my ass. And because he hurt the one precious thing in my life. Alana. He hurt her, and hurting her made me strong enough to fight him. I hadn't been before. I couldn't. Every time I tried, he knocked me down. But then I found her, and I wanted to save her life more than I wanted to live."

"You did a wonderful thing for her. And people will know you saved her life. She will go back to her family and live her life because of you."

He got up and left the room, taking my confession and the deeds of my father with him. I knew he'd come back. That there would be more questions. A trial. So much. But what made me cry, what broke my heart, was he'd said Alana would go back to her family. That she'd have a normal life.

People like us weren't normal, and they didn't understand. They were ripping her from the man she needed in her life. They didn't know her darkness or understand what we had suffered did to the human soul. All they did was send a monster back to suburbia and task me with finding her.

One day I would because she'd told me I had to find a way to get the girl back if I lost her. And she *would* be mine.

# Chapter Twelve

## Nila

### 8 years later

*Patient: Jonathan Ross*

*Patient shows lack of emotion and no regard whatsoever pertaining to his previous victims. When sent to me, patient had recently been paroled after a seven-year sentence for rape. Warden and Parole Board believed him to be rehabilitated. With the utter lack of remorse he has shown under my care, I believe that to be untrue.*

**M**en are mindless, sadistic drones who only think with their hardons, I thought as I listened to my patient ramble about how his urges had become more prominent lately, playing at the forefront of his brain.

Sent to me eight months earlier—believed to have been rehabilitated in prison but still needing some extra care—Jonathan Ross was now on a tangent about how he longed to taste another victim. For eight months, he'd put up a good charade, but as with every man I came across in this room, I had my ways of getting them to speak. A kind word here, a patient soul, a trusting look. Soon, they were spilling all their secrets and I was taking advantage of it, playing the part for my own needs.

As he spoke, I pictured what I would do to him once I got my hands on him. How I would do to him what he'd done to his victim.

"I slash a smile across her face so that even in death she smiles."

The sick bastard got his rocks off on shit like this, and I had to listen to his confession as I bit back the darkness that threatened to overcome me.

*Play the part, Nila. In order for things to go accordingly, you must play the part. You are Nila Winters, therapist. You have friends. You have family. You are happy.*

So I played the part.

"I want to taste her blood. I want to feel it flowing through my fingers, warm, pungent. I need it."

"Jonathan, we've talked about this before. You spent seven years at Metropolitan Correctional Center. You know why. Do you really want to risk everything you've worked for in the last few months to throw it all away on a fantasy?"

"Miss Winters, you don't understand. The urges are taking over me. The voices in my mind are telling me I have to do this. I *have* to."

He was wrong though. I did understand. More than most people would.

"Jonathan, you don't have to. It's your mind playing tricks on you. You've worked so hard to stay on the correct path since your release. I would hate to see you lose sight of that."

"I know, Miss Winters."

"Our time is up for today, but I want to schedule you again for this Wednesday so we can get control of these urges before you act on them."

"Okay. Thank you."

Crossing one leg over the other, my black Calvin Klein dress stretched along my thigh as I updated my patient notes. I knew Vanessa, my receptionist, would soon be sending in my final patient before my day was finished. Day in and day out, I had to hear people spill their confessions. And each one of them would always tell me the same: I didn't understand.

*But I did.*

Once upon a time, I was Alana Masters. I was a girl who had a bright future, a beautiful smile, and a family. Then, I was Alana. Slave. Prisoner. Victim. Girlfriend to Master's son. Once I escaped the clutches of my captor, I was free. And after the nightmare of the trial was over, I changed my name and moved to get away from my past, from the weight of it. I started over as Nila Winters, but the darkness from that nightmare never left me.

Now, I heard patients open their mouths and tell me their dirty desires, the secrets they were ashamed to have. I had to hear in graphic detail what they did to victims or what they would like to do. And I had to do it all while pretending nothing fazed me. That I was the good little therapist doing as I was trained to do.

I was lost in thought, and Vanessa's voice was exasperated by the time I heard it on the intercom.

"Nila, your four o'clock is here."

"Send him in."

Pasting a smile on my face, I rose to greet my newest client before settling in once more to hear all about the darkness rising in him.

*Samuel Edwards, I can't wait to hear your confessions.*

Locking up, I headed to my car. The beautiful, red Mazda MX-5 Miata was a gem. I slid onto the cool, leather seats and started the engine. It purred like a dream. I thought about Jonathan and his confession earlier in my office. Something will have to be done about him. I was smiling as I made my way to Alejandro's Restaurant to meet some acquaintances for dinner.

I always had to think of appearances.

Emma Lane was a wedding planner. Sweet but naïve, Emma was a firm believer in love and romance despite being left at the altar four years earlier. Stupid girl.

Milly Roberts was a designer, a successful one at that. She designed clothes in high school and went on to open her own boutique after college. Her business was booming. Still, she tended to talk too much, and it irritated me.

It was useful, however, to be marginally normal in society. Having women I could meet up with regularly helped, though they weren't ones I called on my days off or hung out with any other time. Typically, these dinners could turn into referrals. But to the outside world, I was coping and developing lasting relationships. I wasn't wallowing in my past and finding it difficult to trust outsiders. After college, I more than understood the psychotherapy of my issues and the standard treatments that would be prescribed. I also knew none of those things would help me. I needed something darker, more twisted, to settle my heart, but those things weren't excepted in society. Most people never understood trauma sometimes damaged one's psyche so much that it fundamentally changed who they were.

I was one of those people.

Arriving at the restaurant, I spotted Emma right away. She looked lovely in a floral sundress, but she always did. A petite brunette, Emma was a classic beauty with starlet looks.

"Where is Mills?"

"Late. As usual."

She was right about that. Milly was horrible about getting anywhere on time. In all the time I'd known her, she never once arrived before Emma or me.

"Sorry. Sorry. I'm here!" Milly came running up beside us. A redhead with the most vibrant green eyes I had ever seen, Mills was eccentric and boasted a big personality. Dressed in a violet silk button-up and black dress pants, she looked absolutely amazing.

"Now that the gang is all here, let's get seated," Emma said.

Once seated, we all ordered our usuals. For me, it was the chef's salad. For Milly, it was always the lemon poppy seed pancakes, while Emma preferred the Reuben.

"Emma, how's the planning for the Waincroft wedding going?"

"Slowly. They each have such different opinions that it's hard to narrow down anything with them. I've had to change the plans three times already."

"Aw, Ems, that sucks," said Milly.

"Yeah, but I'll get through it. I always do."

"Too true. How's work, Nila?"

"Don't ask. Seriously. I had a session with a new client and literally wanted to pull out my hair and bash my head against the wall."

"That good, huh? I don't know how you do it, Nila. I really don't," Emma's voice rang out.

"Some days, neither do I. Mills, what about you?"

"Well … I've been wanting to tell you guys, but I was waiting until I officially knew," started Milly, her voice full of eagerness. "I'm organizing a fashion show for my line. It's a few weeks from now, and I think I may have pulled enough strings to get some talent there to perform while my ladies walk the runway."

"Oh, Mills! That's wonderful," I said.

"That's so great!" Emma added.

It hurt to smile so brightly. Before I could ask another question, our waitress brought our plates and we all went about eating. Forty-five minutes later, food and the last of our coffees gone, we all said goodnight and headed for our respective homes.

Making my way home, I pulled into the drive and shut off the ignition. My house was a fortress. As long as I could get inside, I had a safe haven. I gripped my keys by the pepper spray bottle hanging from them and head to the door.

Unlocking the house, I entered, immediately silenced the alarm system, and turned the lights on. My cat, a black, green-eyed horse named Neko, came slinking up to me. He was my companion. When I had no one else to talk to, he was who I shared my secrets with. The great thing was he couldn't speak back or judge me.

Heading upstairs with Neko in my arms, I came to my bedroom and pushed the door open. After placing him on my bed, I went to my closet and pulled out a pair of black leggings and a black, tight-fitting, long-sleeve shirt before pulling my hair into a bun. Step one to preparing myself was to always dress in black. Less blood showed that way.

Once that task was complete, I layered on my usual eyeliner and red lipstick but made sure they were darker than usual, giving my face a seductively sinister appeal.

With that, I gathered my supplies, including the intel I'd gathered on Jonathan Ross, and headed out into the night.

*Jonathan Ross and his "urges" wouldn't know what hit him once I was finished.*

Jonathan lived in a modest two-bedroom home. Before his sentencing, he was a husband and father. Once his wife knew what he'd done, he was left with nothing. After the death of his father, he received enough to attempt to start over, hoping to win back his family. Once he was free, he was slapped with a restraining order so he wouldn't be able to go near his ex-wife or daughter.

He was the perfect target.

Waiting for him to get home from work, I bided my time patiently, preparing myself for what was to come.

When headlights shone through my car windows, I knew it was time. Slinking through the dead of night, I came up behind him, playing the same trick my captor had used when kidnapping me: chloroform to the face. With my small stature, though, I needed to adjust accordingly. Once Jonathan was down, I looked around to see if anyone saw and ran back across the street to retrieve my car. On nights like this, I didn't use my everyday car, not wanting it to stand out. Instead, I drove a nondescript, black Ford with license plates that could not be traced to me but to several shell corporations as a company vehicle.

Once in the drive, I opened my rear drivers-side door and dragged his body to my car. Getting him in the backseat proved to be a difficult task but something I had become accustomed to in the last few years. Making sure to handcuff him so he couldn't jump out of the car if he woke, I looked him over.

*We've got him now!* my inner darkness crowed.

In the driver's seat, I made one last attempt at surveying my surroundings. I always made sure there weren't any witnesses.

Years ago, I was taken by a monster who became my Master. Where once I was a girl who'd loved life and love, I became a slave—first to my Master, then to the darkness. I had learned what real nightmares were made of since the abduction. They weren't things like the boogeyman that parents told children about to get them to behave. They were monsters disguised as men who preyed on young girls, stealing their innocence like a thief, leaving only blood and pain in their wake. A slave to the inner darkness captivity left behind, I killed the boogeymen.

I was once a delicate doll made of porcelain skin, childhood innocence, and sugary sweetness. I had a boyfriend I thought loved me. Ryan had moved on by the time I'd gotten back to him, and my ordeal made it difficult for him to see me as anything other than a victim. My skin now contained an array of scars from when I was weak, a powerful reminder never to be that girl again. I was dark and dangerous now. You hear about monsters every day, but I was the real threat, the real monster. I was your neighbor, I was your friend. I lived in your community, I counseled you. And late at night, when you thought you were safe and nestled snug in your beds, I hunted you. I preyed on you and your weakness.

*Men of evil, men of darkness, I come for you so you can never hurt someone like me again.*

Letting out a malicious laugh, I drove off into the night, ready for the fun to begin.

# Chapter Thirteen

## Jacob

S he thought there was no one watching. In truth, if I hadn't been on the street, she would have been right. But I spent my nights looking for men like my father. Punishing those who hurt children like Alana and I had been. Ending their fucking existence because they destroyed innocence that could never be recovered. I didn't regret killing them. She'd been finding her own way to deal with the past we'd gone through together. The girl who'd haunted me for years while I was in the juvenile detention center I'd been remanded to for psych evaluation—because chopping that fucking prick to bits had been a bit too much—erased evil too.

Still, Alana, *my* Alana, was so close and yet so far.

"I told you we'd find her, Noel, didn't I?"

Noel didn't answer, but then again, I didn't expect him to. I talked to him because that was the only piece of her that was real anymore. She parked her car on the side of the road and waited. What was she doing? Was this her home? A stroke of luck was all that had put me on her path. A moment of divine intervention said it was time to get the hell out of Texas, following the clues about the girl who'd once been known as Alana Masters. A few deaths and a couple of states later, I came across a newspaper article about a prominent therapist who handled some of the worst cases of male sexual sadism and inmate intervention. When she wasn't doing that, she was donating her time to the lower-rent populace around the Chicago area. With no picture, I wasn't sure it was her, and I hadn't given a shit about her philanthropist side work. No, what got me was the fact she refused to be pictured because, for all the men she helped, there were some she couldn't.

It was enough.

Alana had been careful, disappearing under another name shortly after the trial. Locked up, I hadn't had the chance to follow her or look into what she was doing. But I was here now. Watching her, holding out until it was the perfect time to take her.

But what was she doing? If this was home, she should have gotten out of the car. I slipped further into the darkness, having already disconnected the flood lamps in a driveway. The shady place, along with my dark clothing and black cap, hid me well. When the headlights from a car came up the street and she sank into her car seat, I paid closer attention.

*She's stalking.*

She was smooth and quiet when she got out of her car and darted around a corner to get ready. And then she did something that sent my heart fluttering as much as it pissed me the fuck off. She used my dad's skills, sneaking up behind her quarry and covering his mouth and nose with a cloth. I knew it had chloroform on it without even having to smell it. Her mark dropped quickly, barely able to give a fight, and she rested him on the ground. Her gaze scanning the road, she left him there and went back for her car. Smart, so fucking smart. She pulled her vehicle into his driveway, then she used the car to shield her as she pulled him into it.

She'd done this before. She moved like a well-oiled machine, and I was proud of her. I could respect another hunter. I'd come across a few in my travels, and though I gave them a wide berth to stop any pissing contests, I gave credit where credit was due. She picked a time late at night when porch lights were off, no one was moving, and things were silent. The little neighborhood wasn't the best, but it was quiet. People here probably didn't get into each other's business, and that helped her.

Pride only helped her so much. Because what the *fuck* was she doing kidnapping a man? If she slit his throat where he stood, or even if she shot him point blank and made a speedy getaway, things would have been different. But she took him, and she'd learned what to do with a taken soul from dear ol' Pops.

The bastard she took deserved to die for having the pleasure of her touching him. And, oh, the punishments I'd give her for doing some sick shit with someone else. She was mine. Had been mine for fucking a decade. We were denied eight years because other people didn't understand love like ours, and I wouldn't be denied anymore.

*After* I found out what about this man made her tick.

As she drove away, I fought the need to follow her and headed to the man's house. It didn't take long to circle around the back and find my way in. I didn't often break and enter, but sometimes it was useful. I scanned for any signs of a home alarm system and saw wires from the side of the house leading to a small box near the ground. After a couple of well-placed cuts with my knife, I made it through the main alarm. With that taken care of, the lockpick kit I had got me in his back door.

"Let's see who you are, buddy boy, to have my girl want to kill you. You're going to die anyway, but it'd be nice to know how badly I need to punish her."

The back door opened into a laundry room. No fun places to hide trophies there. After a short hallway, I came into the kitchen. My stomach knotted, but I ignored it.

"I hate fucking kitchens. I really do. Eating out is the way to go, boy-o. If having a kitchen would be an awesome enough reason to kill the entire population, that would be reason enough for me to go on a spree. But let's see if you're a Dahmer anyway."

A quick check into the fridge and freezer told me he wasn't keeping body parts in there. So, unless he had a garage freezer chock-full of lady and boy bits, he wasn't a cannibal. Next room, off to the right of the kitchen, was a parlor living room. No shelving with pickled phallic symbols or nipples.

"Oh, he's fucking boring. At least give me something fun to destroy."

There was a door to the left which opened into a barely furnished bathroom. The asshole had no vision. Just none. A few steps away was the main hall leading to the front door. On either side of the hall were two doors facing each other.

"Eeny, meeny, miny, moe. Catch a killer by his throat. If he hollers, let him choke. Eeny, meeny, miny, moe. And the one on the right is the winner."

Not that it really mattered; it was basically a storage unit full of boxes. A quick perusal of them showed kids clothes, family pictures, and winter clothes. Nothing out of the ordinary. Except …

"Wait, these are all Latino women in these pictures. And not the right angle. Hold on." I looked back over the stuff, realizing the shots were all from outside of the home or on the street. And the main focus of the pictures was the mothers.

"So the clothes and shit are a way to cover this up. Guess you had a family at some point. Worthless fuck."

Stalkers were low on the totem pole for me. All that looking from the outside in and they never enjoyed any sort of fun. I couldn't exactly figure out what about this guy would get Alana up in arms. She'd seen quite a bit worse in her time; stalking shouldn't have even registered. As I dug further into the boxes, at the bottom of one, I found a fire safe that was locked tight.

"Bingo!"

I pulled it onto my lap and took out my kit once more. I was rusty, so it took a few minutes, but it wasn't too long before I had it wide open and was pawing through all his little pretties. Panties. That's what he kept. Thongs, G-string, straight Granny-style, all with the crotch covered in blood. So a rapist then, and he liked to press the cloth into his victims' blood when he was done. That would have sparked a trigger with my girl for sure. Something was nagging, though, about the women.

"Is that all you do?" Backtracking, I found another in one of the boxes I'd already checked. Then I threw it across the room and decided maybe I'd come back later and burn this entire place down.

"You pedo fucking bastard."

I killed, sure. I tortured when I needed to. And every one of the sick fucks I'd sent to their demise had touched kids. I'd have helped Alana bury this bastard into the ground after I finished having a long session destroying his spirit. Pedos got the worst treatment, and I did the world a great service wiping them off the face of the planet.

"I won't punish her for you, but she should have waited for me. We could have shared it. I would have made sure you hurt, and we could have shared it like we did before. But, for now, I'll give her some time. She isn't ready to see me yet, and I need to look into her more. Where she is, where her killing space is. She could have offed you in the house, but she didn't. That means she has a place to go, and she's using the skills my father used against her."

Me? I killed them in their own killing fields. Ultimate gratification. I took away the one place that belonged to them, where they were powerful. I made sure they had all the fear and distress they made their victims go through. Complete anger, then punishment. That was my gift to Alana, to myself. And I thought that maybe she'd see the pattern and know it was me, but she never did. So I had to go searching for her. I needed to see how far she was going with her marks.

"Fuck, I should have followed her, Noel. I should have."

Noel was still quiet, and I shook my head. So be it. I'd have to start with what I knew. If she tracked and stole them like Dad used to, she had a location to take them. Maybe not her own home, because she was a prominent figure in the community, but somewhere. I'd have to go to an internet cafe and look up some abandoned places and see what came up. She'd need space and privacy and distance to ensure no one came or went. Or at least somewhere she could tell they were coming and could get out before they caught her.

That's what Father would have done and how I would keep her when the time came.

Tomorrow would be soon enough. My entire M.O. was attacking killers in their own places of work, so finding her would be a matter of understanding how she ticked, and I knew that. I'd have fun for the moment. I went through the rapist's home, breaking and knocking things over. By the time I was finished, it looked like he had been robbed. I made sure to put the silver and some choice pieces of jewelry in a bag before laying out his pretty trophies with the pictures of the women. The cops could thank me if they came here looking for him.

"Heh, maybe they'll think the robbery turned into a vigilante killing after looking at this shit."

With that done, I grabbed the bag of stuff and ran out of the back of the house. Around the back, I got to my car. It made me smile I was using a similar nondescript car as Alana was. I wondered if she changed out the plates like I did and had the VIN replaced so it came back as a clean vehicle instead of a stolen one. It made it much easier for me to keep the same vehicle across state lines. But then again, her kill car may only come out of the shop when she was ready to take someone, and it stayed where she killed them when it wasn't in use.

Something to think about. I'd make sure I looked into warehouses as well, just in case.

Shit, this was the happiest I'd been in a while. I'd found her, and she was as dark and twisted as I'd always hoped. Fuck, it was going to be magical. Right after I kicked the shit out of her for putting herself in danger and thinking that touching other men was allowed when I wasn't with her.

But I'd deal with that when I got my hands on her.

# Chapter Fourteen

## Nila

*Patient exhibits fear upon waking. He's vulgar and unsure of where he stands in this place, leading to him acting out. It will only be a matter of time before he reaches the pleading stage.*

The problem with capturing was waiting for the drugs to wear off. Biding my time filing my nails, I mentally prepared myself for what was to come. Each patient, each man across my slab, was a battle to me—a war that had raged within me since I was eighteen. An uncontrollable hunger only fulfilled by blood. Never the blood of innocence though. Oh no. My prey was always the weakest form of men—the rapists, the child molesters, the abusers. I took pride in seeing them come apart at my hands. Once men, they were reduced to the sniveling, pathetic wastes of space they truly were. Begging, pleading for redemption, to be spared. Up until the last minute, they truly believed they were worth being saved. That after months of hearing their awful, sinful confessions, I would allow them to breathe the same air as me, as their victims.

He stirred as I headed his way, a strut in my walk as my hips swayed. This was my element. This was where I belonged. Where I once was light, the darkness had gripped me and dragged me so far in, it was now a part of me. As my captive struggled against the bonds that left him with no room to move, I caught his attention.

"There, there, sweetheart," I started. "You don't want to do that."

As my voice registered with him, I came into view, making sure he knew exactly who had taken him. The why would come soon enough, but for now, I savored his recognition of me.

*Come into my web, said the spider to the fly.*

Where once Jonathan Ross was the spider, preying on those weaker than him, the tables were turned and now I was the spider. I was the one in control. Jonathan was weak.

Loosening the gag around his mouth, it gave way and the words spilled over his lips.

"Miss Winters? How could you do this, you fucking bitch! What the hell do you want from me?"

"Ah, ah, ah, Mr. Ross. Remember who's in charge here. I'm the therapist. You're the patient. Same rules apply, despite the surroundings."

With that said, he finally glanced around the room. Not much to look at, the abandoned warehouse did its job. It was quiet with its soundproof walls, in an abandoned industrial district, and far enough from my home that no one could easily trace it to me. These deeds done in the dark of night had no bearing on my daytime life, and I made sure to keep them separate, wanting no hint of the evil lurking within me visible. I wasn't going to let anyone dissect me under a microscope, wondering what made me tick.

In the middle of the warehouse, I had a medical table, reminiscent of the one that I was once intimately familiar with, one similar to where I took my first life. Jonathan looked so weak, so pathetic, strapped down and glaring. As if there were something he could do. He was nothing.

"Mr. Ross, I've spent the last eight months listening to your words … but not the truth. We're here because you deserve to pay for your crimes. The Parole Board may have thought you deserved to be free, but I don't. I've watched the darkness in your eyes. I've bided my time, and today you finally let out a piece. By the time I'm done with you, you'll be confessing to everything. Think of me as your priest. Confess your sins to me."

"You can't do this! Someone will find you. They'll be looking for me."

"Will they? You have nothing, Mr. Ross. A dead-end job, no family, no friends. No one will be looking for you, and by the time they do, you will be long gone, and I'll be back in my office treating another patient. You see, Mr. Ross, I have a reputation to keep up. Nothing traces back to me. *Nothing.*"

For the first time since we began this pointless conversation, realization washed over him and the fear began to seep into his bones. Good. He should be scared. The wimp didn't know what he was getting into.

Heading over to my work table, I looked through my toys. Usually, a punishment was already planned ahead of time, but Jonathan Ross was a special case. He was close to abducting his next girl, if I read between the lines right. That called for a different brand of torture.

Surveying my tools shining against the red cloth, my eyes landed on the perfect tool to start with. Having taken his shirt off earlier, I proceeded to strip off the rest of his clothes. Looking downward, I caught a glimpse of his slight erection. Try as he might to hide it, the situation was making him hot and bothered.

Oh, this was going to be fun.

Grabbing a can and my little friend I'd brought along for the ride, I placed the rat on his stomach and the metal can over it. Jonathan fought to get free.

"You stupid fucking bitch. You'll pay for this! Do you hear me? You will pay!"

"Surely, darling, I'll burn in Hell, but you'll be there far before me."

Holding the can down with one hand, I lit the edge of a tightly bound bunch of herbs and slid it into a pocket inside the can before sealing the top again. I started my interrogation as the smoke curled around the trapped rat. I wondered when he'd start trying to eat his way out. Jonathan's screams filled the warehouse, and the pain that radiated from his face was intoxicating.

"What were you planning to do?" I questioned over his wailing screams of pain.

Another scream, but no response came from him.

"What were you planning to do?" I repeated.

"I-I … was going to take her! I was going to take her, all right?"

"Take who?"

"Some girl."

"Elaborate."

"No. That's all you're getting from me."

I wasn't surprised he was starting to fight back. Jonathan was a man who prided himself on being in control. I was taking his control from him. It was worse because I was a woman, someone he thought was lower than him. It was only a matter of time before he began to fight. They all usually did, but they lost their fighting spirit pretty quickly. Something told me Jonathan, having experienced both lust and rage at the same time, would be a bit harder to break.

That was okay though. I had all the time in the world. I much preferred being able to take my time and savor it. I wrapped a tie-down around the can on his stomach to hold it in place. Pulling plastic gloves over my hands, I poured lubricant on my fingers. Spreading Jonathan's legs, I sodomized him with my fingers as he yelled.

"What the fuck are you doing, you crazy bitch?"

"How do you think that girl felt, huh? What do you think she went through when you pried her legs open and raped her? You *forced* her to have sex. You took something from her. How is it to have your legs pried open and something forced inside of you? How much of a *man* are you now?"

Tears in his eyes, he shook his head.

Pulling my fingers from him, I grabbed an anal plug from the tray.

"I want you to think of her," I said right before shoving the plug in. "Think of poor, sweet Melissa Hankins. Melissa was a college student. A lacrosse player. You raped her, and now she has to live with the memory every day. She dropped out of college, you know? She was a bright star, but now she shoots heroin to get rid of the memory of your teeny, tiny shit violating her."

I always made sure to do my homework when it came to my kills. They needed to go through every torture their victims did. Melissa reminded me a lot of me—innocent and sweet before becoming lost in darkness. She hid in her demons. Me? I embraced mine with arms wide open. A killer. A monster. Dangerous.

Leaving Jonathan to sweat a bit, I walked to the doorway in the far corner and into the small kitchenette area filled with a '70s-style refrigerator and sink. When I bought the warehouse a few years back, I didn't change anything. There was no need. This was the last stop for these men. No reason to make it homey.

If I were going to sufficiently torture Jonathan, I needed to keep him hydrated. I wanted him scared for his life and in absolute agony. I wanted to avenge Melissa. I wanted to take him, break him. Hear his confessions and absolve his sins with a swipe of my knife. But until he confessed, the killing blow would have to wait. In the meantime, though, torture was sweet. His screams were beautiful madness.

I wanted to feast on his fear. I wanted to bathe in his pain. The darkness was such a captivating ride, like a roller coaster I never wanted to get off of. Full of thrills, speed, and ups and downs, the darkness was magnificent in all its glory.

Filling a glass with water, I headed back out to the main area in time to see Jonathan leaning his head over the side of the table, throwing up. I knew it was only a matter of time before the shock and pain overcame him. Watching them shatter was always the best part, and this was only the beginning.

"Here." I thrust the glass toward his mouth, waiting for him to sip from it, which he did greedily. The aftertaste of throwing up was never good, and he was eager to wash it away.

He licked his lips, eyes darting back and forth nervously. "Why are you doing this to me?"

"Men like you are the reason I'm the way that I am. You did this to me, all of you did, with your sick fascinations and

123

obsessions. The way women's screams get you off. Do you think I asked for this? That I wanted this? I didn't! I wanted to be normal, but a man like you destroyed that. Like you destroyed Melissa."

"I'm not the one who hurt you though."

"No, but I'm not going to let you hurt someone else."

With that said, he shut his mouth, giving me a minute to pause and reflect on the past.

> *It had been two months since I was freed and reunited with my family, but everything was different. I was no longer the same, and my family couldn't understand it. They thought I should be happy to be home, and I was, but a piece of me was damaged in a way I couldn't put into words.*
>
> *I should have been happy to be back in my bed at night, but instead, I was as much a prisoner there as I was in my cage.*
>
> *Every time I closed my eyes, I pictured the boy with the sad, tormented eyes. His dad had done a number on him too. I was sorry for leaving him the way I did, especially to clean up my mess. Each night my heart cried out to him, and I clawed at my bedspread to hold myself from racing to find him. My parents wouldn't tell me what happened to him, but I knew by the way they clammed up when I asked, it was nothing good.*
>
> *Another night, another nightmare. I woke up to screaming, but this time it was the neighbor's dog that insisted on howling all hours of the night. I must have sleepwalked here, my bare feet curled against the cold—here where my hands were wrapped around his neck. I was fighting the two sides of myself: one who wanted to drop the poor old scraggly mutt and run back to bed and forget this happened, and another who wanted to squeeze the life out of the annoying, yapping thing.*
>
> *With one loud bark, I knew I would be discovered, so I began squeezing, tightening my grip until the last of its*

*life died out. Letting his body fall to a heaping pile at my feet, I heard the darkness call to me for the first time.*

*This. This is what you need. Embrace the darkness.*

I never killed another animal besides that damn dog. Animals weren't what satisfied my craving for blood. Only men. The worst of the worst. The predators. From that day, I started to prepare myself. I started to train myself to be wiser, stronger. This may have been a man's world, but now I was living in it. I could be as good as them. If I was going to give myself over to the darkness completely, I needed to be smart about it. It was all a game, a mental strategy. The ultimate goal was to never be caught. I'd survived time in one cage, and I would never go back there again. I would die first.

Jonathan was half out of it, his head lolling to the side. I probably wouldn't get much more from him tonight. Leaving him to rest, I took the rat off his stomach and began plotting. I couldn't wait to bring him to the brink, hearing the confessions spill across his lips like a floodgate crashing down. I'd go home for now.

*Tomorrow, your secrets are mine to take.*

There were two reactions to rape, from a psychological standpoint, based on the perceptions of men and their reactions. One, the Madonna Complex, where the victim refuses to have sexual relations and may even find more comfort with the opposite sex of the one who'd hurt them. Two, the Whore Complex, where they sleep with anyone, be it because they need that sort of validation or because a part of them craved what had been done. Like a light switch that was never turned back off.

I suffered from the Whore Complex, with a fixation on those who represented my darkness.

Naked in bed, I laid with my legs spread, fantasizing about Jonathan on my table. His screams stirred my blood, desire dampening my panties. As all my fantasies did, it slowly gave way to Jacob.

His eyes had stayed with me all these years. The connection between us hummed through the air, but I was too scared of what that meant for me. If I thought I could ever be innocent, I was wrong. The darkness had already seeped into my soul, and I could never truly be free of it.

Now, thinking of his eyes boring into me, there was no shame as I spread my legs wider and inserted by vibrator. Immediately, my body clenched, pleasure thrumming through my core. I was a mess between the vibrations working my body into a frenzy and the thought of Jacob's classically handsome face, sharp cheekbones, brown eyes, and the blood … Oh yes, the blood on his face as he stood there. My savior.

I knew it was sick and wrong, but the rush I got from thinking of him, blood-splattered and free, made my toes curl. And when our last kiss, came to the forefront of my brain, my orgasm washed over me, leaving me basking in pleasure.

For eight years I got off to the memory of Jacob. The only way I could come was to picture him.

With an exhale, I dropped the vibrator to the side of the bed and slid down into my silk sheets. Tomorrow couldn't come soon enough.

# Chapter Fifteen

## Jacob

People irritated me. Not really because they were there but because they fucking existed in tiny fucking worlds where how to pay a bill was the biggest worry they had. Could be that my father's wealth had been neatly stashed away, and I had taken the lot of it, so I didn't give a shit about a bill. I could pay for what I wanted, when I wanted, and made sure none of it led back to me.

At least that bastard I called a father was good for that.

I stomached the people for a while so I could search the local listings for abandoned properties. But before that, I needed to find out where the good doctor lived. Wasn't as easy as I thought it would be. There were no listings for her living address on any public sites, so I hacked a few places—like the employee section of her business website. A few more keystrokes and I had her home address in Rockford. My girl lived about an hour and forty-five minutes from where she worked. It was crazy, but that meant she was nice and far away from her killing zone. We'd revisit that later.

Alana was smart, obviously. The way she'd snatched that guy said she had done this a few times. That was hot as hell. And it also meant she took some of what she'd learned at the hand of dear old Dad to keep things running smoothly. There was a caveat, however. She was a prominent figure in the Chicago community and couldn't risk doing the dirty deeds from her own home. Which left me to look at abandoned places for sale. She'd have purchased hers—to make sure a buyer couldn't come through at any time—and would have made sure it couldn't be linked back to her.

Easiest way to narrow it down? Look for places for sale *near* locations that looked empty but weren't for sale. It took about fifteen minutes, but I compiled a good list and printed it out. A few clicks and the browser history was wiped. That wouldn't be good enough, of course, so I took the extra step. Watching to make sure no one was being fucking nosy, I plugged in my USB and booted the ISO image of the program I had on it. After a bit of a wait, and the hard drive was wiped. Someone was going to have the very hard job of reformatting and installing everything on the computer. But erased was much different than deleted, and I didn't want anyone trailing my searches to me or Alana. I powered down the computer, put my sunglasses on, and walked out with a whistle. A short walk to my car parked over a couple of blocks and I was heading out to the first abandoned property on my list.

I relaxed on the drive, enjoying the sights, knowing I was getting closer to Alana. Every mile I passed was a little more distance I closed between us. Thinking maybe I should check on her alibi, I got out my phone and dialed her office.

"You've reached the offices of Winters, Miller, and Sui. How can I help you today?"

Winters, the name she was going by now—Nila Winters. It was sexy, but I liked that I knew the real her. That I knew a part of her many didn't know. Like it was a secret between us.

"Yes, I'd like to make an appointment with Ms. Winters, if I could. She was recommended to me by another patient."

"We'd be happy to assist you. Can I have your name and know if you are a part of an indigent program, have health insurance, or private pay?"

"Jonas Gilden and private pay, thank you."

"Well, Mr. Gilden, Ms. Winters will be out of the office for a conference, but she will be returning Monday. Can we schedule you in at that time?"

"I'd like that. First thing in the morning, please."

"No problem. She has a 9 a.m. open."

"That's perfect."

"Please arrive thirty minutes early to your first appointment in order to fill out paperwork and file your payment options. The first visit is a consultation, which is free. At that point, Ms. Winters will design the program that works best for you."

"I appreciate it, see you then."

"Have a great day, Mr. Gilden."

I didn't answer as I hung up. It was Wednesday. She'd given herself enough time off for the snatch of her victim. A conference was easy to mark as an alibi, especially if she traveled during the day and visited said conference to make sure others saw her. That also gave me—if I found her today—four days of alone time with her.

*Perfect.*

Twelve fucking locations. That's how many places I'd gone in and out of with no fucking luck. The sun was setting, all was quiet, and I was nowhere near close to finding my target. Alana was better than I thought she was, and I had to say it gave me a hard-on for her in ways I couldn't describe. Most of the locations I looked over weren't too far from the water, an easy dump site if I ever saw one. Things were nearly inaccessible. I had to leave my vehicle and go on foot to get to some locations. It made for an exhausting search and an even more irritating, tiring time of climbing in and out of boarded-over windows. She had to have somewhere easier to get into. No way she'd do all of this climbing and shuffling around with an unconscious man.

I was missing something, and I needed to find it quickly. I wasn't going to take time away from our reunion looking for a needle in a haystack. So instead of driving around some more, I looked back over my list of property photos.

"Come on, Alana, show me where you are." There were a few closer to the water, but they might be too accessible. Hmm.

"Noel? I've got to find Mommy. She's all out here by herself, having naughty time with some douche, and we want her back, don't we? Where could she be?"

Noel didn't answer. He never answered. Never got a chance to. I wasn't mad at Alana for that, and I know he wasn't either. The shit he would have gone through if he'd come into that house would have turned both our stomachs. But for both of us, so he wasn't forgotten, so he knew he was loved, I carried him with me. I remembered him and his momma. The woman who should have been mine because she belonged to me. And I would always remember him. The small child who'd died so she and I could both gain the strength to fight back.

"Help me find her, buddy," I whispered.

I stared at the pictures hard, looking for a clue, something that would stand out. There it was. In a subtle, crazy fucking way. Noel had helped me because I remembered Dad, remembered the home I was taken from. The warehouse that was about half a block from the water, deep into the center of several buildings, was shaped like dad's old house. A vacant unit to one side looked like the barn, and an open field, that may have been a parking lot at one time, looked like where I'd buried so many toys—and that asshole.

"That's where you are."

It took less time to get back to my ride and jump in than it had taken to get to the information I needed. Another half hour of slow and careful maneuvering to get in deeper. Under a slim overpass was a good place to hide the car, especially once it was covered with the tarp from the trunk. I snuck around the right side of the barn-shaped building and looked for a quiet entrance to Alana's killing place. I climbed up a side chute until I reached a small opening I had to force my shoulders through.

"Fuck," I grunted as wood caught my shoulder, but I made it. The interior was pitch-black until my eyes adjusted. Then I was heading across the tall walkway overhead and looking for a way down to the ground level. I found the nondescript car Alana drove and knew I was in the right place. She was able to drive it right in.

*Good girl.*

Then I heard it—the sweet sound of screams.

I wasn't as worried about staying quiet anymore. Alana's mark was hurting, and I needed to see this. See her in action. Following that sweet music, I headed down further until the screams were loud enough to echo in the halls. The cold darkness swallowed me, wrapped me in those sounds, and I stopped. My chest tightened, and I gasped. My shoulder hit the wall before I knew it, and I was falling to the ground.

*Fuck, not now. Not fucking now.*

But I couldn't stop it. The memories from the darkness were breaking up and out of my soul. Washing over the fucking worthless little boy. A murderer's son who deserved every fucking thing he got.

*"How many girls did you help your dad kill?" Dennis hollered at me. His red face was pressed against mine, his big body crowding me into the wall behind me. I wanted to rip his head off. Swallow his blood. Twist his arm until it popped off and then beat him with it. Anything to get him away from me.*

*"I didn't kill nobody!"*

*"Liar. I know you did. That girl said you cut your dad into pieces. Hacked him all up with a saw and then ate pieces of him."*

*They came up with new versions of how my father died at my hands every time someone told the story. It was the worse form of the telephone game, and there was nothing I could do about it.*

*"I didn't. And you better leave me the fuck alone before I hurt you."*

*"What, you going to kill me too?"*

*"Or me?"*

*I groaned, curling against the wall. Eddison was here, and he always was worse than Dennis. Brothers who were taken out of a drunk father's home and put into the system for beating the shit out of him and not stopping. They were supposed to keep records confidential here, but everyone learned each other's secrets eventually. The brothers could read me, sense what I was, but I couldn't be that guy. Not without Alana. Not without my fucked-up little compass who gave direction to my life.*

*I was a fucking monster, but Alana was the darkness from which I was born.*

*"If I have to," I said with bravado, but I knew it was a lie. And so did they. Losing her had taken something out of me.*

*"Hurry up, before Ms. Becket comes back and messes things up," Dennis said.*

*"He won't make a sound, will you, Jacob?"*

*I whimpered, but it didn't matter. Eddison swung, and I could have sworn my jaw was hanging. Pain blossomed into the joint where my jaw was hinged, and it locked. My cry was warped, like a wounded animal. Dennis joined the fray, punching me in the stomach. Air rushed out of me, and then I was coughing, fighting to hold down the bile.*

*I didn't beg though. I wouldn't fucking beg. Instead, I fought back. Knowing it wasn't going to do anything. Knowing I wasn't going to win. But I couldn't die here. Not like this. Not until I found Alana. So I bit and scratched, punched until my knuckles ached, and kicked until they gripped my ankles and flipped me over. I fought until they pounded my head against the ground.*

*And then I couldn't' fight anymore because darkness swallowed me.*

*It wasn't until the morning I found I was bleeding from the inside too. Just like with Dad.*

I forced myself to my feet, pushed through. I hated dark fucking hallways. They made me ill. It was why I left those molesters' bodies in those nasty fucking alleys and hallways when I could. To wipe away my fear. To break those memories. But they were still here, haunting me. And I wanted to punish Alana all the more for bringing them back. This time, when I stepped forward, I was more than ready to punish her than to celebrate our coming back together.

But maybe, for ruined souls like us, that was the same thing.

When I reached a heavy door, I opened it as quietly as I could before slipping through a crack. Inside, I let my eyes adjust again to the darker area. Alana had her back to me, dressed in nothing but black tights and a black bra. Her victim was strapped to a medical table and bleeding all over the place. I could see why when I spied the barbed whip dripping bright-red blood in her hand. Fear and despair coated the air thickly, and it tasted good.

In those moments, the anxiety and terror faded until there was nothing left but black lust, anger, and the need for retribution crawling through my veins. I smiled— Cheshire smile that made my cheeks ache. I wondered if her victim could see me, would I look like some dark, avenging demon feasting on his pain? Then, as Alana raised her hand, making the whip swish wetly, I didn't give a shit about him. All I cared about was her.

"I'm your sin eater, Jonathan. The absolver of your black soul. Give unto me your secrets, and I'll set you free. Confess."

She swung wide and hard. The tail of the whip snapped, cracking through the air, and sliced through Jonathan's chest. He screamed long and loud, his voice cracking at the end.

"Please! I have nothing else to tell you."

"Oh, but you do. Tell me about the girl you were going to take. What were you going to do to her? How long did you watch her? Did you fantasize what it would be like to hold her hostage and destroy her? Did you think this one would be the one you'd finally kill?"

"No. No, I swear."

"Yes, you did, Jonathan. You want to know why? Because I already know exactly how I am going to kill you. The smell of it. The taste. How my heart will pound. How my mind will clear. And how I'll come so hard when I'm done I'll be reborn. Confess, Jonathan. From one monster to a worse one."

Fuck, this girl was my soulmate. Demented, despicable, and violent.

# Chapter Sixteen

## Nila

**M**y blood pulsed. The rush of excitement came over me as Jonathan's screams rang out through the empty warehouse. The stench of urine radiated from his body where he'd pissed himself in fear as the first strike of the barbed whip lashed at him. The crimson blood now coating his chest was a beautiful sight.

"Are you ready to confess yet, Jonathan?"

"Never!"

I had to hand it to him, even with the brutality of my punishment, he still bit his tongue. I knew it was only a matter of time before the secrets came flooding through his sinful mouth.

"Jonathan, Jonathan, Jonathan … Give up already. Haven't you learned this can only get worse from here on out? Each time you deny me what I want, you make it harder on yourself."

With another strike of the whip, Jonathan howled.

"Your screams bring me such joy, Jonathan. But what would really make me happy is hearing your sins rolling over your tongue, spilling out from the dark crevices of your black soul."

Covered in blood, Jonathan looked much more handsome. There was just something about the crimson liquid. The knowledge of how powerful blood truly was. It was the center of life, keeping the heart pumping. With one slice of a blade here or a gunshot wound there, you could watch the life flow out of a person—the sweet relief of death.

Contemplating the tools of my trade and wondering what sort of pain I should inflict on him, I cast my eyes around my work table until I came across a wonderful instrument of destruction.

*Ah, perfect.*

Calling out to me from the work table was The Screw. Only used once before, it inflicted the most damage and had my previous victim wailing out all his secrets within seconds. As much as I wanted to get right to it, though, I wanted to savor the buildup. Grabbing a hunting knife from the table, I inched it close to Jonathan's skin, moving the blade up and down like a slow, sweet caress from a lover. Jonathan's eyes immediately locked onto the sharp, six-inch blade, and he began to tremble.

"Wh-what are you going to do with that?" he croaked, voice hoarse from screaming.

"Shhh. I want to play a game."

"A game?"

"A game. Truth or lie, if you will. If you tell the truth, you'll avoid a nick from my blade. Lie to me? You will feel my rage. Understand?"

No response.

"*Understand?*"

"Y-Yeah."

"Good. First question. What was her name?"

"Who?"

"Don't play stupid. What was the name of the girl you were after?"

"Ellen."

"Ellen who?"

"Ellen Morgan."

Examining his body language, I knew I had finally gotten the truth from him. No signs of stuttering, he made direct eye contact with me. He was bold for someone knowing he would eventually die at my hand.

"Good boy. Why now?"

"Why not? I've been craving some sweet pussy since I was released last year. Something hot and wet to pound my frustrations out on."

Rage built inside me, and I bit my tongue, knowing it was a matter of time before I boiled over and Jonathan was left dead.

"How old is she, Jonathan?"

"Fourteen."

*Fourteen?* The same age his daughter had been when he first went to prison. This information surged through my brain as the picture became clear in my mind. His own flesh and blood. A victim of his sickness.

"Did you ever rape Molly?"

"What? No! Never!"

His breathing had become uneven, his eyes turning to the side, away from me. He was nervous. Sweating. He was *lying*. Running my blade across his ribs and over to his side, I thrust downward.

"Holy shit. Motherfucker! You crazy fucking bitch. I'm going to kill you."

"I warned you that you would pay for lying to me. I may be a crazy fucking bitch, but I'm an honest one. You're pond scum. How could you rape your own daughter?"

"She wanted it! Walking around in those short shorts all the time. Teasing me with her virginity."

"She was *fourteen*!"

"She was a tease!"

Thrusting downward once more, the rage boiled inside me, threatening to foil my plan of torture. Faltering for a second, I came back to myself, staring down at the blood pooling around the hilt of the blade. With a quick movement, I removed the blade and held it up for him to see.

"Beautiful, isn't it? The crimson blood. The very reason we're alive. How much blood do you think you can lose before you're nothing but a decaying corpse for my eyes to feast upon? With one thrust to your heart, you would be dead. No more blood pumping through your veins. No black heart beating with evil. You would be nothing but a corpse. Erased from the world like you never existed. That's the beauty of blood. The pureness of it."

"You're one sick chick, you know that?"

"I wasn't always this way."

"Well, someone sure did a fucking number on you, lady."

"Maybe you've heard of me … Alana Masters. I was once an innocent, happy girl. I had just turned eighteen when I was taken. I had my whole life ahead of me until I was kidnapped, forced to be a slave to a man who was like you. A rapist. He blackened my soul and destroyed me bit by bit until nothing was left but the darkness eating away at my soul."

"I remember. He was twisted like his son."

"Don't talk about Jacob that way!" I snapped.

"What the fuck, you stupid bitch?"

"You're twisted too. Did you ever think of that? You get off on raping teenage girls. Making them suffer. Does it make you feel like a man to have a girl half your size and half your age underneath you?"

"It makes it all the sweeter."

With a well-aimed blow to his sternum, I knocked the damn wind out of him. That bastard. How dare he bring up Jacob! How dare he make me think of him while I was in my killing zone! The anger tore at my insides. Every inch of me was on fire, and I knew in that instant I would make him regret mentioning Jacob.

With a powerful strut over to the workbench, I picked the tool that had captured my attention earlier. The Screw—made for maximum pain when punishing a waste of space like Jonathan Ross.

Making my way back to the table, I brought my head closer to the tip of his manhood. Whereas before Jonathan was semi-erect from the dominance I showed, he was now flaccid. Between the pain and the humiliation, he could no longer get it up. I would have to do something about that.

My head coming closer, I blew soft puffs of breath over the top of the helmet, my nails lightly scraping across his scrotum. Tantalizing and sensual, I used my breath and my touch to bring his desire back to life. I would hate to have to give the bastard an actual moment of pleasure from my mouth, so my hand was all I would offer. When that didn't get the desired effect, I gripped his shaft in hand and worked it. Up, down. Slow, fast. Twist to the hand.

*Ah, there it was.*

Taking The Screw in hand, I started to insert it through his urethra while my other hand stayed firm on his cock. The agony in his screams as the device made its way in slowly, inch by painful inch, made my vengeance even sweeter.

Writhing in pain, his body was covered in sweat, blood, and tears. It was an amazing sight. Jonathan was handsome, but he was even more so when he was wrung out from being tortured at my hand. It was a shame he had to die.

As The Screw reached the end of its journey, I gripped the wings more tightly and made the first twist. Face contorting in pure agony, Jonathan's scream ricocheted from every inch of the warehouse.

"One last chance, Jonathan. Tell me all of it. Confess your sins."

"Okay … Okay. Please, please just stop. Please, I'll tell you everything you want to know." His pain and fear reflected in his voice as his pleading eyes bored into mine, seeking mercy I granted for a moment.

"Tell me and I won't remove it. Removing it will cause so much more pain."

"I fucked Molly. I fucked the little bitch and she loved it. She wanted more. She craved Daddy sliding into her. It was mine. She was mine, all mine, and she loved it. She howled like a fucking bitch in heat trying to claw at me. Fuck. She was so damn tight. Such a sweet, sweet sight she was." He paused and took a deep breath, and then he couldn't stop the words from flowing. They covered me like a shroud of darkness.

"Ellen. Ellen was who I told you about in your office." He took another heavy breath. "But you were too late …"

Another heavy breath.

"But you were late. Too late. I had been tailing her for weeks. Waiting for the perfect moment. I didn't want to go to prison. I tried to stop myself, but I needed it. I needed it! She was alone. It was perfect. I came up behind her and dragged her into the woods by her house. Her sex smelled so sweet. Begging me to lick it. Suck it. But I didn't have the time. It was amazing. I fucked her so hard that I lost myself in her. I was choking the life out of her before I even knew what I was doing. I looked into her eyes in time to see life escape her. And then I couldn't help myself. I needed one taste. Just one. It was so sweet."

This. *This* confession. It was what I'd begged for. What I longed for. But every time I heard another, the lost little girl in me, the one I was before I was taken, curled up inside my mind, crying. The bile crept up my throat, but I refused to show one ounce of weakness. This man had preyed on enough girls. I wasn't his victim; I was the predator in this game. The one who would bring him down at the knees. He was my bitch. With a turn of my hand, I turned the wings of The Screw and kept turning. Turning, turning, turning. I wanted him to feel my rage. My pain. I wanted to make him suffer.

For Molly, his daughter.

For Melissa, his first victim.

For Ellen, raped and murdered by his hand.

For me, the girl who had been torn apart and unleashed into the darkness because of a man like him.

With a final grunt of pain, Jonathan passed out underneath my hand. Between the blood loss and torturous pain, his body couldn't take it anymore and began to shut itself down. I knew I didn't have much time if I wanted him to feel his death.

Giving Jonathan a moment, wanting to surprise him when he least expected it, I entered the kitchen area and poured myself Dom Perignon, my favorite. A good torture session always left me with a craving for a glass of fine Champagne. Toasting myself on a soon-to-be-successful kill, a sensation washed over me, prickling awareness over my skin.

*Someone is out there.*

Impossible. No one knew of my warehouse. I went to great lengths to hide any trace of it, and for all anyone knew, it was still abandoned. Looking around, nothing caught my eye, so I shrugged it off, thinking I was being paranoid now that I was so close to the so-called finish line. With one last sip of my Champagne, I licked my lips and left to get reacquainted with Jonathan before he took his last breath.

"Jonathan. Sweet, sweet Jonathan."

Shaking himself from his stupor, his eyes opened into slits, his gaze meeting mine.

"Wha- what?" he slurred, voice filled with misery.

"Have you confessed it all? Have you given all your sins unto me?"

"Yes … Yes."

"Good. Are you ready to repent?"

"Repent?"

"Don't make me repeat myself, Jonathan."

"S-s-sorry."

"Tell me, Jonathan, are you ready to repent for your sins?"

"Yes."

"Very well. It's time."

"Time?"

"Yes. In order to repent, you must die. The only way those girls can be free from pain, free from your destruction, is for you to die. Melissa is too weak. Not strong enough. Ellen is dead. And Molly? Well … Molly …"

"Wh-what?"

"Molly's locked up. Not in prison though like dear ol' Dad. No, she's locked up in the nuthouse because Daddy was a naughty, naughty boy who liked to touch her. She still has nightmares, you know. She still dreams of Daddy creeping into her bed at night and touching her with his perverted touch. I should know, I'm the one who treated her. Why do you think I requested your case, Mr. Ross?"

It was almost comical the way remorse flew across his face. Too little, too late though. Jonathan Ross may have been tried and sentenced for the rape of Melissa, but he'd never paid for Molly.

"Goodbye, Jonathan."

Plunging my knife into his heart, his life was snuffed out in a flick of an eye.

*May peace be with his victims.*

# Chapter Seventeen

## Jacob

We were sick, twisted fucks. So much like my father, even though we hated him. From him, we learned to enjoy the beauty of death, and that beauty could only be achieved by the destruction of perfection. Jonathan was in his prime. Fresh off a kill. Invincible to the world. It was a perfect time to take him and break him. To snap every part of his psyche, and then, in the end, show him he was nothing. I was on her like a peeping Tom through the slat in her door. Watched her eyes dilate, her body quiver, and her nipples harden.

She was so fucking beautiful.

Covered in black and wearing a dangerous smile, she was my perfect woman. Fashioned by the devil, born of a demon, and tested through the fire, she'd come out made of pure stone and as pervasive as whispers in the dark. And I wanted her so much I could taste it. As my gaze traced her, I released my cock from my pants. It was thick and solid in my hand, swelling at the sight of her.

When she licked her lips, chuckling darkly, I twisted my hand around the end, the motion smooth and hot. Perfect, like her mouth would be. Blood covered her hands as she dropped the tool on her work table. I imagined her palming my balls, the warm stickiness coating me. My free hand found its way to my balls, cupping them. My hands were hers. My pleasure belonged to her.

I pumped my shaft, from base to tip, envisioning her graceful, deadly fingers gripping my length. She twisted her hand, grinning at the liquid leaking from the tip. And then she breathed over me—hot fucking fire—and it shot through me. Nerve endings pulsing with pleasure I turned my head and bit the black leather of my jacket, imagining it was her neck. Somehow, though, her mouth was still on me. Still taunting me with her tongue, her hot little mouth.

Pumping my hips, I stilled my hand so it was like I was fucking her face. Pushing my way, forcing myself between her lips and into her throat. So fucking good. So tight. The death grip I had on my length was better than anything I'd ever had. I couldn't get hard for anyone else. Didn't know what it was like to take a woman to my bed.

I'd saved it all for her.

She'd forgive me for training my cock with my hand. Teaching it to withstand pain. To last longer. To revel in darkness. She'd appreciate that I'd done so much for her. Waited when no one else would have. Proved I was all she ever needed, like I'd already promised her. And it would come soon. I'd have her. Be inside of her. Possess her. That thought was enough. My balls tightened against my palm. Throbbing, muscles clenching, I bit harder into my jacket. Swallowing the moans, I stayed quiet. I was close. Just there.

She pulled a large, square tarp next to her victim on the table before removing his straps. All it took was a push and he fell wetly onto the tarp. The sound. The smell. The vision. All of it pushed me harder. I choked my shaft, punishing it. Faster. I jerked my hips in an erratic rhythm. I needed to take her soon, but I needed this relief. This moment.

*Please, Alana. Please, baby. I need this so much. I need you.*

"I loved killing you," she whispered.

It answered my prayers. We might be the death of each other, and that was the most beautiful thing I'd ever heard. Maybe we would go down in flames, but it would be our way. Pleasure violently swelled in the base of my stomach, spiraling and tingling its way through my body until I froze. On a precipice. We were stuck in a tableau—me on the outside looking in, her head bowed over her victim, and the dead man sweetening the atmosphere. There, right there, I came, spurting white shit across the dark hallway. The pleasure chased away everything but the three of us bonded in this moment of violence and pleasure.

It lasted until my legs gave out, and I used the wall to hold myself up. I stayed there, trying to control my breathing. To stop my shaking hands so I could put away my still-hard cock. But it was amazing, so amazing. A few steps and I'd have her. I was right there. Finally calm enough, I stuffed myself back into my pants. With the door cracked, I'd be able to get through easily enough.

She tucked the body into the tarp and started pulling toward the door where I was standing. Shit. I sprinted away and pushed into a darkened alcove off to the side of the end of the hallway. A few seconds later, I had a black mask pulled down over my face and neck and tucked my hands into black gloves. Pushing as far back into the darkness as I could, I banked on her being preoccupied with moving her victim.

She passed right by me.

I stayed in place as she dragged the man to her car and popped her trunk. It took a few minutes of her struggling with the weight of the body, but she got him in there and slammed her trunk closed again. She stopped to take a breath before getting into her car. From my vantage point, I could see her back out through the singular entrance into the warehouse on ground level. Once her car was out of sight, I left the alcove and ran to where she'd disappeared from. I could then see her take the path out toward the water I hadn't been able to find.

"Clever girl, moving around the container units like that."

Good to know. I wouldn't be keeping Alana here for long. She had to know who was boss and get acclimated to me being back. Once she did, we'd be able to go home, to the house she'd bought, and live like we should have been. I needed to make sure I knew how to get us out of here.

"Now it's time to get ready."

Back in her killing room, I looked around to get to know her tools and move them as far away as I could from her capture zone. Wouldn't want her getting her hands on any of that stuff when I snatched her. Then I went searching for her cages. She had space to eat in off to the side of her killing area. Not bad. It wasn't for long-term stays; it was for coming and going, and that would work well enough for me.

There was nowhere to sleep, which told me she came and went when she was finished torturing her victims for the day. There had to be a cage room, and it could only be so far from where she broke them. She wouldn't have the strength to move them long distances without risking them fighting back. I went back to the first room and looked for some sort of entrance. There wasn't any.

"What the fuck? There has to be something here. I'm not looking hard enough."

I shuffled around the edge of the room, and my shoe got caught on a handle. "What's this here?"

When I lifted it, I found her cage. It was deep enough that a man could squat but not stand, and it wasn't wide enough to lie down. There was nowhere for him to use the bathroom, so he was stuck in filth if he didn't wait until she opened it and let him out. No, I was wrong. There as a bedpan off to the side, but it would be exceptionally difficult to use. Near the cage was a dart gun.

"So she knocks them out and drags them to the table, waiting until they wake up. Yeah, I officially want to marry this girl."

And now I knew where I was going to keep her.

It was two hours later before I heard the sliding of her entrance gate, but I waited. No killer left their space unkempt if they had to come back and use it again. The time after the murder was the most important time to remove all traces of evidence. I had already done it for her—everything was pristine and perfectly clean. Aside from moving them around to better accommodate me, I took very good care of her tools. Now, I waited on the blindside of her door for her to enter. I tracked her progress toward me due to her lack of concern for the noise she made. My hands were cool and steady, my mind clear. I knew exactly what I was going to do, and I had her cage open and ready for her.

I was going to have my woman. My toy. Finally, after all this time.

First things first, though, I slid a few pastries into her toaster. Blueberry Pop-Tarts. I wondered if she'd remember me by the smell. When the door opened, Alana walked through confidently, cleaned of the blood and now wearing a simple, blue sundress. Easy to remove. Nice. She paused when she saw the slab was gleaming silver, and then she sniffed. Her eyes widened, but she didn't react. That was all the time I needed.

"Honey, I'm home. Would you like a Pop-Tart? They're blueberry, of course."

She spun around, sinking into a crouch, but I was bigger, stronger. I spearheaded her, taking her down to the ground. Air rushed out of her in a loud *whoosh*, and then I was on top of her. She wasn't that young, high school girl now. She was a killer, and she didn't give in easily. Balling her fists, she swung hard and fast at my stomach. I caught the hit, grunting, but I didn't let her go. In the morning I'd be sore. She kicked and raged, but she couldn't break my hold.

"Get the fuck off me!"

"Now, that's no way to welcome your man home, Alana. You're my toy, and you know the proper way to greet me. Or do I have to punish you already?"

She froze, eyes wide. For a few moments, I saw fear—pure, unadulterated fear—before rage replaced it. And then she was wilting under my hands and staring at my face in wonder.

"Jacob?" Her voice was disbelieving.

"In the flesh. I told you that you belonged to me."

"I don't belong to anyone."

"That's where you're wrong, Alana. You will *always* belong to me. And that shit you did was a no-no. You don't kill anyone without me. Ever again." The anger was back, and she bucked, trying to throw me off. It wasn't enough.

"I won't belong to anyone again! Never. I'll kill you first."

"Oh, sweetheart, that's why I came back to you. You say the nicest things. You promise?"

Her confused gaze met mine. There was so much there—anger, fear, and, under it all, some sense of hope. The need for someone who understood her. Could handle her. Love her. I could do that. I could be that man. But she had to be broken before I could build her up again. She couldn't see past the history that bound us. It was ruining what we could have. I wouldn't have it anymore.

She didn't answer my question, and I didn't think she would.

She did come back to life in my arms, a knife in her hand I didn't know she'd been hiding, slashing toward my face.

I slammed her wrist against the ground until she released it.

"Noel, Mommy's back now," I said.

Tears filled her eyes and she swung again, going wild. "Don't you say his name. Not his. Jacob, don't do this. Don't."

"You have to fall down, Alana, before I can pick you back up. But I promise I will."

And then I punched her in the temple. She crumpled, and I stood up. It hurt to bring her pain, but it was good too. My body was alive, enjoying what was to come, imagining all the things I'd do to her. The shit she'd do to me. I opened the cage door and pinned it so it wouldn't fall, then I went back to her.

I picked her up in my arms and looked at her. Her golden hair, the large crescents of her eyelashes shielding her green eyes. Her soft strands of hair caressed like air against my arm. Her skin was smooth and clean, so clean. Shifting her weight, I stood her against me and pulled the dress from her. The thin straps ripped, and then it puddled to the ground.

She was so beautiful. Her heavy, full breasts were still tipped with slightly darker nipples. The hair covering her mound was trimmed, but it wasn't to my liking. She needed to be bare. Clean. I'd take care of that on her first day of training when she was awake and would have to listen to my orders. We were here, together.

I carried my precious cargo into her cage and laid her on the disgusting ground. She was an angel about to be trapped in hell. I couldn't wait to see how she came out of it. I wondered if I could control Nila—that dark side of her, that murderous bitch who would bend to my will—or if I would have to break that out of her and only leave Alana.

I hoped I could have them both. That we could face the world together and get rid of so much filth. There were so many people to kill. So many who deserved retribution. And Alana and I were the two to do it.

As I closed her cage door and locked it, I hoped we would survive the path to that glorious future.

# Chapter Eighteen

## Nila

**N**ot again. Not again. Not the fuck again.
I was trapped in a cage, my worst nightmare. The cage before had suffocated me, but this one here? It was made to torment. And now my own cage, the one I used to break others, was being used on me. Trapped in the darkness, the silence threatened to break me, so I made fucking noise. I screamed and kicked. Banged against the bars with pure rage. Fuck him and men like him.

How was it possible that Jacob was here? Nila Winters was a new start after the trial. Alana Masters no longer existed, and I had no ties to who I used to be. How did he find me? And why did it make my heart skip knowing he went to so much trouble to do so?

Young Jacob had been a sight. Good-looking, Jacob could've had any girl he wanted if he would've been a normal teenage boy. But grown-up Jacob? He was a whole other breed of man. Handsome, with movie-star looks, a hidden darkness peered out from his eyes when he gazed at me. I lost all sense of reason underneath him. But what he'd said about him being my master and me being his toy filled me with an uncontrollable rage and made me crave his blood on my hands.

I was no longer a toy, and he sure as hell wasn't my master. I was older, wiser, and much, much darker than he could imagine. He entered dangerous territory when he walked into my killing ground and had the audacity to knock me out as if he had some sort of control over me. Wait until I strangled him with my bare hands and sucked the life out of him. He'd see who was in control then.

"Alana, time to wake up."

Glaring, I didn't say a word to him. The bastard wanted something from me, he could damn well work for it. I was no longer that sweet, naïve eighteen-year-old. I was a grown woman who left bodies in her wake. I would not bow down to him so easily.

"Alana. Come on, baby. Noel, tell Mommy to be nice."

"Jacob! Stop. Stop using Noel against me. That's a dirty trick and you know it."

"No, Alana. Someone has to remember him. Remember what we lost."

"What *we* lost?"

"He should've been mine! You were mine. You were always mine. Father gave you to me. Then he stole you away. He fucking stole you out from underneath me!"

His words took my breath away. My stomach turned to stone.

"I was supposed to be *yours*?" I scoffed. The bastard had another think coming. "I'll gut you, I promise."

"You were promised to me. A sweet blonde. And how sweet you were. Too sweet. Of course, Father had to keep you for himself. But it's all right. I'm here now. We can finally have the life we were meant to have. It's okay that you left … if you accept me now."

He was delusional, absolutely delusional. Sure, we'd always had a bond. We were drawn to one another because of what his father put us through, and yet here, now, he was talking as if we had a future.

We had no future. I was a killer. A woman who lusted for blood and made men pay for their sins. And he was the son of the Devil, the man who took me and made me this way. I should hate him. I should want to see him dead.

And yet … I didn't.

*What the hell is wrong with me?*

Jacob shouldn't have been able to affect me any longer. What we had was support and emotion triggered by immaturity and a need to survive a horrendous situation. It wasn't real, and it was nothing we could find again. Even now, years later, I was drawn to him, despite his delusions. Despite telling myself there was nothing between us. While we may not have a future, our connection thrummed in the air. This couldn't be right.

"What are you going to do with me?" Knowledge was power, and killers tended to like to brag.

"What should've been done from the start. I'm going to make you mine."

"Don't do this, Jacob. You saved me. *You* saved me. I'm alive because of you. You don't want to do this to me."

"I've always wanted to do this to you, sweet Alana. I've dreamt of this moment. I know you never meant to leave me behind. You were scared. I've been waiting for us to be together again. You told me, remember? That if I ever lost the girl, I had to find a way to take her back. I'm here now."

I ran away back then. I ran and left Jacob behind to pay for our crime. I could've looked him up and found him before, but I didn't. He wasn't a part of my new life. I did what I could when I didn't implicate him in my treatment. While Jacob may have played a starring role in my fantasies, I never wanted to go down that path again. My feet were firmly set on the path of darkness, and there was no time for love or relationships. Love was a nuisance. Not that it existed for monsters like me anyway.

"We were children, Jacob."

"And I *loved* you, and *you* left me behind!"

I sucked in a breath, closing my eyes against the anger and pain in his gaze.

"You left me. Alone. I couldn't find you. My girl, my Alana. The woman I learned to change for. We were together for over a year, we killed my father together. Did that mean nothing to you?"

"We can talk and spend time together. You don't have to hold me prisoner."

"I trusted you to come back, and you didn't," he whispered.

I couldn't help but look at him, at the dip in his shoulders, the closed-off way he held himself. I'd hurt him, I could read it plainly on his flesh, the scarring I'd left behind. But he shook and changed, surety replacing confusion in his gaze, along with that cocky grin that took my breath away when we were kids spreading over his face.

"Can you feel it, Alana? Your soul calls to me like a whisper in the dark. We were made for it. We were made for each other."

"I don't feel a thing but irritation. You're bothering me, shoo."

It was a lie. He *scared* me. Fucking terrified me in ways I hadn't known for so long.

He smiled, a brilliant fucking smile that set me afire. *Evil can be gorgeous.* I'd learned that before. But made for each other? *Hell. No.*

For a therapist who dealt with some of the worst, most stubborn patients on a daily basis, I couldn't find the words to respond. Eight years since I last saw him and now he was here, standing before me, wanting to turn me into the same thing his father had years earlier.

*Would you be my girlfriend if I learn how?*

The memory swirled in my head. We were so lost then. Fucked-up and twisted, looking for something normal to hold on to. But he wanted things I couldn't give him, wanted to bring out cravings inside of me that once I released I wouldn't have any strength left. I couldn't let that happen. I couldn't be that broken girl again.

This time I was prepared to fight, but Jacob did not make it easy. While he may have spoken nonsense, he was right about one thing: the connection was still there, stretching between us as if no time had passed at all. Torn, half of me wondered how he had spent the last eight years after getting out from underneath his father's rule. The other half of me, though, was too nervous to know. Too angry that after all this time, this was how he came back into my life. By taking me against my will and locking me in a cage, knowing everything his father had done to me.

He truly was his father's son.

"Jacob, it's been eight years. I'm not that girl anymore."

"You'll always be Alana to me no matter what your name is. No matter who you are. You can try to escape, but you'll fail."

Coming closer, he stroked my cheek with his palm. Gazing into my eyes, he whispered, "This time there is no running. You're mine. You've always been mine."

*You're mine.*

Spoken once before. Then, it had been from his father. Now Jacob. The apple hadn't fallen far from the tree. No matter what we did, no matter that we had broken free, Jacob turned into the man we despised.

But then again, so had I.

Our mutual hatred for one man led to his downfall, but in killing him, we gave ourselves over to the darkness. Thus, leading to our own.

In the corner of my subconscious, I had been waiting for it.

I had been waiting for him to strike. To kill me. To be like his father.

I never expected him to want me, not after I'd left him behind.

"It's time for some fun, Alana."

Unlocking my cage, he grabbed me by the wrist. My eyes locking on his hand, a quick glimpse of his other caused me to shiver. In his hand he held a neck device I'd used to tether victims before—a pole leading to a collar of sharp spikes on the inside.

I jerked my head forward, striking him in the mouth.

"How's *that* for meant to be?" I taunted.

He spat blood, but he didn't get angry. No, he gave me that same smile that twisted my stomach.

"Now, now. This is for your own good. We can't have you running off, can we?"

Turning me so my back was to him, he pulled the collar around my neck. Before clasping it shut, he pulled tightly until my breath was almost lost. The sharp spikes digging into my throat, I winced in pain.

With one hand gripping the pole, he turned me once more, his other hand pressed to the middle of my back as he led me around the warehouse. Back where he had gotten the jump on me, my tools were there, shiny and bright, calling out to me like a beacon. Oh, how I wished I could grab my blade and hold it to his neck. How I wished I could make him bleed for me.

"Turn around."

Doing as he said, I waited as he turned the collar around my neck before pushing me down into a chair resembling something a prison would use for executions. I feared what he could do to me, but my black heart pitter-pattered with something resembling lust and my insides grew wet. Wondering if he could smell the arousal coming off of me like waves, I pushed my thighs more firmly together.

"Alana, Alana, Alana. Do you know how long I have searched for you? Waited for you? And now you are here in front of me. A succulent feast all laid out for me. Utter perfection."

His gaze roamed over me from head to toe. From my blonde locks to my perky breasts and down to my core, everything was bared to him, and there was no mistaking the lust in his eyes. The desperation. Rubbing my thighs together, I refused to get lost in his brown eyes. He was my enemy. Nothing more.

It was hard not to be captivated by Jacob though. For so long he had starred in my fantasies, the only thing that could bring me to orgasm time after time. And now he was here, and while the rest of me was an inferno of rage, I desperately craved for him to make me come.

Here, captive once more, I was a sick, sick woman thinking of the things Jacob's wicked tongue could do to my body. Having found my release last night thinking of him, the reality of him standing before me made me even wetter.

That damn connection still confused me. My body, traitor that it was, reacted to him, even when my mind screamed for me to kill him. Every inch of my body was consumed while a mental battle raged inside of me between fear and lust. The excitement wanted to beg for it, beg for Jacob to make me come. The fear of him left me silent. I was afraid he was more like his father than I could imagine, especially after the blow that knocked me out earlier.

I knew darkness. I lived darkness. But when my kidnapper could make me want to spread my legs and beg for him to eat me, I knew I was completely fucked.

"I told Noel we had to get you back. We had to have you with us so we could finally be a family like we were always meant to be. Don't you want that, Alana?"

"What I want is for you to quit fucking mentioning *my* son. Noel was my son. What gives you the right to casually throw his name around?"

Pulling on the pole, the collar dug deeper into my neck.

"I'll tell you what gives me the right. You. Are. Mine. Noel was meant to be ours. He may have been my brother, but he was always meant to be my son. I remembered him. While you were living your life as Nila Winters and fooling every fucking person around you, I was carrying Noel with me. Not abandoning him like you did."

"You think I don't think about my son? My child? I think about him all the time. All the damn time. That first year I couldn't even breathe without remembering him. Even after I was freed, all I could think about was him. Every fucking month he would've been born I think about him. Every fucking anniversary of his death I think of him. That monster deliberately told me the date of his death so it would stay with me. But Noel has always stayed with me no matter what, so don't you dare *ever* use him against me again, you bastard!"

Spitting in his face, I couldn't control the rage that had come over me. I'd trained myself to be calm, cool and collected through every situation, but with a few casual mentions of my son, the darkness in me came flying out.

Jacob backhanded me, and my head jerked to the side. But he didn't let me go for long. He was there, grabbing my cheek and forcing me to look at him.

"How dare you fucking hit me!" I yelled.

"You need to learn how to speak to me with respect. I am your Master now. You are the toy. Remember your training now or remember it after I'm putting you through the same paces dear ol' Dad did. Is that what you want? You want me to train you? Is that what it's going to take to get it through your head that this is it, baby. The big picture. You and me. And the darkness."

His words sent my heart stuttering.

I wanted to keep fighting. I wanted to hurt him. Claw his eyes out, make his blood pour onto my hands and suck the life out of him with my kiss, but this was still Jacob. My heart may be black as the dead of night now, but somewhere there remained a speck of the girl I used to be, and she was screaming to be let out. To hear Jacob's story. To soothe his pain.

*Stupid girl, he has you captive. He's trying to break you. Make you weak. And once your guard is down, he'll kill you.*

Not saying a word to him, I simply stared, trying to see into his mind. I wondered what made him tick. I had so many questions I wanted answers to, but I knew if I even showed the slightest hint of curiosity he would think he won. He could never win. I would not be his puppet, his toy. Things were different now. It was time to figure out a plan.

"I thought you would be ready, but I guess I was wrong. You've really disappointed me, Alana. Truly. I hate to punish you and mar that beautiful skin before I'm ready to take you, but you need to learn. Until you can treat me with respect, you won't be leaving your cage."

With a rough grip on my arm, Jacob grabbed me from my chair and pulled on the pole, leading me around as if I were a dog. Taking me back to my cage, my own personal brand of hell. Oh, he was punishing me all right. Knowing my only weakness was this cage, he knew he would start to break me. Or at least he figured he would.

*Oh, Jacob. Silly, beautiful Jacob. Don't you know I'm much stronger now?*

# Chapter Nineteen

## Jacob

She was fucking weak. Completely and utterly weak. Why? Because she gave up. On us. On *me*. After everything we'd shared. Where was the Alana who'd gripped my skull and kissed me with Dad bleeding like a stuck pig between us? Where was the girl who'd thanked me for freeing her but stayed with me the whole way to make sure my sperm donor got his just desserts? Or the girl who had taught me how to love?

Hell, where was Nila, the one who'd torn Jonathan apart?

Neither was there, and it pissed me off. Royally. I couldn't take her home or make a life with a woman I had to train all over again. She had to be in there somewhere. And I had to find a better clue than locking her in a cage I knew she despised. That was her kryptonite. Thinking, I turned in a slow circle, looking around. What had I missed? What wasn't I understanding?

I tore through the warehouse, looking through rooms and her belongings. Everything appeared exactly as it had before and didn't help me a fucking bit. I ran the pass again, taking it slower this time. Looking under crawl spaces, through her fridge, in the overhead walkways—everywhere I could—until my eyes rested on the car. Maybe that's where I would find more about Alana. I made a beeline for her vehicle and was thankful she'd left the doors unlocked. No reason to worry about a break-in here. She had brown file boxes in the back seat.

"Heavy sons of bitches." I knew why the minute I opened the lids. There were many folders, each having a name labeled on them. Jonathan Ross's name stood out, and I picked up his file.

"Well, lookie here." It looked like copied versions of patient notes.

"Jonathan Ross, forty-year-old white male, divorced, who currently lives alone in the North Lawndale area of Chicago. Mr. Ross is a new patient in our office for evaluation of threat due to past history of sexual violence against women. Recently paroled and deemed safe from prison psychiatrist. Mr. Ross was interviewed about his past, and his reliability therein is considered fair."

I scanned the document, noting where he was listed to have sexual deviance under rape and incest. He was also listed under delusions to have a sense of absolute right to the women he raped. Believing every single one of them had enticed him, begged him for it, and their fighting back was only a way to spice up the consensual sex.

"What a fucking idiot."

I dropped his folder and looked through others. Most of the names I didn't recognize, but a couple I did. I'd seen some of them on the news about their disappearances over the last few years.

"My, my, my. Alana has been busy."

I wondered how long she'd been taking men off the street and punishing them, and maybe what punishment she thought I deserved. Every man in her file had either kidnapped, raped, or brutalized teens or women younger than twenty-five. Physically, the types some of these men preferred didn't look like Alana, but the needs they had, the perversions, were close enough to what she'd been through.

"There it is. I think I may have found the switch. But can I make you face it?"

I hefted the heavy boxes back into the killing room and thought of what to do. I wanted to know more about what Alana was doing here. Having her share her secret would only bring us closer together. The more in her life I was, the harder it would be to get me out of it. And that was most important.

Needing to make sure she was amenable to my questions, I went to her workstation and looked for a blade. Finding one, I placed it on the slab, within reach of the strapping chair, and got ready. I moved the straps from the legs of the chair so they were higher, and looped rope around them so I could stretch the tying further. A quick jaunt to the kitchen area and my hands were cleaned, my shirt was off, and I was ready to play with my toy.

When I opened the cage hatch and dragged her out by the pole connected to her neck, her eyes shot fire at me but she remained stubbornly mute. She was at a full stand outside of the cage before she looked around. When her eyes landed on the knife, they widened for a moment, but then her face was back in the determined mask. If I wasn't looking right at her I may have missed the moment of fear. But it was there, and I was watching.

*She's afraid. No matter how strong she gets, she is still afraid.*

And she shouldn't have been. My girl should welcome the pain. Love it. Trust me to take her to the ends of the earth if I had to, but it would all be for the pleasure she could find there. Even if it killed her. Shit, especially if it killed her. She would die a happy fucking woman.

"It's time to answer some questions, Alana."

She still said nothing, but she would soon enough. I sat her down in the chair and looped ties around the pole holding her collar so her head was forced back and up. I could see the pinpricks from the needles pressing into her throat and the throb of her heartbeat covered in dried blood. I liked blood on her. Once I had her in place, I strapped her arms down. When I went for her legs, she lifted her hips and kicked me in the shin.

"Bad girl."

My punishment was swift and sure. I punched the inside of her thigh, right in the center. She grunted, breathing through the pain. I hit her again in the same spot. Her muscles clenched in a spasm. Her wrists were white as she strained against the ties holding her down. Her neck bled where she forced her head against the spikes, trying to free herself.

"I am going to kill you," she promised. Her voice throbbed with hatred, but there was something else. An emotion I would explore soon enough.

"Maybe you will. Maybe you won't. Until then? You're going to do whatever the fuck I tell you."

I tied her ankles to the slab, using the ropes looped around it so she was open and spread for my inspection. I secured her knees to the legs of the chair, forcing to keep them open.

I lifted the blade and waved it in front of her face. "Rule number one, I like my toys nice and bare. You've grown a patch down there, and I don't like it. I want to see everything I do to my pussy. Rule number two, it hurts when you don't do what I want. It's bloody when I want it to be, and doing what I want won't stop the pain, but it will make sure it doesn't get worse. Tell me you understand."

Stubborn bitch didn't say a thing.

"So be it."

I pressed the flat of the knife between her breasts and dragged it over the slope of her stomach. As it reached far enough, I flipped the knife and the tip bit into her skin. Like butter, her skin gave way. I was so good with the knife. So fucking good. She should have remembered that.

"I'll take my pound of flesh now."

I saw the knowledge in her eyes as she shook her head. "No, Jacob. Don't."

I didn't listen. Instead, I pressed the knife edge against her skin, at the fleshy part of her stomach. Slowly, centimeter by centimeter, I removed one layer. She screamed as the blood flowed, and I smiled. I could do this all day. I'd learned this skill for her, and now she'd taste it. Time and death, it's what I always could give her.

"Don't make me ask again, Alana. Tell me you understand."

"Fuck. You."

"Oh, fighting only makes me hotter."

That connection between us blossomed. Through the anger and the rage, it pulsed in the room. I could smell her blood, and I wanted to taste it, take her into my being and combine us. Her hands gripped the edge of the chair until her knuckles were white, and she bit her lip, but she didn't scream anymore. She dared me to cut her again. Willed my hand to give her more pain, and that's what I did. This time under her breast. That thick swell that was so pretty. So perfect. My knife cut through it. I was only taking small layers, sections that would bleed but heal in no time, but the pain wasn't any less. Her back bowed, her mouth opened in a silent wail, her eyes were wide with fright, but she took it. Held it. It was like fucking sex. We were trapped together, chasing that elusive orgasm but knowing it was around the corner.

"I understand!" she finally screamed.

"Good girl. Now you're going to answer some questions."

She panted, her breasts quivering with each breath. She was magnificent as I ducked under her leg and got between her and the medical table. Cocooned between her legs, I couldn't help stiffening. I palmed it through my pants and groaned. Alana changed. She froze at the sound, her eyes pressing down to the bottom of her sockets to see me.

"Do you like it?" Her hips shifted, and I looked down between her legs. Wet. Her thighs gleamed in the light.

My fucking nasty girl.

"You like it." It was a statement this time as she closed her eyes against my words.

"No."

I slapped the inside of her already bruising thigh with the flat of the knife. "Don't lie to me."

She remained silent. Fuck it. I watched carefully as I shaved her, dragging the knife and cutting her hair with precision. She held her breath, her body rigid, as I got close to her lips. I could barely hear her breathing, but she didn't fight, didn't try to get away. She minded my rules, and it made me so fucking hard. She was so perfect. So sweet. I let go of myself long enough to hold open her lips and remove the rest of her hair. She was so hot inside, like an inferno against my fingertips. Her labia got red and engorged, and her clit peeked from its hood.

"You want me. You won't deny it. Tell me about your patients. Why you have those notes, and how many you've already killed."

"I'm a psychologist, I always have patient notes," was her answer. It was a fucking lie. It soured the air and pissed me off.

"Wrong move."

I moved the knife away from her body but kept my other hand pressed against her. I played with her folds. Using my thumb and forefinger, I pushed the hood of her clit back and exposed that sensitive bundle of nerves.

"Lying to me only makes it hurt more." And then I pinched her. Tried to fucking make my fingers touch.

"No!" Her back bowing again, she strained against the collar, and her legs locked. I held on, never letting up the pressure. Leaning forward, over her breast, I nuzzled the flesh above her nipple.

I was alive for the first time in eight years. With her, joined by pain, we were pulled together by a connection she could never deny. Because even as I brutalized her clit, she was leaking against my hand. I groaned and released her clit. Her pale skin was flush with a red blush, and she shook in her bonds. Her eyes followed my every move. I didn't let her see my hands. Instead, I kept them out of her limited sight.

That was part of the fun. She would never know what was coming.

"The patients, Alana. Why do you have their records with you?"

"Because I study them."

It was the truth, I knew it, but it wasn't the answer I wanted. She knew it. But she had answered my questions, so punishment wasn't in order. Unless I decided to say fuck it.

"There are twenty-six bones in the foot and ankle, Alana. That's a quarter of what's in your body. There are thirty-three joints, over a hundred ligaments, muscles, and tendons. Do you know why I'm telling you this, Alana? Because there are so many I could break, dislocate, and cut, and you'd still live. Such delicious pain to make you wetter, and you'd answer every question I have."

She watched me with wild eyes, like a brand-new colt unsure of the world and terrified of every sound.

"Confess your sins unto me, Alana Masters. I'm your sin eater, and the only way to absolution is through me."

She closed her eyes, breathing roughly. "You'll kill me anyway."

"No, Alana, I won't kill you. I'll do something so much worse. I'll keep you, and I'll make sure you love me for doing it."

She opened her eyes and glared at me. "Never."

Said the woman whose pussy just quivered.

# Chapter Twenty

*Nila*

Alana. The name he kept referring to, my God-given name, was not me anymore. I buried Alana years ago, gave her a proper goodbye and stepped into the darkness, never to emerge again. I was no longer Alana: weak, innocent, happy. I was Nila: dark, seductive, and full of rage. With every reference to Alana, to Noel, I was back in that cage hoping to be let free.

Jacob, for all he had claimed to want my love, was enacting his father's plan for me. He was turning me into a toy for his sick pleasure. And yet my darkness was calling out for more. What the hell was my problem? My fascination with Jacob ran as deep as my blood, flooding my senses, calling out for more.

More of what? I didn't know, but I knew nothing could come of this. For fuck's sake, I was a prisoner of my original kidnapper's son. And here I was, bared to his eyes, to his touch. Wet, I shivered in anticipation of what would come next.

I hated that he made me feel like this.

"Tell me what I want to know, Alana," Jacob demanded, knife to my neck and hand caressing my thigh.

"Don't call me that!" I snapped.

"It's your name."

"No, it's not. My name is Nila. Alana is a weak, insignificant girl."

"She's a part of you. I'll always think of you as Alana. Innocent, young, and pretty, waiting for me to feast upon your flesh. The one I asked to be mine, and she said yes. Alana is everything to me."

"Don't, Jacob."

"Don't what? Tell you the truth. Tell you who you really are? You may dress yourself up and play a part, but underneath all that hatred is Alana Masters, the girl who ran from me. I took the fall for you, sweetheart. You owe me."

"I don't owe you a thing!"

"You helped me kill my dad. You ran. You left me to take the fall, and I ended up in a hell hole biding my time until I could come for you. You fucking owe me."

Maybe he was right, maybe I *did* owe him. Maybe he owed me. Hell, maybe we were in debt to each other, never to be free of one another until one of us was dead at the other's hands. Maybe our debt was made to be paid in blood.

In any case, Jacob may get my blood stirring, but he was my enemy. At one time "the enemy of my enemy" rang true, but now no one stood between us. We were each other's greatest downfalls.

"Maybe you're right," I said, surprised at my admission.

"Now we're getting somewhere. I want you to tell me about these patient notes."

"What do you want me to say, Jacob? Do you want to hear about every man I have killed? How I tortured them for sport and got off on their pain, their agony? Do you want to hear about their screams echoing through this room or how they begged, pleaded for me to spare them? Is that what you want to hear?"

"Yes! I want to hear about it. You shouldn't have been doing it on your own."

"You were gone! I did what I had to do to survive. The darkness ate up my insides like acid until I gave myself over to it. I would've gone crazy. I would've killed myself if I hadn't started to kill others! The kill, the blood … it gave me the willpower to survive!"

"I should've been here."

"But you weren't! The men who preyed on weak, pathetic girls like I used to be. I used them for my pleasure. For my pain. I used them to forget about Alana. I never wanted to remember her or how fucking weak she was. And now you're here! Here, dredging up those memories. You just couldn't let me be free. You couldn't let me exist on my own."

"When are you going to realize you've never been alone? Your pain has always been mine. Your darkness? Mine. Everything about you has always belonged to me. Your soul is a part of mine, and I *will* have your heart."

I clenched, the wetness sliding between my thighs. Jacob immediately homed in on it as he started to bring the knife from my neck to my mound, a caress between old lovers. I bared my teeth at him. The edge of the knife so close to my delicate skin held me on edge, but every nerve in my body was poised to combust. Try as I might to think otherwise, Jacob was captivating me, and my body was having a reaction to him in every way.

"See there? See how wet you're getting for me? You want me, Alana. Now tell me about the fucking patient notes before I use this knife again."

Was it him or the darkness exuding from him I wanted? I was so confused, so torn. The cage had fucked me up and torn me apart, only to leave me the thing I once hated. Now I was teetering between showing how much I hated him and how much I craved him. For a therapist, I was truly fucked up. I had no answers for myself. Only more questions.

"Tell me what I want to know, Alana," Jacob snapped, taking the blade to my shoulder and making his mark across it. Not deep, but enough that I knew he was in charge.

*For now.*

Biting my tongue, I refused once more, only to feel the searing bite as he dug the blade into my chest. Feeling the sharp edge dig deeper than before, he carved something into me. One word. Four letters.

*Noel.*

My son. Jacob's brother.

I now bore his name on my chest, carved by a knife, sealed with blood.

The blood flowed, my anger simmering alongside it. That bastard did this on purpose, knowing perfectly well it would be a crack in my armor. Son of a bitch, that asshole was good.

I would still make him bleed though.

"Tell me, Alana. Tell me right the fuck now."

"They are the men I killed, okay? Are you happy now, Jacob?"

"No," he raged. "I won't be happy until you fill me in on the details."

"They're my kills. They were my patients. Day in and day out, I had to hear their wicked little secrets. Their lusts for their daughters, for neighborhood kids, for the women they work with. Their sick desires, their plans. I snapped, and I killed them. I laid them out and feasted on their fear. I made it my own. I tortured them. I broke them. I made them bleed for me. I made them beg for me. And then, as they confessed their sins to me, I forced them to draw their last breath at my hand. I murdered them, and I loved it. I fucking loved it! There's my confession, Mr. Sin Eater."

He yanked me back and shoved something into my mouth. Jacob's cock was being pressed between my plump lips. Hard as a rock, Jacob looked down at me with a frantic look in his eyes. My rant had overcome him, and the lust shone all over his face.

His forced erection in my mouth brought me back to the first time his father did this. How he pushed himself on me, leaving me to gag around it until vomit threatened to come up. Jesus. Like father, like son, that was for sure. But I wouldn't let Jacob do this to me. Not now. I bit down, hard.

"You bitch! You fucking biting bitch!"

Fisting my hair, he tried choking me on his length once more, but each time I threatened to bite down again.

"Take it, Alana! Fucking take it."

His father had taken a lot from me, and Jacob was doing the same. I may have been Jacob's prisoner, but it was time to remind him I wasn't a timid little girl anymore. I was a grown woman filled with hate, pain, and rage. I had killed men a lot bigger than Jacob. I had brought them to their knees before taking them out of this world. The son of a bitch was easy on the eyes with his dark features, honey-brown eyes and a dimple that actually made me want to swoon, but I'd be damned if he forced his dick into my mouth one more time without consequences.

"Fight it as much as you want, but you're going to be begging to suck me soon enough." With one hand fisting my hair, the other went to his cock. It was pure pleasure and pure torture at the same time. On one hand, the gratification on Jacob's face sent spasms through my body. But on the other, I hated how it made me feel to see him like this. I wanted to fight him, but I was becoming a victim of my body's needs.

*The betraying bitch.*

Something drew me to him. Something dark and primal, but I was drawn to him in a way I couldn't explain. I was mesmerized by a boy who, by all accounts, could be a monster himself—the flesh and bone of the devil. Yet there was something in his eyes, in the way he carried himself, that called out to me.

Maybe his father had fucked me up worse than I thought.

My pain recognized Jacob. My blood called out to his. The darkness that slowly crept into my mind and soul ached for this boy.

*Oh, how precious is he. What a wonderful specimen. Handsome. Dark. Dangerous.*

But the side of me with some sanity left sickened at my thoughts. He'd flat-out told me he wanted me. He wanted my body. He wanted me as his toy. But the thought didn't disgust me as much as it should. What the hell was wrong with me?

His hand worked his hardness in fast motions, then slow. A twist here. Faster, faster. With a groan of my name, his cum painted my face and he swiped his shaft across my lips. Even as sick as it was, my tongue came from behind wet lips to lick the head of it. The salty taste of his release slid down my throat, and I immediately found myself craving more.

I was a nasty, vile woman getting off on the taste of my captor's seed, but I loved it. The darkness howled at me to be released. To let this man eat me. Fuck me. This would be no ordinary sex. This would be dark, dangerous, kinky sex. The kind you only heard about in fucked-up books and movies. If I weren't careful, this man could literally be the death of me. Better yet, I would be the death of him. If I could only convince him I was on his side, I could get the upper hand. But first …

"Noel was never yours."

"I know. You were the most beautiful girl I had ever seen. Delicate. And you said we were together. In my mind, through it all, Noel became mine." Jacob shrugged as if it all made sense.

"No, Jacob, he was *mine*. He's *always* been mine. You may have deluded yourself into thinking otherwise, but don't get it twisted. Noel was *my* baby, *my* blood. Never yours."

"My blood ran through his veins! He was my brother."

"Exactly. Your brother. Not your son. *Noel is mine.*"

Mine. Mine. Mine. Noel was mine, and I wasn't going to let what he meant to me be tarnished by Jacob. Noel was all I had left of Alana. My dirty little secret. My shame. My love. Jacob could take many things from me, but he could not have Noel.

I'd kill him first.

# Chapter Twenty-One

## Jacob

Where was Alana? This woman, this fucking Nila … she didn't love me. She didn't know me. Alana was buried so deep in there she wouldn't come back out. I needed her. I had to know everything I had gone through, everything I'd suffered, was for something. I stumbled away from between her legs and left her tied to chair, covered in blood and cum, and ran to the kitchen.

"What a fucking mess. A *fucking* mess," I said. Groaning, I sank into the chair at the table and rested my face in my hands. They smelled like her blood and my lust. Combined, perfect. Why couldn't she see how well we fit together? How perfect we were? Why didn't she pay me back? She should have been waiting for me. After everything I'd sacrificed, she should have been begging for my return, so fed up with a fucking normal life that she came alive under my hands. But she fucking didn't.

"Eight years, and this is what I come back to. A broken woman who hides behind the mask of her darkness because she doesn't know how to accept it. Won't accept it."

I refused to talk to Noel. Yeah, I'd used him against her, but it didn't feel right to bring him out now. I was tarnishing his name.

I'd held on so long. Through everything. Through that fucking juvenile home for psychotic children. What a fucking joke. It was an orphanage filled with kids who took their hate, anger, and pain out on others. Who mimicked what they went through at home, or sick fantasies stuck in their heads, on others around them.

The memories rushed in, pushing through my barrier, ripping away at the cracked protection I had on my soul. I slammed my head to the kitchen table, over and over. As the pain grew, the memories faded. I wanted her. Needed her. She saved me from the darkness as much as I saved her.

Only to be turned away at the fucking gates.

No. No fucking way. I wasn't going to lose everything and sink under all the pain I'd endured for her so she could go on in life without me. We either lived together or died by my hand. That fucking simple. If I had to kill her, I'd make sure I died with her, but she wasn't going to be without me.

"Never. She owes me. Fucking owes me for loving her. For saving her. For giving her freedom when I was held prisoner. I traded fucking places with her."

Standing, anger and resolve coursed through me. It was time she understood. Time she knew what she'd done to me. How she had no choice but to splay open her heart and give it to me. I deserved that. My mind raced as I headed back to her, grabbing a little something on the way and tucking it into my back pocket.

"Where's the shower?"

"What?"

"You're not hard of fucking hearing. Where is your shower?" My voice vibrated through the room, my anger at a boiling point.

"I don't have one."

"Liar. I'm going to pay you back for every lie, you know that? Your marks would die of infection if you didn't have ways to clean them up or a doc on hand. Remember the doctor? The one who took Noel from you? He'd been working for my dad for years. When he was a young doctor, he killed a girl on his table. Botched abortion. A young woman pregnant with his child. His daughter."

"Sick fuck," Alana said harshly.

"Aren't we all? Dad helped him clean it up, and in return, he helped Dad. Wouldn't want anyone to know what he did. After a while, he was so wrapped up, telling would only give him an appointment with lethal injection. I took care of him, too, you know. Performed surgery without anesthesia until he was no more. Left him on his desk like that. You're welcome."

"I didn't ask you to do that."

"Yeah, well I fucking did. No one was ever going to hurt you again, and if they ever had, they deserved it."

"*You* are hurting me, Jacob."

"No, I'm loving you. The only way fucked-up people like us *can* love. Now, where is your fucking shower?"

"You don't love me, Jacob. You're obsessed. You're preoccupied with the idea of us, the love you've imagined we shared, and you can't let it go. We kissed, Jacob, and we shared a bond people won't understand, I'll give you that, but it isn't love."

"Don't psychoanalyze me with that bullshit. One last time, Alana. Where. Is. Your. Shower?"

"Let me go, Jacob. If it's love, *real* love, you'd free me. Because you know what the cage does to me. I could never love someone who put me in one. Never."

Her words were like daggers in my chest— sharp stilettos that burrowed into my lungs and deflated them. She stole my breath. Turned me inside out.

"Love or obsession," I said as I walked toward her. "Either way, they both say you belong to me. And you, Nila, Alana, whoever you are today? That body and mind of yours knows it. You want to know why? You could have bitten my dick off if you wanted to. But you didn't. You tortured me, punished me, but didn't maim me. That connection, that moment of hesitation. Find our love there. And, hell, maybe obsession is what we'll share."

Her mouth opened on a sigh. She still hadn't answered my question, though, and punishment was in order. I pulled my knife from my pocket and slit the ropes off her legs. Then I unstrapped her, gripping her collar to keep her in place. I forced her to stand up before I kicked her feet out from under her.

"Ah!"

Her scream was magical as she fell to the floor. Then I was dragging her, the sharp points of her collar starting to dig into her neck. She hollered at me, but I didn't care. I allowed her to stick her fingers into the collar and hold some of the pricks away from her skin, but she couldn't stop them all.

"We're going on an adventure."

"Fuck you."

"Oh, you will. Trust me."

I dragged her down the long hallway toward the entrance, knowing the shower wouldn't be that way, but I proved my point. She'd be filthy, and each tug on the pole for her collar would be agony. She stayed stubbornly silent as I pulled her, but the way her chest rose and fell in rapid succession told me how badly it hurt.

"Over a hill we go." I climbed up on the hood of her car and jerked her up with me before going down the other side.

"Damn, no shower here. To the next location. Maybe if I'm up high enough?"

She didn't answer, and I didn't expect her to. Fucking stubborn woman. I found my way to some stairs to the back—the ones I'd used to get into this place the first time—and yanked her up those. Her hip hit a rung hard enough to vibrate the metal and she whimpered. I steeled my heart from her pain. She needed to come back to me, I needed her to be Alana again. I'd do whatever I had to do to Nila to get her.

"Just ... oh, I don't know ... twenty more to go?"

"Wait. I'll tell you. Dammit, wait," she said with a moan.

"What? I didn't quite hear you."

"On the other side of the warehouse, across from my car."

"Good girl."

I dragged her to the shower. She cursed me the whole way, but my point was made. Don't answer my questions and it hurts. Answer me, and it can hurt in a good way—the way that would make her pussy weep for me. Those were the only two alternatives. The rules, so to speak. She understood all about rules.

I pushed through a door and found an open, tiled area. It was grungy, but it had four showerheads, locker-room style, poking from one wall. Once I was close enough to one, I saw she had plain soap and a rag there to be used. I ignored the rag, but the soap would work. Bracing her under the water, I turned on the hot and cold to adjust it.

"Too cold," she said, but I ignored her. I would get it to a good temperature in a minute.

"If you weren't such an ass, I'd have let you do this yourself. But since I can't trust you to cooperate, you'll deal with it."

I didn't leave it freezing though. She sighed as hotter water rushed over her, sluicing away the dirt, blood, and grime. She tilted her head back, and it ran over her face and hair. I was entranced by the water running over her features. The way her dry lips plumped and smoothed out under the water. How her eyelashes clumped together and looked darker. Every part of her was delicately formed, but I knew of the steel inside her. A perfect blend.

It was then I saw the cuffs embedded into the wall, a way to keep a prisoner held under the water. That would work. I stood her up and turned her into the spray before I cuffed her hands. Then I locked her ankles too.

"I can't run with this thing on my neck, you know."

I removed the pointed collar. She blinked before looking over her shoulder at me. I held her gaze as I dropped the collar and reached for my back pocket.

"Twenty-five," I said.

"What are you talking about?"

I let her barbed whip uncurl, the end falling loudly to the wet floor. "Twenty-five lashes for lying to me."

"No. Fuck no. Don't do this. It'll ruin my body."

"Nothing could ever ruin you. Each mark, every scar, is a badge you wear for the darkness inside of you. And each one is going to belong to me."

"Jacob!"

"Say my name again."

"Please."

"Beg me and I'll stop." Her mouth clicked shut and she glared at me, murder in her eyes. "Then we will go ahead with the twenty-five, won't we?"

I swung. She screamed, and the blood flowed.

Forgive me.

# Chapter Twenty-Two

## Nila

My screams ricocheted off the walls. Blood ran ruddy down the drain. I was completely shattered, but I would not give up. Jacob could dish out the torture, I could give him that, but it was nothing compared to some of the things his father had done to me.

I would fight until my last breath if that was what it took to get out from under Jacob's thumb. Obviously, he had a plan for us floating through his deluded head, and I would have to hold on until I could figure out his plan and make my own. I'd defeated Jacob's father, surely, I could defeat the son.

My screams were my outlet, a release of the rage and pain wreaking havoc throughout my body. My senses were on overdrive between the anger and pain, but simmering underneath it all was a hint of lust.

"Come on, Alana. Be a good girl and cooperate."

There was that word again. Cooperate. As if I were a child meant to be tamed. I wasn't a child nor was I Jacob's toy.

"Never."

Jacob chuckled coldly in my ear. "This could have been a lot simpler, you know."

As he adjusted his stance, his erection brushed against my thigh, and I wanted to spit in his face. With all the willpower I had left, I held control of myself. Another lash hit me, this one unexpected. I screamed, but it didn't matter. I picked this place because no one would hear screams, even if the soundproofing failed.

But as his erection once again dug into me, I immediately knew what he had planned.

With a swipe of my hair to my right shoulder blade, Jacob rained kisses to my shoulder in an affectionate gesture. It was so contradictory to the fact he had beaten me bloody.

I was barely standing. In fact, if I had not been trained to tolerate the pain, my body would be a heap on the ground. As it was, my legs quivered, trying to hold me steady and beginning to fail.

"Don't do this, Jacob," I barely managed to get out, my voice hoarse from screaming.

"Don't do what? Love you?"

"This isn't the way to show it!"

"I didn't ask you to talk."

Shoving me against the wall, his body crowded mine.

"You're going to take it, Alana. You're going to take my dick in your tight little pussy and love it. You're going to beg for more like the little slut you are and never make a fucking sound unless it's to moan in pleasure."

"No … No … No. Jacob, don't do this!"

I heard the smack of something hitting the ground. Looking down, his shirt laid upon the wet shower floor. His pants followed, and his naked body pressed against mine for the first time, making me wince in pain as his skin rubbed against the welts left behind from the lashes. Although it hurt like hell, there was something about it that was so damn good. His cock dug into my pert ass while he licked across my neck. One strong arm wrapped around my waist and I was thrashing, throwing my head back to try to slam against his nose. Something to cause damage. Something to hurt so he wouldn't go through with this.

"You bitch!" he cried out, wrapping his arm around my throat. I sank my teeth into his forearm, biting down until blood was drawn. "Oh, you fucking cunt!"

No warning came before he thrust into my ass, and I screamed from both the lack of lubricant and for the fact that no one, not even Jacob's father, had dared enter there before. I may have been forced to lose my virginity, but this was one thing I'd kept. Once more, I was violated by a man who thought I belonged to him.

Thrusting harder, deeper, I was being torn apart. My ass was on fire, the burn spreading down to my toes. I could no longer keep myself standing and fell slack as Jacob's arm stayed wrapped around me. He followed me down, thrusting faster. There was an ache spreading through my insides. I had been violated by a monster. I had been raped repeatedly, but this time … Oh, this time evoked something brand-new.

I wanted to hate Jacob. Part of me did. But another part pitied him. I had been the only connection Jacob had ever made. He had latched onto me, and now his brutal, so-called love bruised my skin.

Pulling my hair back, Jacob's hips jerked as he rode my ass deeper, sinking every inch of him into my tight hole. I wanted to scream, but I was afraid if I opened my mouth, I would throw up and give away my weakness. Tears streamed down my face as I gave myself over to them. I cried for myself, for Jacob, and for who we were before we became these sick, damaged things. The pain spread over my back, burning my soul.

"I've never had this." Jacob's words were barely a whisper. Awe, wonder, and fear all wrapped into one.

His hand went to my pussy, spreading my folds, and my nerves came to life under his fingertips. Circling my clit, my body began to spasm. The burn started to leave my ass and pleasure took over. As sick as it was, I was beginning to enjoy Jacob's brutality. Within seconds, his masterful touch was sending me over the edge. I'd always known I needed it dark. Vanilla sex did nothing for me, and I'd given up on being with a man. But having this, with Jacob, was wonderful. Absolutely wonderful.

"Good girl, Alana."

His voice sounded mocking, and it made me want to fight. Made me want to tear him apart from limb to limb, but then he was pulling out of my ass and invading my pussy, and my mouth flew open in a moan instead. He filled me in every way, and it burned away the past. His hands on my hips, him fucking me harder than ever, I was on the brink of my second orgasm.

What had happened to me? Why was I enjoying this? I was a therapist, for fuck's sake! I knew I was being raped. I was being forced into this and yet I couldn't stop my body from responding to Jacob's touch. Try as I might, I couldn't bring myself to stop him.

I could use sex to get Jacob where I wanted him. I could pretend to love Jacob. I could build him up, like I did with my patients, but this time with some smooth touches and submissive behavior, I could gain Jacob's trust and make him mine. I could own him. I could make him bleed for me and send him to his grave.

And I would take pleasure in it.

*Game on Jacob, game on.*

With one last thrust, I clenched around Jacob's cock as my orgasm rushed over me like a tidal wave. The thought of defeating Jacob turned me on more than ever, giving me the orgasm I so desperately craved.

"Don't you see how perfect we could be, Alana? We could be brilliant together."

"You're demented."

Brilliant. That was one word for it. Twisted was more like it. Jacob and I were one side of the same coin. We were dark and evil. Twisted and broken. But we both had a hidden glimmer of light left in the very deep crevices of our souls. No one but us could possibly recognize it, but it was buried under the rubble of the mess his father had left behind.

I remembered an old tree in my backyard growing up. It was struck by lightning and left for dead. It was blackened and mangled, but my family kept it. I once asked my dad the reason for this, and he explained, "You can always find beauty in the brokenness. This stump is a reminder that this tree once stood tall and proud. It may be broken now, but if you look closely, you can see its beauty shine through." That was Jacob and I. Twisted, but we could find something beautiful in one another.

Face down in the shower, I remembered my Jacob, the one I knew at eighteen. Not this man claiming to know me and following his father's lead on how to treat me. Pulling out of me, Jacob planted a kiss on my neck, a parting gift to soothe the pain. If he wouldn't have come back, I would've been fine. Free to live my life as I damn well pleased. My act would have gone on forever. The after show, the murders, they would've continued to go smoothly. But no, Jacob was back. Jacob was here.

And Jacob raped me. Brought me to tears. He'd coveted me, and I was his. For now. My plan was cemented, and all that was left to do was follow through with it.

"Why, Jacob? Tell me why."

"Because you were the only one ever there. You and Noel. Even in my dark times, even when you weren't physically there, I had you. I had Noel. I had no one before you. No mom. Fucked-up dad. But I had you. And that bastard tried to steal you from me."

"I'm sorry your dad ruined you."

"He didn't ruin me, he created me!" Jacob screamed.

It was as if he was a different person when his father was mentioned. Who could blame him? I remembered Jacob's confession. I remembered vividly killing the man who'd spawned Jacob. It was a wonder Jacob lasted as long as he had. Now though … Something had snapped in Jacob. He was darker and more dangerous than ever before.

"I'm sorry, Jacob. I'm sorry."

"No. You don't get to apologize. Shut up, Alana. Shut the fuck up! Shut up, shut up, shut up."

Jacob had himself backed into the wall, tears in his eyes and hands covering his ears, afraid to hear my words. I was powerful as he fell apart. I was once again back in control, but …

This was Jacob.

The boy who helped free me.

The boy who gave me my last kiss.

The man who found me.

The man who claimed to love me.

And now he was falling apart, lying at my feet after raping me. After stealing what his father hadn't even managed. Jacob wanted to make me his in some way. He'd succeeded, and now he was broken. The reminder of his father was too much for him to bear.

I remained still as a statue, waiting to see Jacob's next move. All too soon he was yanking me up by the hair.

"Don't you ever mention my father to me again. Don't you *ever* apologize, or I *will* kill you."

My therapist brain was supplying *overcompensating, manic, daddy issues* as Jacob raged on, a war within himself.

"Wash the fuck up. We're leaving!"

"Where are we going?"

"Home. It's time for us to be the family we always should have been."

Not another word was spoken as I washed up, ridding myself of the blood, the cum, and the filth. Once I was finished, Jacob took me into the other room and started rummaging for something.

"What are you looking for?"

"First aid kit," he snapped.

"It's in that drawer."

Following where my finger was pointed, he opened the drawer and removed my first aid kit. I only kept it in case one of my victims was dumb enough to bite or scratch me. Fishing through it, Jacob walked back over to me until he was standing behind me.

Pulling my wet locks aside, he rubbed cream on my wounds.

"Learn to be good, Alana. Learn to submit. I hate hurting you, but as long as you keep taunting me, fighting me, I'll keep punishing you. Got it?"

"I understand, Jacob."

It was time to put my plan into action. If Jacob wanted me to be submissive, I would be submissive. I would follow his lead, and right when he left his guard down, I would kill him. I may be connected to him in ways I couldn't explain, but this was too dangerous. Anytime genuine emotion was involved, life became too complicated, too messy, and I wasn't about to go down this road. And sure as hell not with him.

"That's a good girl. Real good. Are you ready to go home?"

"I'm ready."

*But are you, Jacob? Are you ready to meet your end at my hand?*

# Chapter Twenty-Three

## Jacob

I fucked up. No one had to tell me. Taking Alana the way I had may not have been the best idea. But she was so beautiful. So perfect. And I couldn't help myself in taking what had always been mine. But it was not enough. I didn't take my time with her. Taste her, lavish her with so many things that I wanted to.

And then I thought we didn't need those things.

Round and round. Always round and round in my head. As she slept wrapped in a blanket beside me in my ride, passed out from the meds I gave her, I wondered how far she'd go to get away from me. I knew her. She wouldn't give up easily. In all the time my father had her, he'd never broken her. He'd never forced her to see things his way. He'd made her his toy to play with, beat, and fuck, but he never broke her.

And I realized I didn't want to break her either.

"How much of a piece of shit am I, Alana? I don't know any other way to love you."

I fingered a lock of her hair. It was so soft between my fingertips, fine and almost white. But there was strength in it. Just like her. Fuck. I messed this up and I needed to fix it. Needed her to behave so I didn't revert back to some piece-of-shit asshole who took from her until she begged for it, instead of making her beg for what I could take from her. Alana and me? We were ragged pieces of a messy mosaic of pain. We needed it. It validated us and bound our souls together. But our pain didn't have to fucking destroy. Did it?

I wasn't so sure I knew the answer. Really didn't know if I could do what I wanted. But I was at least going to try. That was why I made the plan to move her from that disgusting warehouse to the home we should have shared. The warehouse would always have a special place in my heart. I'd never forget the first time Alana clamped around my cock. How I took her ass and knew, *knew*, I was the first to do it. I'd stamped her, made her mine in a way she could never take away. Sex had never been good until her. Until I had a choice, and she was it.

Now I understood what all the hype was about.

I needed her underneath me so I could do it again.

Two hours later I was pulling into the long drive that led to Alana's home. There was a gate with a call box, but I'd snatched everything from Alana's car, including a wireless signaler that was attached to her visor. The large, wrought iron gate slid open silently as I drove up to it. The drive curved up and to the right, blocking the house from view on the main street. Sweet. Then I got the first glimpse of what Alana had made her home. It was beautiful, like her, and what I would expect from a monster of the dark.

"Holy shit. Bring the darkness in."

The house was glass, steel, and open. There were no lights. Absolutely no "I'll be home soon" porch illumination. Instead, recessed lighting around the bottom of the house showed me where to go. It was large, bigger than my father's. Some rooms had solid walls, but the rest were open glass. I did see thick shutters folded up against the roof of the house and wondered if she could put those down when she needed to.

As I pulled up, a single light turned on above the door, illuminating a smooth, black pad where the doorknob should be. I parked the car and got out, wondering what the scanner was. Figuring it had to something to do with the fact Alana had no keys in her purse other than for her car, I pulled her out of the vehicle. She wasn't heavy in my arms, even completely passed out. But this small slip of a girl meant more to me than anything in the world.

Once we go to the door, I saw a slight green line that ran up and down the center of the scanner. I shifted Alana and reached for her hand. Pressing her palm and fingers straight against the glass, the green light lit up and the door slid open with a *whoosh*.

"Oh, I love that shit. Gonna have to calibrate my hand to it, too, of course."

A meow inside the door caught my attention.

"A cat, Alana? Seriously?"

Once inside, I carried her upstairs, searching for the master suite. I wanted to explore, but I needed to make sure she was taken care of first. Whip lashes could be nasty things if they weren't properly cleaned. I may want to punish Alana, but I wasn't going to let her die of a fucking infection. I swept past the stainless steel and granite kitchen and the parlor room that housed a grand piano. The stairs were in the center of her living room space. Once upstairs, the house extended over the bottom floor.

That fucking cat followed me all the way.

Up here, things were different. The ground was covered in soft carpet, and the individual rooms had solid walls around them, except to the outside. The first three doors I checked led to a linen closet and two spare bedrooms. Then I saw what looked like an office before I found a full bath. The next room was magic though. It was dark and clean. The carpet was a rich dark-red, almost black in the dim light. In the center, a large bed took up a bit of space and was covered in black—ebony pillows, midnight duvet, and raven sheets. The bedside tables on both sides were polished and looked like they'd been carved out of obsidian, and there were no lights on the stands. To the left of the bed, against the wall, was a large mirror and vanity area where Alana had set up a chair and laid out her makeup, hair products, skin products, and more. Beside that was a door leading into what I hoped was the bathroom. I shuffled Alana in my arms and headed for the door.

Alana had made a fucking palace out of the bathroom. In the right corner, a large, garden whirlpool tub rested, surrounded by black and gold marble. Beside it, in a misted fog case, was a shower. The rest of the bathroom had his and her sinks, wraparound mirrors, and two more doors. Toilet and closet, I guessed. Resting Alana on the side of the tub, I balanced her as I turned on the bathtub faucets to a nice warm temperature. I needed to wash off the blood that had seeped through on the ride before I could put more antiseptic on it. I'd made sure to bring the first aid kit in and figured she'd have more here. Plus, a quick stop at a corner store before we got here nabbed me some bandages and extra care products.

Now it was time to strip the cover off Alana and get her taken care of. I slid her into the bath. She hissed before relaxing into the steaming water, but she didn't wake up. For the next half hour, I touched her the way a man is probably supposed to touch a woman. Soft and easy. I washed the blood and the smudges from her face and arms. I cleaned her until the bath water ran red and I had to drain it out. And then I lifted her out of the tub and climbed into the shower with her. I didn't care that I got soaked. I needed to wash away the pain, the blood, the anger. I knew when she was awake it would all start again, but we were clean for now. Her brows furrowed and she shook her head. She'd be awake soon.

I got her out of the shower, and it took a little time to get out of my wet clothes and put medicine on her wounds before wrapping the bandages around the gauze I'd put on the welts. I made sure they were tight to stave off any blood flow and stop them from opening again. For now, she was resting comfortably on her stomach, naked and bandaged. She looked fragile, broken, and I had done that to her. I felt sick. Alana never should have looked fragile or broken. She should always look like a fucking avenger waiting for a chance to take my head off.

"Fuck, Alana. I'm sorry. I won't tell you while you're awake. You'll look at me with rage and anger in your eyes and I won't know how to react. I won't know how to deal with the fact that even you won't love me, and I'll forget I'm supposed to be soft before I can be hard with you. Dammit, I'll fuck it up again because I want it so badly. But I can't let you go. I can't. I've never been strong enough to."

Sinking to my knees at the end of the bed, I gripped her ankles and pulled her off halfway. As nicely as I could, I put her feet on the floor.

"Wh-Where?"

"Shhh, Alana. For a few minutes. Let's …"

I didn't finish what I was going to say. Didn't have the heart to. Instead, I pressed my mouth against her folds. In those moments between when the drugs still had their hold and she wasn't exactly clear-headed, I give her what I normally couldn't. I sucked her lips before tracing my tongue around her clit. She tasted like rage and desperation. Like my fucking dreams and my worst nightmares. It terrified and exhilarated me, and I couldn't get enough.

I pushed her ass cheeks apart and dragged my tongue from her clit to the tender flesh of her anus. I knew it still hurt. Saw the red angry flesh that puckered from my possession. I soothed her there. I gave her everything I could. Then I was back to her clit.

"Jacob," she moaned. Her fists bunched in the covers. She couldn't pull away, couldn't fight. Her limbs would still be loose after what I gave her, but she could enjoy this. I wrapped my arms around her legs, forcing her wider, and nipped her clit. She screamed, her back bowing. I loved it. I loved that fucking sound. Loved how she screamed for me. How she was so wet and ached for my touch. How her body betrayed her and reminded her that she was mine.

"Just a bit more, baby. You taste so good. I want you to come against my lips. I want to drink you. Give it to me."

I resisted the urge to smack her ass. To pull her hair and force her to give me what I wanted. I curled my fingers against her thighs and pressed my nails into her flesh. That was the only free rein I gave my need to punish and hurt. But it twisted something. I could smell the blood as my nails broke the skin, and instead of shuddering away from me, Alana flew into the sky. She bucked her ass against my face, fucking my tongue as I jabbed it deep inside of her. I let her move, gripping her tighter, pulling my tongue away and biting her again. This time it was harder, letting her show me the way.

She reveled in it. Screaming. She needed that beast. She tried to fight it, acted like she didn't need it, but she did. I didn't stop myself from smacking her ass this time. Or raining those hits until her ass was bright red. Nor did I stop when I bit her clit around the little bundle of nerves. I didn't stop myself as she screamed and came all over my face, her essence coating my cheek, her thighs, and dripping to the floor. Fuck, I didn't even stop as I lifted to my knees and pushed myself inside of her.

Her molten insides took me by storm. I fisted her hair, yanking her head back, but she was gasping, clawing at the covers. I wanted her nails scoring my skin. I wrapped my free arm around her neck, and she immediately answered my need. Her nails dug gouges down my forearm.

"Fuck yeah. Just like that."

We fucked hard and rough, leaving behind the rainbows for barbed wire fences and bullet wounds. For shattered glass and serrated blades. We left the niceness behind and came together like we were meant to—in rage, need, and fucking violence. But instead of one of us ruling the other, we combined, lifted, and ripped apart into bloody fucking pieces. In the morning, when it was over, and the drugs were gone, she'd hate me again.

But I'd love her a little more.

# Chapter Twenty-Four

## Nila

Jacob had made me scream in ecstasy and I didn't know how to feel. Every moment spent with Jacob left me more torn than before. I wanted to get to know him, what made him tick, what made him who he was. I wanted to dig deeper into the mystery of Jacob and sink my darkness into his skin. I wanted to make him mine. But at the same time, I wanted to make him scream.

I was so damn confused.

To make matters worse, I was now confined to my house. Once a sanctuary, now a prison. Jacob molded me into his perfect housewife—the pretty princess I should've been had my life not gone astray.

Instead of pure nakedness, I was now allowed to flaunt around the house in heels and an apron, like a demented 1950s housewife in stripper form.

Jacob was determined to make us a family, to make me his wife. I still didn't think he knew what his emotions truly were. He was lost, confused, and I became his anchor. It was comical, really. The fucked-up doctor and the man who should've been a patient.

But Jacob didn't know how to love. Didn't even know where to begin. He took me prisoner, kept me in a cage knowing full well what it would do to me, tortured me, and now he had me playing a game of dress-up and pretend.

I was being blackmailed by him.

His words echoed in my head.

"You obviously don't understand, Alana, so let me make it clearer to you. I have evidence of your crimes. You think I cleaned your workstation to make you happy? I did it so I would have evidence. Top to bottom, I inspected every inch of that warehouse, collected every piece of evidence I could, so I would have it to use if you ever thought of leaving me. You are mine. And if you think otherwise, you will be left rotting in a cage the rest of your life."

"What is wrong with you? You know you can go down with me?"

He smirked at me, standing tall and beautiful.

"I'm taking care of loose ends, don't worry. Don't think you need to worry about kitty kitty anymore."

"What the fuck did you do to my cat?"

"Got rid of him. You didn't need him."

"You killed my cat?"

He rolled his eyes. "I'm not an animal. I took him on a bit of a drive. He won't find his way back. Case solved. You've got much bigger things on your plate.

What else could I do but bend to his demands? I wasn't strong enough to fight him physically, but mentally I could come out on top when the time was right. For now, I would play the submissive housewife.

For eight years I had been meticulous in my life. Nothing out of place. Nothing changing. Work, home, kill. Then Jacob shook up my world and left me a weak-willed prisoner in my own home.

For fuck's sake, I was dusting my own damn bookshelves in a skimpy apron and six-inch heels. This get-up was atrocious. But the way Jacob's stare lingered, the way his eyes caressed every inch of my body and his hand palmed his erection, I knew he liked what he saw.

"You missed a spot."

Fighting the urge to roll my eyes, I turned back to him. "Where?"

"Over there," he directed, pointing at the left side of the shelf. Moving my feather duster back that way, I made sure it was spotless so Jacob had no other complaints. Suddenly, not having more meaningful relationships in my life was a mistake. If I'd cultivated more with Emma and Milly, maybe I'd be looking forward to them coming to check up on me or call. I'd unwittingly helped Jacob isolate me.

His attention fell to the book in his lap. Glancing at the cover, it was *The Things They Carried* by Tim O'Brien, a book I'd read more than once. There was a quote among the pages, "I survived, but it's not a happy ending," that was my life. That was Jacob's life. We'd survived, but it was no happy ending, especially not this sham of a fake family. After everything we'd seen and done, Jacob and I were not meant for a life of happily ever after. Jacob was deluded to think we could settle down and live a life together. The thirst for blood would always hang over our heads, forever taunting us and teasing us back into the darkness. We could never be happy. We could never be free.

Jacob's father had made sure of it, the bastard.

Looking up from his book, Jacob's eyes caught mine.

"I want you to make us dinner tonight."

"Dinner?"

"Yes. The meal that comes after lunch." Sarcasm dripped from his words.

"What would you like to eat?" I asked in my best submissive voice, averting my eyes.

"Steak. Rare. Some sort of potato."

"Yes, Jacob."

"*Now* you get it. You're finally cooperating."

*So you think. Really, I want to gouge your eyes out with my nails and carve my name into your neck.*

Back to cleaning, I made plans on how to escape. But each time I thought I'd cemented a plan, something held me back. Something was keeping me here. The part of me that wanted Jacob … I wanted to cut it out of me and mutilate it. Chop it into hundreds of tiny pieces and scatter it into the wind.

"Yes, Jacob. I don't want to be punished again." Classic good-girl smile in place, I didn't stop when Jacob's eyes narrowed. I could play this game.

He relaxed with a sigh. "I'm so happy to hear that. I hate punishing you, Alana."

"I'm sorry I haven't been as understanding as you need me to be."

*Step one: Show remorse. Make him think I'm starting to come around and understand.*

"You need to learn to trust me, to love me. But you will. You will."

"Of course, Jacob."

*Step two: Be agreeable. Earn his trust.*

"Shall I go prepare dinner?"

With a glance at the clock—five thirty—Jacob looked back up at me. "Yes. Go get dinner ready."

Strutting into the kitchen as if my so-called outfit no longer bothered me, I took out the steaks I'd left in the fridge a few days ago. Hard to believe it had only been a few days. Time passed funny with Jacob.

Preparing a marinade, I soaked the steaks in it. Turning on the stove, I waited for it to preheat while I began chopping up vegetables and potatoes to make a grilled vegetable stir-fry to go with our dinner. I'd always loved cooking, before and after my kidnapping. Cooking was like a skill of its own. Everything had to be perfectly measured and timed. Without that strictness, you would burn your food to ruin. Being in the kitchen helped give me the control I had lost.

And made me wicked-skilled with a knife.

I wanted everything perfect for Jacob, and my reasoning for it was so fucked up. Of course, I wanted to follow through with my plan to escape, but a small part of me whispered, *I wonder if Jacob's ever had a home cooked meal?*

I may not be able to give Jacob the love he so desperately sought from me, but I could give him a good meal. I could provide him with something his father never had. I wished it was good enough for him.

*No.* He was getting to my head. That was the only reason this knife wasn't buried in his gut.

But as he'd pointed out before, I left him to take the fall after he helped me escape and kill his father. I owed him something. I owed him everything. But what he wanted from me was much more than I could give. I couldn't even remember how to love my own parents or brother anymore. I was twisted. I was broken. I played the role of Nila—put together, bright, beautiful, and perfect. I pretended otherwise when, emotionally, I was a robot. I had no soul left.

Jacob wanted me to love him, but I couldn't. I had no heart to love with. Broken, shattered, and left in the past, I was now Nila. Unbreakable, unshakable. Alana could love. That was her downfall. I was stronger now. Jacob would see that soon enough.

As the timer dinged, I plated everything to a chef's perfection.

"Jacob, dinner is finished!"

He strolled into the kitchen with his head held high, only to wrap an arm around my waist and inspect our dinner plates. "This looks incredible, baby."

"Thank you."

His praise warmed something inside of me in a way I wasn't prepared for. Shaking it off, I took our plates to the table. Jacob wanted a housewife, I would give him one.

"I hope you enjoy it."

"I'm sure I will."

He cut into his steak and took a bite, and I wondered what was going on in that mind of his.

"This is delicious."

"Thank you. I've always enjoyed cooking."

*Step three: Give him something personal.*

"Really?"

"Yes. During the trial, I cooked or baked something almost daily to keep my mind off of things. My mom thought I should've gone to culinary school."

"Why didn't you?"

"I wanted to know why men like your father did things like what happened to me. I wanted to get in his mind. Find out what made him tick. Find out how to help myself. I didn't want to be dark. I tried fighting it for a long time, but then I couldn't any longer. I wanted to know why."

"Did you ever find out?"

"No. By then I had already grown to love the darkness in me. It's funny, really. Did you know I used to be a cheerleader? A dancer?"

"No, I didn't."

"Yeah. I used to be a normal teenager. And then one day I wasn't. I was lost."

"I should've been there."

"You were going through your own problems, Jacob. He may have been my kidnapper, my rapist, but he was your father. You lost your family."

"What about you? Did you lose your family?"

"I lost myself and, in turn, lost them. We used to be close. I loved my parents, we had a great relationship. The week I was taken, Dad and I were supposed to be going to the father-daughter dance. I was thrilled. And even though my brother got on my nerves a lot, I loved him."

"So why did things change?"

"*I* did. I wasn't happy anymore. I went through the motions of life, but I wasn't really living, and when I saw how torn apart they were, I slipped into Nila's personality. I gave them a well-adjusted girl. I played a role. And while it made them happy for a while, it was an act. They wanted their little girl back and I couldn't give them that. They tried to help me deal with what had happened to me, but I was still stuck back in that cage, and I couldn't be Alana again."

"I understand."

"I thought you would. What about you, Jacob? What happened to you?"

"Life. Foster homes. You're a therapist. You know what happens to kids like me."

Patting his hand, I apologized to him, even though I knew he didn't want it. He was right, though, I did know what happened to kids like him in the system. If I had to take a guess, I would say there were fists involved for sure. Possibly even rape. Foster homes weren't good to anyone. Especially if you were a serial killer's son.

"We're more alike than I thought, Jacob."

"Why do you say that?"

"Eight years later, we're still broken and living in the past. Do we ever really get over it?"

"I'm not sure. I think that's why I'm here."

"To get over it?"

"To reclaim my life. To reclaim what was stolen from me."

To him, I would always be the girl his father had stolen from him. Sometimes, I wondered what would have happened if his father would have allowed him to keep me. Would I have ended up resenting Jacob? Hating him? Would I have developed Stockholm Syndrome and fallen for him? And if we would have run, what would his father have done to us? Kill us, most likely. No matter what would've happened, Jacob and I would have come out of our situation twisted and broken. And that was if we lived to tell the tale.

Knowing his father, we would've been forced to dig our own graves and die at each other's hands so he could get his jollies off on our pain. That was who the sick son of a bitch was. I was so glad to be rid of that bastard, but oftentimes I found myself wishing I could kill him all over again. He took pleasure in my pain, and I took pleasure in his death.

I had a new problem on my hands. I was finding myself even more attracted to Jacob and wanting to know more, even though I planned to escape him. Problem was, I wasn't positive I did want to escape him any longer.

*I think I may just want Jacob.*

# Chapter Twenty-Five

## Jacob

Dinner was bittersweet. Alana said all the right things, went through the correct motions, and even prepared a meal unlike any I'd ever had before. The two of us, eating the results of her culinary art, in her kitchen, was comfortable, sweet, and family-like.

It didn't erase the fact I knew it was bullshit.

There was only the connection, nothing beyond. I could see it in the slight warmth of her eyes and the way she answered my questions too sweetly. Although she maintained eye contact, she never really looked at *me*. I was crazy, I knew it, but I couldn't let her go. I would never be able to, and maybe that's what was between us. The fact she didn't love me was the elephant in the room, pressing his fucking foot into my chest and forcing blood into my lungs. Maybe she was right and I was obsessed with her and she couldn't love me. Maybe I was idiotic for believing that showing back up in her life meant everything would be okay.

Still, if she wanted to play the perfect housewife, so be it. I'd bank on it. As she cleaned up the remains of our dinner, I grabbed her cell phone from my pocket and put it on the counter in front of me. At least we'd see how invested in this act she truly was.

"Call in for a few days. Don't want them worried about you not showing up."

Her hands stilled in the soapy suds, and I bit back a smile.

*Gotcha.*

But I was on the side of fucked up enough to enjoy our push and pull. To like the idea of breaking her down and forcing her to face what we shared. She wanted to play a game, then I'd be willing to play along with her and see who would come out on top. I let the smile peek through as she rinsed the last dishes and turned around.

"Okay. That would work. I'd be coming back from the conference as far as they are concerned."

"Conference?"

When she narrowed her eyes before smiling brightly, I knew she'd let me in on too much.

"When I take my victims, it either coincides with a conference I've been scheduled to attend in advance, or it's during times I have light casework in the building," she answered.

"The perfect alibi. Makes sense. That's the one thing easier about killing the way I do. I don't have to check in with anyone, I'm a ghost. No one knows me, I've got aliases, and I never leave any evidence behind."

"But after being in the system, they have to have files and information on you."

I lifted her phone and held it out to her. "We both know Child Protective Services has too many kids to keep in line after they've gone through foster care or have been adopted. They can be good people, but there are too many children and too few workers. Make your call."

She took the phone from my hand, and I pulled mine out too. Her eyes darted to the screen as I laid it on the table and opened the gallery to bring up photos. I kept my eyes on her as I swiped the screen through pictures of her files, bloody workstation before I'd cleaned it, and the image of the location listing. A pinched state of her lips was all the evidence I got that my threat of revealing her had sunk in. She pressed a few buttons on her screen and put the phone to her ear. It was late, so I didn't expect anyone to pick up, but the message would be enough.

"Hey, Vanessa, it's Nila. I'll be taking a few days after returning from the conference. Move my appointments from this week to next or call them to reschedule for a better day. I'll be available by cell if you have any questions."

I shook my head at her last sentence, and she rolled her eyes before speaking into the phone once more.

"On second thought, I'll be available by email."

She hung up before I could say anything. "Give me back the phone," I gritted out.

"Look, I've never been completely unavailable to my patients. There are emergencies and the like that come up."

"Then you could have referred them to another doctor."

"This isn't a damn hospital, Jacob. Some of my cases have long histories and don't deal well with new people. I've worked my ass off to get where I have with them. It's more natural to keep myself available if they need me."

I chewed on her explanation for a moment. I didn't like it, but it was plausible. "Emails attached to your phone?"

"Of course," she said.

"Fine. I'll scan them first and will type for you if you are required."

"Jacob." She sighed my name and I liked it. Wished we could do this more. Fight like a normal couple. Fuck like the dark pair that we were and maybe kill a few assholes who deserved it. Was that too much to ask?

"What is it?"

"This thing we are doing? It's not going to work, you know? Eventually, we will kill each other. I can't be caged. I can't be owned. That is something you've never understood."

"I don't want to just own you, Alana."

She harrumphed and stared at me.

"I don't. I want to free you."

"You have a funny way of showing it."

"Let me ask you a few questions, and if you are honest, completely honest with me, I will let you go."

"You're lying."

I shook my head. "I've never lied to you. Ever. You are the one person in my whole life I've never lied to. And if you give me this, I'll walk away. I swear it."

She looked at me, peering into my eyes. I wondered if she thought she could read my thoughts. I knew she would fail. I knew she would turn away. Because somewhere, deep inside of her, she didn't want me to go. She couldn't.

"Okay," she said. She sat primly on the stool across from me and folded her hands on the countertop.

"Do you enjoy killing, Alana?"

"Yes," she answered quickly. Tension sat in her stiff shoulders and focused gaze, but she relaxed at my question. Even she knew there were some things she'd fight to tell me.

"Do you think you could ever be normal? Loved for who you are?"

The tension came back as she rolled her shoulders. "No and no."

She was answering but gave nothing else away. I shook my head, smiling sadly. A twinge of loss filled my heart. She was right in front of me, but the girl who'd helped me kill my father, stole my heart, and kissed me with such passion, was gone. I saw it now, and I ached for her. This woman was destruction's roadmap, and she had no way to navigate back to who she'd been. Perhaps I didn't know this new her. I didn't know how to bring us back around. I knew I would try. I would give everything to keep her. Time. We needed time.

"What happened to you when I was gone? Where did you live? How were you?"

"That's more than a few questions, Jacob."

"We're almost done."

"I went back to live with my family. Finished high school and was tossed from therapist to therapist until I learned to fake it. And then the town provided me with a full ride to college, so I took it and ran. After getting my doctorate, I opened my practice. End of story."

No, it wasn't. Those few scant sentences didn't tell me if she had nightmares. They didn't describe the struggles she had with fitting in. Or how she may have viewed the world. They gave me nothing of her. But she answered. She gave the truth, no matter how dry. So I asked the question I knew she wouldn't answer, that she would refuse to give truth to, and our game tonight would be over.

"What would you need from me to love me?"

"To let me go."

"No, that is what you *want* from me, so that you can escape. Not the truth. I'll give you one more try."

"Being free is all that matters to me, Jacob. When I was in that cage, I wanted nothing more than to get out. To get my revenge and go back to life. And when you put me back in that cage, I wanted the same thing."

I looked her over, memorizing the emotion on her face— hope, anger, need, and the desperation in her eyes. All emotions that were directed at what she wanted, not what she needed. But I'd take her on her bed. And she'd cling to me. Bite me and make me bleed. She wouldn't try to fight her way away. She wouldn't scream and rage. When she called her job, she didn't attempt to leave a cryptic message. By the time they came for her, or anyone heard that message, we would be long gone. And I think she knew that. No. She didn't want to be freed from her cage.

I stood and paced around to her side. She pressed her hands on top of the counter, a slight tremor in her arms. It was probably hard for her, staying like that—not swinging, not fighting back. But her mouth was slightly parted, her chest rose and fell with rapidly, her pulse thudded in her throat, and her eyes dilated. She breathed me in as I came closer, and all those signs told me what she didn't want to say aloud.

I pressed against her back and placed my hands on hers. We molded, fitting together and synchronizing. My heart galloped to match hers, my blood rushed, and I couldn't fight the urge to run my teeth against her shoulder. She balled her hands, and I gripped her wrists to keep her in place. But she shifted, her head falling to the side, her eyes sliding closed. As a moan slid passed her lips, and I bit the soft flesh where her neck met her shoulder, I knew wildness and dark places. Blood and agony. Pain and pleasure. Need and craving. We were all of that, and she didn't realize it.

"Alana," I whispered against her neck, "you lied, and I'm going to keep you. What you need is not to be free. Cages are in the mind. It's a state of being and you're trapped there. Held in place by fear and fighting what you think will destroy you."

She pushed against me, but I didn't break my hold. "No, what you want is to be free, you're right, but your context was wrong. You need to be *freed*. To be that bloody little sociopath that's locked in your heart. You want to forget your worries, your cares, and your emotions for anything except the rock you'll cling to in a sea of blood. I'm your rock, baby. The man who's going to blow the doors on your fear wide the fuck open. Crack up the world and present you with its soft underbelly for you to gut. Because I'm the king to your wicked fucking empress, and I'm going to put you on that fucking throne."

She moaned before she could cut it off, but I heard it. It sang to me. Lifted me up and sent me burning into the sun.

"I …" She cleared her throat and tried again. "I'm …"

She couldn't finish her sentence and shook her head instead. I was afraid once too. Knew what it was like—the absolute terror of stepping too far into the darkness and losing that little bit of light. Letting go of the past so you could move on to the future. I knew it because I'd done it. The only memories I'd given a shit about had included her. The me before she was taken to my father's home faded into the black void. She needed to do that. Let go of family and friends and the pretense of living normally. I'd help her. I'd teach her.

"In the orphanage, Dennis and Eddison were my worst enemies. Two fucked-up teens who liked to beat on me because daddy liked to fuck them over. Then they started fucking me, taking from me, because they liked the control and violence. They needed it. And I wasn't strong enough. Losing you and everything else had broken me. I wasn't strong enough to protect you, and I knew it. I raged about it, but I couldn't get tough. It was like I needed you to set me off. So I used you. Found a way to pull you tighter and tighter inside until I finally snapped. Killing them was my first time after my father. No one has found their bodies yet. I guess if they figured it was me, they'd know to go back to the ranch and look there."

Her head rested on my shoulder, and her nipples pressed against her apron. It was a fucking beautiful view. My little messy girl was getting hot hearing about death.

"Did they suffer?"

"More than Dad, I'd say. I took my time. I had days to work. Then I disappeared. Looking for you. Trying to find you. Always you. The talisman that made me strong enough to survive it."

"You don't love me, Jacob. Not really. You love the *memory* of me."

I shrugged. "Maybe. But then two seconds ago is a memory. This morning is a faint thought. You're a walking memory, Alana, and I'm okay with loving that."

"It's not enough."

"Then we'll make it, Alana. Fuck, we'll beat love bloody and pull its fucking fingernails off. We'll hold it down and strip it to tears and a visceral mess. We'll fuck its head up until what we have is the only kind of love it understands. And then, Alana, love will mean *us*, what we are, what we've created."

When I kissed her, finally, we were brand-new, a beginning. The fucking world opened and wept. Love needed to be terrified of us.

# Chapter Twenty-Six

## Nila

His words and behavior confused me. I was a killer; I shouldn't be getting close to someone who could bring me down. Who had, in fact, *threatened* to bring me down. There shouldn't have been anything between Jacob and me. I'd worked so long to harden the walls around me, to become cold-hearted and protected. People like me didn't love or get hurt. And yet here we stood, the two of us, kissing, and this time I wanted more. More Jacob. More kisses. Just … *more*.

And it terrified me.

Shaken to the core, my heart thumped heavily in my chest, wanting to kiss him, wanting to heal this broken man standing before me. But my head was telling me to run, to get out, to kill him.

For once, I listened to my heart. My face in Jacob's hands, his eyes penetrated mine and I was staring into his gaze, searching for the truth behind his words, and right there, clear as day, I saw them.

"Tell me."

"Tell you what?"

"Tell me about your first kill, Alana. Tell me why you became Nila."

"I think we need to get comfortable to have this discussion. Follow me."

Leading him through the kitchen into the foyer and down the hall, we passed several closed doors until we got to my favorite room, my sanctuary. Behind the door was my safe haven and I was inviting Jacob into it. Turning the doorknob, I led Jacob inside. Decorated in tones of black and white with pops of deep, dark-purple and gray, this was my library. On one side of a decorative rug was my desk with a chandelier hanging above it while two walls were filled with floor-to-ceiling bookshelves. A ladder rested against them to reach the books on the highest shelves. And on the other side of my desk were glass doors overlooking my outdoor pool. A chaise lounge sat near the doors so I could curl up and read near the beauty of my garden. Walking into the room, I immediately headed to the chaise to sit. If I was going to have this conversation, for the very first time at that, I needed to be comfortable. And while this may not be the ideal situation, this could give me some of the comfort I needed.

Before speaking, I collected my thoughts so I knew where to begin. Jacob knew the starting point, but should I tell him about that time from my view? Or do I start after we were separated?

I looked at Jacob. For the first time, he didn't have the same air of confidence or control, so I reached my hand out to him.

"Come."

Placing his hand in mine, he walked closer until he was right in front of me.

"Sit down, Jacob. I'm ready."

As he sat next to me on the chaise, I opened my mouth and the words began pouring out.

"Becoming Nila wasn't an easy feat. It wasn't something I'd planned. The trial took a toll on me. I couldn't sleep, and when I did, I sleepwalked. One night, I woke up choking the neighbor's dog, this yappy thing that never quit barking. Up to that point, I kept trying to rein the bloodlust in. I knew there was something wrong with me though. I couldn't adjust well to life back home.

I was irrevocably damaged and nothing, absolutely nothing, could change what I had been through and the demons that lived inside of me. I was tortured, I was lost … And in an instant, I was found. In a sea of darkness, in a world of endless night, the veil was lifted, and I could no longer fool myself into believing I was Miss Innocent Alana. I was Nila. I was forged from the blood, pain, and misery of my captivity.

And when they suggested I get away from the public, change my name, and start over, I wanted a name that captured the change in me. Like a phoenix, I had risen from the ashes for my second life. I wanted to be a strong woman who would never be controlled and held against her will again. Thus, Nila was born. I made the right connections, I went to school, I made friends. Everything a normal person is supposed to do. But I wasn't normal."

Taking a pause, I remembered my first taste of darkness. And my inevitable first kill. Jacob watched me, savoring my words and taking it all in. Finally, he was getting what he'd wanted from me from the very beginning.

"In my junior year of college, there was a serial rapist on campus. He was drugging and raping girls, and they would wake up the next morning with a rose next to their pillow. Like a sick thank you for letting him rape them. I went to a party with my friends. Rachel, who is a sweetheart, met a guy there. She thought he was so nice. I, however, could see the sickness radiating off of him.

"I tried warning her, but she thought I was jealous. It caused a fight between us, and she ended up spending the rest of the night with him. He drugged her drink, raped her, and left her a rose. But it didn't stop there. She was the unfortunate one. He set his sights on her and began stalking her. She opened her dorm room to find dozens of roses one day not long after the rape and had a nervous breakdown."

It was hard remembering what happened to Rach. She was so sweet, so innocent, like me, and that monster had stolen that from her. She didn't deserve that. Not at all. My poor, sweet Rach. I tried to save her, and save her I did. She tried to apologize to me for not trusting me. It wasn't her fault. She shouldn't have to apologize for a man's wicked ways and slick tongue.

"His name was Peter Barnes. He'd graduated the year prior and was an insurance broker who liked to get his kicks by coming back to campus for keg parties with his old fraternity. When he wasn't at work or out partying, he was raping girls. It didn't matter what type of body or hair they had. As long as they were female, they were in danger. The campus was in a frenzy. Girls were sticking together.

"And Rachel, she was docile. Like a kitten. She lost herself in painkillers and antidepressants to numb herself. Her brokenness made the darkness in me rise, and I knew Peter Barnes needed to die. I hadn't known his name before, only his face. But I started going to parties, and when I saw him again, I did what he had done to Rach. I stalked him. I found out every little piece of information I could, every skeleton in his closet. And then, when his guard was down, I struck."

"How was it?" Jacob's eagerness at hearing the rest of the story compelled me to share it.

"Sloppy but satisfying. It was my first kill, so I didn't prolong it. I lured him to the waterfront and killed him right then and there with a knife to the heart. I pushed him into the water so he wouldn't be found. I was glad I got rid of him for Rach's sake, but the darkness in me crowed because I hadn't taken my time, I hadn't prolonged it or given it the attention it deserved. Peter deserved torture, and even though he died with a blade to the heart, he should've suffered."

"Damn right he should've suffered! What did you do afterward?"

"I studied. I studied serial killers. I studied how to get away with murder. But my favorite thing was torture techniques."

"I've noticed."

"There was something that grabbed my attention. It was the perfect way to fuck with someone's mind. To bring them to the brink of insanity, to the point where they craved death. Where they begged for it. And then I want them to think of their victims, what they put them through. It's why I always ask for a confession."

"I wondered about that. About the confessions."

"Somewhere out there, a girl has been hurt. Raped. Violated. Like I was. Some come out on top, but some sink to the very bottom of despair. The become addicts, prostitutes, and some kill themselves to get away from the memories and the pain. This, *this* is for them. Some of the girls were murdered and are already long gone. I like to think if there were a God and Heaven, those girls are watching down and seeing these bastards get what they deserve because those beautiful girls sure as hell didn't deserve to die at their hands."

"You're passionate about this."

"Of course I am, Jacob! Your father raped me. He tortured me. He killed Celia right in front of me. He raped you. He impregnated me. He killed Alana, the girl I used to be. I was a shell, a fucking shell of decay. I would've been one of those girls if I didn't have the craving for blood. I would've been found hanging in my closet or in a tub full of my own blood, wrists slashed. That's what your father caused. So you're damn right I am passionate about ridding the world of fucking scum."

I stared him down. Sitting next to me, hand on my thigh, dressed in a black t-shirt and jeans, Jacob's eyes seared into mine, and then he was pulling me into his arms, holding my body tightly. For the first time in a long time, I had a sense of security.

"I understand your reasons, Alana."

"Nila."

Pulling back to look me in the eyes, Jacob looked directly at me as if trying to look into my soul.

"Alana. You were Alana when I met you. You're breathing. You're alive. He may have killed a piece of you, but he didn't kill all of you."

"Because you saved me."

"I'll always save you," Jacob whispered, lying back on the chaise with me in his arms. Nothing was better than his arms around me. Holding me. Keeping me safe from the outside world. In here, we were in our own little bubble and were an everyday, normal couple.

"You can't save me from myself," I whispered back.

"I can damn well try."

"You don't know me, Jacob." Once again, I was trying to talk reason into him. No matter how my thoughts drifted toward imagining us as a normal couple, we barely knew one another.

"I fucking know you, Alana. We are one. Quit pushing me the fuck away."

"I don't know you!"

"Then get to know me. You're a damn therapist, ask some fucking questions."

"Tell me about your kills."

"And then you'll tell me more about yours," he returned.

"Perhaps."

"I'm still in control here, Alana. You want me to open up, tell you about me, fine. But you'll do the same."

"I told you about Peter."

"But there's been more," he insisted. "I want to know it all. I need to know it all."

"Tell me about your kills and I'll tell you about RJ."

"RJ?"

"RJ Campbell. My first torture."

"I kill pedophiles," he said.

"Like your father?"

"Just like him. Men who have to hurt little boys. Fathers who hurt their children. I put them all in the alleyways, leaving them with the trash and filth they deserve to be in."

"It's you, isn't it?" I questioned, already knowing it had to be.

"What?"

"The Molester Killer."

"I hate that name. Like, they couldn't come up with anything cooler than that?"

"Tabloids love their names."

"Idiots."

"Is that why you think we're somehow alike? Because you kill degenerates too?"

"Maybe." He shrugged.

"Maybe?"

"They shouldn't be allowed to walk the plane of the earth, it's that simple. I don't do it to save little Johnny from his dad. I do it so I don't—"

"So you don't have to what, Jacob?"

He sighed roughly and gripped me closer. "So I don't have to be afraid of kitchens anymore." Where his father had hurt him the most.

He clenched down around me, not letting me go.

"I was lost, Alana. So fucking lost. I was looking for you, and I was small. Always so small. Late bloomer, they called me. And each time, I was angrier and angrier. Do you know how many kids in the system hate kitchens?"

"Shhh. It's okay."

He buried his face into my neck and inhaled deeply. "I need this, Alana, with you. I'm not afraid when I'm with you."

"But I'm not yours to own, to cage and do whatever you want."

"Of course you are."

I clawed at his arms, and he sank his teeth into my neck. This was us, a battle of wills and differences. Wrong and rationalized wrong.

"How are you any different? You still kill, Alana. It doesn't matter if they deserve it or not. You're still a fucking killer. And you want the pain I give you. Lie to yourself if you want, but you can't lie to me."

"And the world is better off without them. "

"You're still a killer, for your own pleasures. And you don't have to punish them like you do. Guess who else is like dear ol' Dad? And training? Bullshit, Alana. You want it from *me*. You always have."

I was too tired to take up the fight, and his words rang too close to home. "Tell me about the first one," I whispered.

"I'd only been out of the home for a few weeks. It fucked me up. I didn't know where to go next. My dad was dead. I didn't know where you were. I was sitting in a diner. It was raining, and this guy walks in wearing this hideous poncho, holding a little boy's hand. I could see it, you know? The way the boy shook, his wide-eyed stare at everyone in the room. He needed help, but he didn't know how to ask for it. I didn't need to be asked. I let them eat and followed them out. Didn't let them get too far before I grabbed that fucking prick and forced him into the backseat of his car. I strangled him, and then bashed his head in against the car door. I dropped off the boy at the nearest church. Figured a police station was pushing it."

"That's a hell of a lot of rage, but he deserved it."

"Every fucking minute. But I wish I had more time, like my dad after hurting you."

"I'm nothing special, Jacob."

"You're everything. Every fucking thing."

"But why? Why me?"

"Because you gave me the courage to kill him. You gave me something to live for. Despite the hellish circumstances, all I thought about was you, and it gave me the strength."

"I'm sorry."

"For what?"

"That I left you to deal with everything on your own."

"You said it yourself. You were young. My father had done a number on you. He would've killed you, you know?"

"I know. I wanted him to."

"You wanted him to kill you?"

"By that point, I was so tired of the torture, not just your dad's torture, but the mental anguish of thinking about what I had done to Noel. I deserved to die."

"No. *He* did. My father always deserved to die. Never you."

"I killed Noel."

"You had a good reason."

"Did I? Did I really?"

"Look at me, Alana. Fucking look at me." Standing up, Jacob stretched his arms wide. He was seething mad. "Look at me! I'm that prick's son. His flesh and blood. I killed him. I killed others. Fuck, I captured you and did exactly what he did to you. Did you want Noel to be like me?"

"No. Never."

"Then you did the right thing. Because this, me, this is what your son would have been like if he had been raised by that monster. He would've been psychologically tortured, emotionally abused, and if he stepped out of line, he would've ended up raped like me. My dad was a sick fucking monster. Noel deserved better."

I never thought of it that way. I'd thought of a monster raising my son. I'd thought of him having a chance to become like that monster, but I never thought of him being Jacob—the son of the devil. Noel wouldn't have stood a chance.

Jacob was right. I killed my son, but my son had deserved better. I wouldn't have been able to save him from a cage. I would've watched the abuse from the sidelines and have been tortured over not being able to save him. And Noel, poor Noel, would have been a mess. I did the only thing I could have done.

I loved my son. I *still* love my son.

And Jacob loved Noel.

He thinks he loves me.

He wants to know me.

What do I want? What do I really want?

Freedom.

I'm a bird in a gilded cage.

*But do I want Jacob to free me, or do I want to be free of Jacob for good?*

# Chapter Twenty-Seven

## Jacob

The pain in her eyes was real. I knew it, breathed it. There was no artifice or subterfuge, but there was more. Deep in the pit of her gaze, I saw questions I couldn't answer for her. Worries I wouldn't be able to assuage because she wouldn't ask them. She kept them locked inside, even while she opened parts of herself to me. I wouldn't kid myself into believing we were perfect now, the way I wanted us to be, but things were different. She didn't have so much rage or hatred in her eyes. Was I a fool to want more of her so quickly?

Probably, but that didn't stop the urge. It only intensified it.

Alana was an airborne infection I'd breathed in so long ago, and I was dying to have her again—to have her breath searing my face, her walls clamping around me, and her sharp nails gouging my flesh. I was sick from her, pulsating with fever and delirious vision, but what a fucking way to go. Perhaps dying at the hands of my vicious little vixen wouldn't be such a bad thing, but for the first time in my life, I wanted to truly live.

Instead of surviving to get back to her, I wanted to create a life, a world where our sick, twisted ways were okay. That we didn' have to apologize for being a black stain on the world because the fucking world hadn't apologized for making us that way. None of those godforsaken therapists, orderlies, foster parents, or bitch analysts had ever truly been sorry for what I had gone through. And why? Because how the fuck could they have understood? When in their fucking lives had they ever had someone reach into their chests and rip their souls out and kept them alive on hatred and fear?

Never. Fucking never.

They couldn't save the Alanas and Jacobs of the world because they didn't *get* our world. They couldn't redeem us or make us pretty and perfect again. They left our shattered fucking pieces out in the wild, wrapped us up in fragile paper called medication, and hoped it was strong enough to hold the tsunami of the abyss at bay. The fucking idiots knew it would never work, but they did it anyway.

But Alana and me? We were here now, in this moment of absolute silence. The world was quiet and waiting to see what we did next. In these few minutes, we were broken souls mending ourselves with dirty needles and coarse yarn stitches. It hurt so fucking good, each puncture and tightening, and it made us stronger. I could breathe a little deeper, the tension ebbing in my shoulders with each next moment. Fuck the shitty doctors and their empty promises. Sometimes pain was the *perfect* way to heal when pain was what had destroyed me.

I gazed into Alana's eyes as the change came over me. From eager listener to dark lover. From the man who was understanding what our love might be, to the one who craved to drag her love out of her, kicking and screaming, while she bled for me. Alana went still, her gaze locked on mine.

"Stand up Alana."

"Jacob," she started, but I shook my head. It was halfhearted at best, but it was still a warning. I immediately hated it. There would be nothing like the word "no" between us.

I leaned forward and wrapped my fingers around her throat. I didn't squeeze, but the threat was there. "You know what your problem is, Alana? You're afraid of what you want."

She blinked at me, gripping my wrist in her hands. "Tonight was enough, wasn't it?"

I shook my head. "No, but it will be soon. I need something sharp."

Her eyes widened, and she dug her nails into my skin. Yeah, that sort of looked like a no. I hate that fucking word, even silently. Squeezing her throat, I pulled her to her feet before I turned to look around the room. This was a library and relaxation room, and I knew it meant something to her. I wanted to put my stamp on this room, but if she didn't want to answer me, I'd take matters into my own hands. I dragged her out of the room and toward the kitchen.

"Letter opener, on the desk," she said, but it was too late.

"Change of plans. The kitchen will do better for what I have in mind. You need to learn saying no to me isn't possible, Alana. You *want* me to do the things I do to you. If you didn't, I'd have to damn near knock your ass out right now."

When she went quiet, I knew I'd struck a nerve and smiled over at her. She bared her teeth in response, and it made my dick hard. Fuck, I wanted this woman. Once we were in the kitchen, I went to her knife collection and pulled out a thin filet knife.

"I'm going to tell you one time, and one time only, Alana, before I take the choice from you. I want to know you're mine now. I want to see it. You can fight me every step of the way, but you and I both know I'm not going to let you go, and you don't really want me to. I want sterile supplies, gauze, and salve on this kitchen table within five minutes. If I have to come looking for you, you're not going to like it."

I tightened my fingers on her throat, testing her willpower against my own. This was a test, another step toward the direction of what we could be.

*Do this for me, Alana. Choose me.*

It was pathetic how badly I wanted this, for her to do this on her own two feet, but I couldn't help myself. Her gaze traveled toward the knife and back to me before she licked her lips.

"What are you going to do? That's all I want to know," she said.

"Mark you as mine." I was honest. That's all I wanted to do. Make her mine. See it on the swell of her breast, right next to Noel's name, every time I stripped her. No one would ever be able to take that way. Ever. I needed it like I needed my next breath.

She sucked in a breath before releasing it. "And what about you?"

"What *about* me?"

Letting go of my wrist, she moved her hands to my chest and dug her nails in. "Will I be able to mark you?"

Fuck me running. I hadn't thought about that, but the idea made me shiver. Bonded. The two of us. How could I deny that shit?

"Yeah," I said, my voice hoarse. The woman tore me to pieces.

Her eyes lit up with fire in a way I'd never seen before. It wasn't malicious or foul. It was right. So fucking right. The idea of marking me, giving me pain, gave her pleasure?

"You want to hurt me?"

"Yes." The wildness was still in her eyes, but I wasn't afraid. My little torture queen needed to see me bleed, too, and I'd give it to her. She'd learn all she had to do was say it and it was hers, as long as it wasn't letting her go.

"Get the stuff, Alana."

She took a few steps before looking back over at me with an expression I couldn't fathom, but it made my heart race. Wonder. She looked at me with wonder … and a bit of need. I could read it in her as she turned and raced away.

In preparation, I placed the blade on the coil on the stove and turned it to high. Removing my shirt, I tossed it aside. Then, I went in search of a bowl I could fill with water to cool of the knife when we were finished. On second thought, I needed another blade—for her. It took a minute, but I found another filet knife, this one with a wider blade. I'd let her use that one on me. It was on the coil, heating next to the other one when she came back in.

"I've got a first aid kit, Bactine for disinfection afterward, and some gloves, if we need them," she said in a rush. Dropping her stuff on the kitchen counter, she came back to my side.

"Why?" I hadn't thought she'd be willing to take this brand, let alone mark me too.

"Will you ever let me go?"

"No."

"Will you stop me from killing?"

"No. In fact, I'll join you," I promised.

"Then trying to stop you from having your way with me will only make things hurt more."

"And branding me?"

She stared at the knives slowly turning orange. "Because we both need the pain, and you were the one who kept me alive these eight years too," she whispered.

"A confession," I said. I knew the truth before she nodded. We'd found a way to break into each other's armor. Maybe it wasn't love yet, but we were digging our way toward it. Step by painful fucking step.

"Remove the apron." She did, and it was like magic. She was left in her black heels and nothing else. I could choose anywhere on her to place my mark, but I wanted it somewhere I could see easily. I washed my hands, and she did hers as well, before I blocked her against the counter, my lower body pressing into hers,

"Lift your arm," I ordered. Looping her left arm around my neck, she waited. I cleaned the area over her ribcage that would be mine. I made sure a sterile pad, gauze, the Bactine, and water bowl were near me.

"Ready?" Instead of answering me, she gripped the edge of the counter with her other hand and tossed her head back. "God, you are amazing."

"God has nothing to do with this. This is retribution. For Noel, your father, and everyone who has ever hurt those like me. What I will accept from you is a bond to be the killer I need. But that's all I can promise."

I gripped the knife, waving it between us. She followed the glowing tip of the blade with her gaze but didn't flinch away. "We are more than that, Alana, and one day you'll admit that. One day you'll see the real reason you're letting me brand you and why you wanted to brand me too. But if you want to believe it's to cement the start of our journey, so be it."

She opened her mouth to respond, but I didn't let her. I angled the blade and cut her. The heat cauterized the wound immediately as I traced a jagged J on her body. I didn't want it to be beautiful and perfect. I wanted it wounded, like we were, and angry. It was so fucking perfect against her white flesh. She bit her lip until it bled, a strangled scream coming from her. She panted through the pain, and I dumped the knife into the cool water. As it sizzled, I sprayed disinfectant on the wound before covering it with the salve-covered gauze. Once it was in place, I taped it down, then wrapped gauze around her chest and over the bandage. I wanted to make sure it was secure.

"My turn," she said.

Her voice was thick with pain, and she was breathing heavily, but her nipples were hard, her eyes were wide, and when she licked her lips, I saw sex. I wrapped my arms around her and turned us so I was leaning against the counter and she was resting on me. She cleaned my left pec and gripped her knife. I held on to the counter, urging my body to remain still. This moment defined us. She could hurt me before I had a chance to react, we both knew it. If she took this step, she was mine by choice, and I wasn't going to let her forget it.

She waved the knife between us like I had, smiling a cruel smile.

"Jacob?"

"Yes, Alana."

"I want a confession from you."

"Anything."

"I want you to scream it out when this blade touches you. Tell me, and the pain will stop."

I swallowed before nodding. This was the killer, Nila, rearing her head. Her coldness seeped through, as well as her eagerness to give me pain. She was as tragically beautiful in this moment as she was when she told me how she'd ruined her first kill. I kissed her, ignoring the hot blade inches from my face. I traced her bloody lip with my tongue, tasted her, and swallowed her. Then I set my teeth against her bruised flesh and bit down harshly. She screamed but didn't move away. She let her blood fill our mouths and our tongues played with the fluid; we mixed it with our saliva and swallowed it. Then, and only then, did I finally release her.

"What do you want to know, Alana?"

"Will you break me into loving you?"

I didn't get a chance to respond before she dragged the knife against my chest. It was agony, and the smell of burning flesh filled my nose. But she wasn't stabbing me, wasn't killing me. Instead, she traced letters slowly across my chest. I panted and held on before I couldn't take it anymore.

"Fuck yes, I'll break you! But I'll put you back together. I fucking swear. I'll shatter that fucking armor you've put yourself behind to keep from loving me, but when I do, I'll take its place. You'll be safe in loving me because you'll know the only person who'll ever hurt you again will be me. And the pain I'll cause, baby, you'll crave so much you won't give a fuck. You'll need it. And you'll know who you belong to every time you scream."

She didn't pause tracing across my chest as she looked up at me. "Promise?"

"If I don't, I'll break open my chest for you to pull my heart out."

"Good boy," she said and stabbed the blade in at the end of the last letter. The heat sliced into my chest, but it wasn't deep enough to be life-threatening. It was a point to seal the deal. The last step on the road to accepting who we could be together. As promised, she tossed the blade into the cool water and started caring for her artwork. I finally looked down and smiled. *Alana & Noel.* She'd claimed me for both of them. Bound me to their names and his memory, like I'd bound her to his and mine.

"You break your word, you aren't fit to bear our names, and I'll carve it off your fucking chest before I take your heart out," she hissed at me after she was finished patching me up.

I didn't answer her. Did I need to? I was never going to leave her. Fucking death couldn't stop it. I'd find my way out of hell and be her personal demon on a leash to slay her enemies. I'd frighten her nightmares and take them over. I'd steal her soul and drag her to hell with me. No, I didn't need to assure her of my place. She knew it. I saw the knowledge in her eyes as I picked her up and slammed her on the table. Holding her by her neck, I forced myself between her tensed legs and ground my jean-covered hardness at the juncture of her thighs. I could see the wetness, the need, the way she dampened the blue denim until it was dark.

"Take my fucking dick out so I can fuck you," I demanded.

Her fingers were fast on my belt as she worked it free. Leaving it angled, she opened my fly and my cock fell out into her hand.

I wanted to burn her insides with my heat. Brand her walls until they only worked for me. Hurt her until she could only stand my touch. I released her neck and ripped the belt from my jeans.

"Line me up, Alana."

She did as I asked, stoking the fire by pumping my shaft against her. The head swiped through her wetness, throbbing with need. I grunted, looped the belt, and threaded the end through the buckle. I slid it over her head and down to her neck before I tightened it.

"I won't let you go," I promised her and slammed into her body. She screamed, clawing at my arms. Fuck, she was tight, so tight, and I hadn't prepared her, but she was molten. Fingering her clit, I pumped into her. She was mine. Fucking mine.

But she followed me, face turning red as I pulled tighter on the belt. Her core tightened and released as I punished her. Fucked her hard enough to make the table move with each thrust. As we scooted across the floor, the screech of the table legs dragging along the hardwood was music. Violent music of our lovemaking. She couldn't scream as she choked out noises, her eyes wide and helpless, her body thrust back up against me. I knew it hurt. I knew it was ecstasy. I knew it was everything because that was how it was for me.

Bending over her, I sucked a nipple into my mouth and flicked the tip with my tongue. I lashed it and battered it, only to bite it with sharp, unforgiving teeth. She only got hotter and wetter around me. I rocked into her, nipping and sucking hard on her flesh. Switching between one breast and the next, they weren't safe from me. They bore my bruises and indentations of my teeth marks, but it wasn't enough. I needed more.

I nuzzled the underside of her right breast and bit down hard enough to draw blood. To scar. To wound. She bucked underneath me, and then her hands wrapped around my throat. The angle was off, but she didn't try to push me away. Instead, she tightened her fingers, cutting off my air. I released her wounded flesh and lifted to look into her eyes. We rode the wave together as pleasure licked over my balls, drawing them up. I held the belt, keeping her on the edge, as darkness swam on the edges of my vision. Somehow, she knew, like I did, and didn't tighten her grip. I could barely suck in any air, but it was enough to expand my lungs a little.

The pleasure was sweeter, hotter. Forbidden. We held each other—her with the belt molding into her neck, me with her nails digging into my flesh—until she exploded. With her pussy clenching around me, I ripped the belt from her throat and gripped her hips. I set a punishing rhythm, rocking into her and jamming the table into the wall where it had stopped. We held there, me battling for that final moment. She moaned, voice hoarse, and stared into my eyes.

"I'm here, Jacob. Right here."

She placed one hand over her brand on my chest, and the other on mine on hers, and it was enough. It tossed me into the darkness so fast I couldn't catch my breath. One minute I was fighting my way to her, trying to catch up, to explode, and the next I was there. Right there. My cock swelled, balls drew up against my body, and I was coming in thick ribbons deep inside of her. For a moment I wished I could get her pregnant, bind her to me forever. And then I thought maybe it wasn't time, we weren't ready yet for the pain it might bring her. The memories would destroy the fragile thing we were growing.

I shook the thought from my head, lounged in her heat, and luxuriated in the throb of my chest. We were going to get there, one bloody step at a time.

# Chapter Twenty-Eight

## Nila

I'd already missed work for four days. Submissive. Meekly obedient. Passive. I became submissive to Jacob, yielding to his demands and desires. As much as I wanted to fight back, to control him, part of me like submitting to him. Part of me liked letting go of control for the first time in a very long time.

Could I trust Jacob? I didn't know yet. I couldn't deny he was sincere in his desire for me, his want for a life with me.

And that freaked me out.

I could control many things: the way the blade cut across skin, the fear of men, the ability to seduce. But Jacob, oh Jacob, there was something out of my control when it came to him, whether I wanted it to be or not.

As his blade marred my skin, I knew I was so far out of my comfort zone, but watching the blood droplets come to the skin, seeing his brand on me, I was intrigued by the idea of giving myself over to him. It was foreign and yet … it was right.

I still couldn't believe I'd told him about Peter. That I trusted the information to him, especially after he admitted to gathering evidence against me. Even though he'd forced the information from me, somewhere inside of me I wanted to tell him, to confide in him. Safety hadn't been part of my life. Always the good girl. Always the good friend, therapist, daughter, sister. Never evil. Never dark. And now I had someone who knew everything about me—good, bad, and ugly—and he accepted me completely.

I once had a mission, but Jacob had turned it completely upside down, and here I was, flipping eggs like a housewife.

"Over easy?"

"Hmm?" Glancing up from the newspaper, Jacob regarded me with a look that had my insides quivering.

"Are over easy eggs good?"

"Sounds delicious." With a lick of his lips, he returned to his paper, leaving me to get my hormones under control. Jesus. The man had taken me captive, took advantage of me and fucking branded me, but I was swooning after him like a lovesick teenager. I needed to get control of myself.

Plating our eggs and toast, I crossed over to the table and served him.

"Thank you, baby."

"You're welcome, Jacob."

We sat down to eat as if we were a normal married couple. But we weren't married, and we sure as hell weren't anywhere near normal. We were completely and utterly fucked up beyond repair. Jacob's father had done a number on us, and we would never be able to return to what we once were.

"Jacob?"

"Yeah?"

"How do you think your life would have been if you had a normal father?"

"I don't know. I never really thought about it."

"Did you have any interests when you were younger?"

"Usually when I developed an interest, Father would shut it down quickly. I guess, if I thought about it, I would've gone to school. Maybe been a football player. I was always interested in sports but never got to play them."

"I'm sorry."

"What for?"

"That you weren't able to have a normal childhood."

"You did. That's enough for me. Tell me a happy moment, Alana."

"Happy?"

"You do remember what that means, right?"

"Of course I remember what it means. I'm just not used to it."

"Think about it."

I tried to think of a happy moment. I had so many growing up, until I was taken. I used to love life, live for all the moments that came along with it. But once I returned to my family, things were different. I'd changed, and so had they. My disappearance took a toll on all of them, not knowing if I was dead or alive. My brother grew up quickly after my disappearance. My mom totally shut down, became dependent on pills. My father? He was broken, shattered, relying on alcohol to dull his pain. I had gone from a happy, loving family to a fucked-up situation to a fucked-up family.

"Ten."

"Hmm?"

"I was ten. My dad took us to the circus. It was my first time at one and I was scared of the elephants."

"Scared of the elephants?"

"Don't judge me. They were huge."

Letting out a laugh, Jacob's eyes lightened as a smile came across his face. He was handsome when he smiled.

"Anyway, my dad took us to the circus. We all laughed and spent time together. Dad bought me this jumbo cotton candy and a huge inflatable unicorn, and I got to see little dancing monkeys. It was amazing seeing all the animals. But I loved spending time with my family. Being together."

What I didn't tell Jacob was it was one of the memories that kept me going when his dad locked me in a cage. I didn't tell him how I would picture myself right there in that red and white circus tent, the smell of popcorn and hot dogs wafting through the air and sticky cotton candy on my fingers. I didn't tell him how much I loved that purple and blue unicorn, how I slept with it every night, and once I was too old for it, it became a permanent fixture on my dresser. Because, even two years later, it was still inflated.

Jacob being who he was couldn't leave things be. Where one question was, another would follow. Like a dog looking for a bone, Jacob sniffed things out. In another life, he could've been a detective instead of a murderer.

"I want to hear about RJ."

I raised a brow at him. "Jacob, we're having breakfast. What do you expect us to do? Discuss torture techniques over coffee and eggs?"

"I asked, didn't I?"

"Fine."

"Go on."

*RJ ... RJ ... RJ.* I held a fond spot for the man in my heart. My first torture. My first bloody kill.

"He was local. A traveling salesman. He was never in town for too long. Around the same time he was traveling, a string of unsolved murders cropped up. Never in one place but always the same M.O. You may have seen it on the news. The Time-Traveling Killer?

"Yes. It was all over the news. Everyone knew about it."

"What they didn't know was that he was a patient of mine. He kept it under wraps, paying in cash. The moment he offered cash and wanted to go by an alias, I knew he had secrets to uncover, but I didn't know exactly what they were."

"When did you know?"

"About three months into our sessions."

*Four Years Ago*

> *Patient Notes: RJ Campbell goes by the alias of Kenneth Scott. Confident, to the point of delusion, and speaks in a way to appear smarter. His predilections were singular, but he hid them well.*

The urge to kill was burning me from the inside out. It had been too long—two years since I'd killed Peter. I had taken my time researching and maintaining my cover so when the time came, no one would even suspect me. And now I was a licensed therapist.

"Miss Winters, your next patient is here."

"Send him in."

RJ Campbell, known to my secretary as Kenneth Scott, had been coming to see me for three months in between his traveling schedule. Kenneth was charismatic and suave, but he had secrets. Dark ones. The demon in me longed to know them all. I wanted to eat his sins and watch him bleed.

As he walked in, I noticed the cut on his lip first. Second, I noticed the scratches on his face. A long-sleeve shirt in summer? Something wasn't adding up.

"Have a seat. Would you like some water? Tea?"

"No, thank you."

"How have you been since we last talked, RJ?"

"Fine."

"Just fine?"

"Yeah. Just fine."

"RJ, this doesn't work unless you communicate with me."

"I'm paying you, aren't I?"

"Yes, but—"

"But nothing. I'm paying for your services, so I'll answer however I want."

"Once again, RJ, it does not work like that. I'm a therapist. You can either open up to me and be polite when I ask a question, or I can fill your spot with a patient who needs my help."

"I didn't say I didn't need your help."

"You don't say much of anything when you're here. That's what needs to change. Where were you this week?"

"Detroit."

"Ah, Michigan. Do you like doing so much traveling?"

"I prefer it, actually."

"Where'd that split lip come from?"

"Got hit."

"I see. Did you have someone look at your face?"

"No need."

"RJ."

"No. You don't need to know everything about me, and you sure as hell don't need to know my personal shit. Mind ya own business, doc." The sophistication he usually spoke with had completely faded from his tone.

"Hey! What did I say about being polite?"

"Oh, fuck you."

Getting up off the couch, he carried his weight as if he were a second away from hitting someone. Pulling my door open and walking out, the sound of the slamming reverberated around the room.

Dammit, all the progress I started to make with him was gone. With another half hour to kill before my next patient, I turned to the newspaper.

## TIME-TRAVELING KILLER STRIKES IN DETROIT

Detroit. The Time-Traveling Killer had been killing women for the last nine months in different cities, usually a week to a week and a half apart. Aptly named the Time-Traveling Killer, not only were his kills in different locations, his victims were dressed from all different eras as if a vintage shop had been robbed. And now my patient, a salesman with all his secrets, just admitted he was in Detroit and looked as if he was in a fight.

"What did you do after you started to piece the clues together?" Jacob questioned, pulling me out of the story

"I turned to my patient notes to see if there was a pattern."

"Was there?"

"Every location RJ dropped into conversation had been a location where the killer struck. Once I knew that, I began investigating him more thoroughly and started uncovering skeletons from his past."

"Did he come back to you for another session?"

"Surprisingly, he did." I sighed, taking a minute to process my thoughts. "He hadn't been happy with me and how I handled his case. He was pissed I was digging. He had his last session with me and then I had two patients after him. By the time I finished that night, he was waiting for me in the shadows. He thought he could sneak up on me in the cover of darkness. Little did he know, I lived for it."

"What happened?"

"He didn't know I always kept mace on my keychain and my car key between my fingers, so when he stepped up behind me, I maced him in the eyes and stabbed him straight in the eyeball with my key. Once he was doubled over in pain, I opened my car door, shoved him in, and handcuffed the bastard." Looking at Jacob, I could see the lust written all over his face. "Why are you looking at me like that?"

Smiling, he answered, "You're pretty fucking badass. It's sexy."

"Oh hush."

"No, really. Thinking of you one-upping a guy double your size is hot as shit."

"Oh really?"

"Seriously. You getting the best of some poor fool, and as he's bleeding at our feet, I fuck you, so his last thought is of me sliding into you? Sounds like an epic time. Now, tell me the rest."

## Four Years Ago

Motherfucker. I wasn't ready. I had a plan, but the bastard couldn't wait to try to get the jump on me. Hearing him groan in the backseat, I drove faster. My only thought was getting to the warehouse.

Once I was there, I reached into my glove box to grab a syringe. "Always be prepared" was my motto.

Bringing it with me, I opened the back door and jammed the needle right into RJ's neck. That would knock him out for a while and give me adequate time to drag his heavy ass into the warehouse and set things up.

I had purchased the warehouse six months earlier in preparation for when a moment like this would come. Secluded, soundproofed, and all set to go, I was ready to break the building in.

Dragging RJ inside, I deposited him onto a bed with metal railings so I could chain him up. I cut off his shirt and removed the rest of his clothing. Naked and bared to my gaze, I thought of how to begin. Taking a page from my captor's playbook, I attached nipple clamps to him and started to drip hot wax down his abs. As he stirred from his stupor, he woke to me leaning over him, the hot wax sliding down and covering his body.

"Oh good, you're awake for the fun."

"What the fuck, bitch?"

"Says the man who tried to take me from my office. How does it feel to be on the other end?"

"You're a fucking cunt."

"Oh no, honey, I'm your worst fucking nightmare." And with that, I picked up the whip from the table next to me and began wailing on him. Hit after hit, his skin turned pink, and he clenched his eyes tight to keep from crying out.

"Do you like being hit by a woman?"

No response came from him. I was in control, I was powerful. This is what killing gave me. I took the sharpest knife from my table and, beginning at his groin, I started cutting his leg from upper thigh to knee. Slash after slash. Some thin, some deep.

His screams were perfect. They made my insides clench and the darkness inside me dance in glee. I was doing it. Finally. I was making this man bleed by my hand. His screams were so tortured, raw. I loved it. Every single moment of it.

"Tell me your sins."

"Huh?"

"Tell me your sins or face your next punishment."

He was barely coherent, but when the threat of more torture hung over him, his words came flowing.

"I killed them. I killed them all. I dressed them up. I posed them, and they were all were mine. They were magnificent. My work isn't finished. It's not finished!"

Too bad he would never have a chance to finish his work. At the last moment, with my face right in his, his eyes boring into mine, he heard my words.

"This is for the girls you destroyed. Your sins are not forgiven."

And with a slash from one side of his throat to the other, he died.

"You're beautiful."

"I told you how I tortured and killed a man and you think I'm beautiful?"

"Your madness is exquisite. Your darkness is gorgeous."

"I think only you can appreciate those things in me."

"My opinion is the only one that matters," Jacob murmured, leaning in to kiss me. His lips on mine were pure perfection, a heaven within our personal hells. Pulling back from the kiss, Jacob whispered, "Let's go hunting. I'm in the mood to kill. I want to see you bloody."

As my lips curled into a wicked grin.

*Oh, Jacob, you sure know how to sweet talk a girl.*

# Chapter Twenty-Nine

## Jacob

Alana was smart. Fucking hella smart. She came and went to work as if nothing were wrong, all while searching for our mark. I followed her to work, watched her throughout the day, and followed her home. If she really wanted to get away she could have, but I would have made it hard for her or killed her before anyone could take her from me. She knew it, and so did I. But she didn't test me.

She hunted for me.

For weeks I studied her as she met with patients and helped them with their nasty little problems. It was a game we played. She acted like I wasn't hovering in her bathroom or closet—that I wasn't breathing steps away from her—and I didn't reach out between her clients and fuck her on her desk. Some days were harder than others. She appeared almost bored with some clients, notating on her little pad while the patient droned on. Those were the days I couldn't fucking stand. Then there were others, like the one she sat with today.

"Mr. Miller, you are a bit preoccupied today. Want to tell me what's wrong?"

Donovan was a big man, even sitting down—probably pushing about six foot three and thickly built. Should've been out playing rugby or some shit. But the way Alana's skin was slightly flushed told me something else. I knew her; rage and lust almost appeared the same in her. Sometimes they were the same fucking emotion when she was looking at me, but right now, her eyes were focused so hard I was surprised Mr. Miller didn't have a hole in his fucking head.

No, the idiot was licking his lips and staring at Alana, *my* Alana, with lustful, beady eyes. But he answered her question, finally, taking a long look up and down her body before running his fingers through his artfully cut, dark hair.

*Bastard probably got manicures and shit and thought it was amazing. Fucking metro bastard.*

"I've been a little pent up," he said.

I took a second to breathe through my agitation as Alana shifted in her seat and cocked her head sideways. Her expression was thoughtful, open, and it soothed my urge to rip Miller's head off his fucking shoulders. He'd been coming to Alana for months, and he always did have a chip on his shoulder. As if the world owed him something and they'd better damn well pay it.

"Your job getting you down again?"

Yeah, Donovan Miller, the public defender with a job that didn't do shit for his fucking ego when he thought he should have been some hotshot prosecutor.

"My job is easy and dead-end. Always dealing with these nobodies who believe being innocent actually means shit," Miller said.

"Doesn't it, Mr. Miller? Mean something to you, I mean."

"Not really."

"Why not?"

"You ask weird questions sometimes."

"How so?"

"Why not ask me why don't I believe in innocence as a defense attorney? Or what about my job isn't fulfilling?"

"Because that isn't what matters, is it?"

Alana stood and laid her pad on the desk, dropped the pen next to it, and sauntered over to the closet where I was hiding.

When she winked at me, I let a light chuckle rumble out of my chest only for her. *Vixen.* Then she turned, but I loved it when she leaned against the closet, closer to me. I couldn't help but lean back against the frame, taking in her heat as she talked to the man she'd chosen as our mark. Asshole. I'd been waiting for him.

He stood, too, reading her change of mannerisms the wrong way. "Okay, I'll bite. What do you think matters?"

"That you're a coward, Donovan Miller. A coward who couldn't get into a more prestigious school with such a low GPA, but your LSAT was good, so you were a decent splitter for your school. You don't achieve anything on your own merit because you don't want to work hard. That's you. It's why your wife left you in college, after you cheated on her repeatedly, why you hate your job but can't get into anything better. And you have a need twisting up inside of you that brought you to me. It has fuck all to do with your job or problems and everything to do with that little itch you have to mutilate in your dreams. Why don't we talk about that since it's what's important."

I wasn't sure what her game was, pushing Donovan like that, but I let her play it. She'd been doing this long enough, and no one had ripped out the room yet. He bunched his fists at his side and tossed Alana a vicious look.

"You bitches are all the same. Always looking at me like you want me but belittling me as soon as you don't get what you want. Well, fuck you and your high-and-mighty job serving sick fucks like me. I like to dream about pulling off toenails and cutting fingers off one segment at a time. I like the idea of needles poking holes in labia and cutting off the eyelids of my victims so they can watch. Pretty bitches like you, with too much mouth and not enough power."

"Yes, Mr. Miller! *Now* we can talk. *Now* I can help you. The first part of realizing you have a problem is admitting it. I wasn't going to be able to help you if you weren't more honest with me about why you had those dreams. Now we know. And you're still a piece of shit."

I shifted in the closet, bothered by the violent gleam in his eye, but Alana turned again and rubbed her hand across the closet before returning to her seat. I read the sign—understood I needed to stand down—so I tried my best not to reach for the knife I always kept on me. But if that bastard took one step the wrong way, I was going to flay his ass.

"Excuse me?" he thundered.

"You heard me. Yes, I found you attractive, even breathtaking, when you first walked into my office. You have a mannerism that says you are commanding, important. A style that's classic and hard to imitate. Then you open your mouth and all that beautiful packaging crumbles. You use big words but not the correct ones for the moment. At times, you veer the conversation to what should have been *given* to you because of your intelligence or something or other. And then you even create total fictions as to why you didn't achieve anything, but you've been telling the lies for so long you actually believe them."

"You know what, bitch? This asinine conversation is over. I hope you will be *discrete* about my time in your office"

"There, right there is what I'm talking about."

"What are you talking about?

"That slight inflection on the word *discrete*. I believe *that* discreet, spelled d-i-s-c-r-e-e-t, is what you meant. To be reserved, prudent in speech or manner. To not tell anyone about the things I've learned here. But you said it as d-i-s-c-r-e-t-e, and you wrote it that way on some paperwork you handed me before."

"So I misspelled it, what are you implying?"

"You didn't misspell it. You used it incorrectly because you thought it would be different. To elevate you. Discrete, as you said, means something distinct, separate, or unrelated. It's a homophone many people get incorrect. Like the dreaded their, they're, and there."

"I'm not here for a fucking English lesson, and you're a bitch. A total fucking bitch."

"And you're afraid of your dream, what you want to do. You're too chicken shit to do it."

"That's where you're wrong."

Bingo! I didn't need to see the triumph on Alana's face to know she'd pushed him to open up. Alana wasn't looking for the ones who *might* be killers. The only ones she cared about were the ones who were *already* killers. Who deserved to be punished for what they had done. Alana would make sure she knew what he did before she gave him the hell he deserved.

"I think I'm not."

"Shows what you know, bitch. But I'm untouchable. Patient-doctor privilege and all that. You understand. But I think I'll keep you on the payroll," Donovan said. He came closer to Alana, within touching distance, and leaned over her. Alana stared him straight in the face, not flinching. "Maybe I could tell you how fucked-up I've been, then you'll regret ever fucking talking to me the way you did."

His threat delivered, Donovan stalked out of the office and slammed the door behind him. I stepped out of the closet, rage bursting through me.

"We take that one tonight."

"I thought you'd never ask."

Patient Notes: Donovan Miller suffers from grandiose delusions, negative views of women, and a dominant personality to hide his actual weakness.

"No, no, no, please don't, please."

It was so different now, in the warehouse. Donovan was a punk with a superiority complex, but he'd made women suffer because of it. Alana hurting him was magical.

"Oh, Donovan, don't beg. It's unbecoming of a man. A man takes. He makes his way with his own two hands, and he doesn't apologize for what he's done. Isn't that right, baby?"

"Yeah, vixen. It is," I agreed.

We were different, and so was this kill. Alana and I circled Donovan with long needles we'd purchased with cash three towns over before snatching Donovan. As Alana had suspected, he'd already found a woman to vent his anger on, but we hadn't given him a chance to hurt her.

"Who was she, Donny? I can call you Donny, right?"

"Hey, fuck you."

I punched him in the gut and then gripped his chin. "Fine, we'll do this the really fun way." Raising a brow, I turned to Alana. "Wanna do the honors?"

She chuckled as she gripped a syringe off her workstation and padded softly over to Donovan.

"Don't worry, *Donny*, you won't miss a moment. And you'll still be able to talk."

She was fluid and quick, jabbing the syringe and depressing the plunger to put all the drugs in his veins. I'd made a point to pull out every single one of the needles we'd been working on already and then stow them to the side. He'd be ready for them again in a minute. Alana, though, she went for her trusty whip. She allowed me to administer the torture, so I grabbed the cutters. It was about to be hell.

"Needles first, love. Want some time with him," Alana whispered. For her, I'd do anything, so I shrugged and dropped the cutters. There would be time for that.

"I want your confessions, Donovan. I want to know what you've been doing and with whom," she said.

"Fuck you."

"So be it," she said and nodded at me. As she lifted her arm in the air, readying the whip, I pulled the skin of Donovan's scrotum down and readied a needle. As one, we struck, and the sound of his screams was magic. He couldn't move, but he was aware of what was happening. There was no way to battle against the pain.

We took our time the first day. By the time we were finished, he looked like fucking Hellraiser, with cuts between the protruding needles. And then we pulled them out, dragged him off the table, and locked him in the cage. He wasn't meant to live through the next week, so we didn't give a shit about his injuries or disinfecting them. I made love to her that night when we got home, barely able to keep my hands off her.

The next night, she let me use the cutters. It took hours to cut his fingers by small segments and then burn them at the end to stop the bleeding. Even longer to remove each of his toenails before removing the toes. I liked to call him Stubby now.

"Still with us, Stubby?"

"Please. Just let me go. I won't tell anyone."

Alana shook her head. "Is that what Lynn told you, Donny? Did she beg for her life as you cut her up and played with her for days?"

"She was a whore who thought she could make fun of me."

"Donny, you have a small dick. It happens. Well, not to me, but I know it's an issue for some men," I taunted.

"She laughed at me. Told me she would never be satisfied. I loved her. Fucking loved her, and she laughed at me," Stubby cried.

"So you tortured her for three days until you did what?"

"I stuffed a sock down her throat and taped her mouth shut. Then I covered her nose, and well … I'm sure you know the rest."

He hung his head when he was finished, and I looked up at Alana. She glared at him before she gripped his chin and forced him to look at her.

"You're a fucking liar. You like your victims to suffer horrendous pain and die slowly. Something that takes hours. You'd lie to me? Even now? I told you if you told me everything, the pain would stop."

"I don't have anything else you can take from me," Stubby argued.

"Your life," Alana whispered.

"What sort of life will have if I live now?"

"Then your death," I answered. "You want to die fast, or agonizingly slow? I know which one *we* would enjoy."

It took the rest of the day to get him to agree to a quick death. And by then, he was half dead anyway.

We didn't even make it to the car before I had her bent over and taking my cock. Fuck, I wanted her, needed her. Seeing her like this, being with her, drove me wild. I wanted to see her get darker. To see her kill this man and destroy him. I wanted to see how dark we could go together.

"If it keeps happening like this," she panted, leaning against the car, "we won't make it out of the kill room tomorrow night."

I shuddered. Tomorrow, Donovan Miller was going to die, and I was going to have the killer Nila in my arms. I was going to be with her as Alana and Nila merged, became one, and both belonged to me. Another step, another rite of passage. And she was so right. I wasn't going to let her get out of that fucking room before I fucked her harder than I ever had before.

"You're going to love every minute of it."

"Make it hurt?" she asked in a whisper across my lips.

"Absolutely," I promised.

# Chapter Thirty

## Nila

I was turned on, intrigued by the notion I wouldn't be on my own for the next kill. I would have Jacob by my side, like my very first time all over again. The heat radiating from his body behind me had me clenching in anticipation. I wanted him. All of him. And tonight, I would have every little piece of him.

Donovan would die. He would pay for his sins, and I would eat them up and absolve him before putting him out of his misery. What would it be this time? Blade? Strangulation? Whatever it was, I wanted to hear my name as a whisper on his lips before he died.

*Whispers in the dark.* A game played with my victims, their confessions spilling off the tip of their tongue like ink dripping from a pen.

"You've got that wicked grin, baby," Jacob murmured as he kissed my shoulder blade.

"Just anticipating tonight."

"That's what I like to hear. I can't wait to see you, blood dripping over your body. So damn sexy."

Sliding beneath the sheets with that same wicked grin, I showed Jacob how sexy I could be as my mouth sank down on his length, the tip of it hitting the back of my throat, his balls heavy in my hand. My tongue slid up and down his cock, like licking a popsicle. Up, down, around the base, up once more. I started tracing patterns along his skin with my tongue, spelling out my name and words I knew would get his juices turning: *kill, torture, blood*. My hand alternated between a silky caress and a squeeze to his balls. As I drew him to the edge, I brought my hand to the base of him, pulling my mouth off with a *pop*. Leaning down further, I sucked his balls into my mouth. I was determined to be covered with Jacob's seed this morning as I wrung every bit of pleasure from him. As I deep throated him, my throat burned with each suck.

I lived for the control of making Jacob beg. His moans were such a sweet sound to my ear. As I looked him in the eyes, his dick hitting the back of my throat, I could see his pleasure reflected back at me. With a groan and a pull of my hair that left me wanting more, his cum spilled down my throat. Gagging, memories of his father threatened to take over. I tried to keep it down and hurriedly to swallow every last bit. I wouldn't let his father tarnish something I wanted to give Jacob.

Licking my lips, I stared up at this magnificent man who was all mine.

"We've got work to do." I winked and headed for the shower. As much as I loved stealing a moment with him, I needed to get my head in the game.

"You ready for this?"

"Of course I am. Donovan thought last night was rough, well, wait until he sees what I have in store for him today."

"You're evil."

"You love it."

"That I do."

Donovan was barely hanging on, but he would sure as hell get the punishment I was going to dole out, no matter what I had to do. A cock ring would be the perfect tool to start with. But not your average, everyday cock ring. This one was made just like the spiked collar Jacob made me wear when he held me captive. With spikes on the inside, it was guaranteed to draw blood and cause the wearer agony. Some may call me evil, some may call me a bitch, but I preferred to think of myself as a wicked do-gooder. While my methods bordered on insanity, I was ridding the world of filth like Donovan, one man at a time.

"Donovan, Donovan, Donavan," I started mockingly. "How have you been? I see you're a little tied up. Are you ready for it to all be over?"

After last night's session, it was no wonder he could barely speak today. Trying to push the words past his lips, the most he managed to do was drool.

"Ah, good boy. You've decided to cooperate today."

Placing the cock ring around his dick, I watched as tears immediately began welling in his eyes.

"We're going to play a little game. I'll ask a question. Look left for yes and right for no. And Jacob here is going to hand me a knife. If the answer is yes, you escape punishment. If you lie, it will be worse. Keep that in mind."

"Did you enjoy killing those women?"

He looked to the left.

"Ah, you did. How does this feel?"

With the knife, I made a slash along his right cheek. Shallow, but it would sting. I was saving the best for what came next.

"Did you get off on it? On seeing their pain?"

Once again, he looked to the left.

"If I let you go, will you do it again?"

Look to the right. I guess he hadn't entirely given up on the lies, especially when he thought they would save him.

"Wrong answer, sweetheart. Jacob, why don't you help get Donovan set up on the other bed."

As Jacob manhandled Donovan over to the bed and threw him down, I made sure everything was in order. This was sure to be my best kill yet.

Dragging the coolers Jacob and I had purchased earlier in the day, I began packing the bags of ice around Donovan, watching as the shaking started.

Arching my eyebrow, I couldn't help myself from asking, "A little cold, are we?"

Jacob smirked from the other side as he helped me set things up perfectly.

"I must say I'm quite disappointed in you, Donovan. You lied to me."

He shook his head forcefully as he tried to deny it.

"Save yourself the trouble, Donovan. I know if I were to let you go, you would keep on killing. Do you know how I know?" Pausing, I let my words sink in. "Because I couldn't stop killing if I tried. The darkness calls to me too much to be able to stop."

He lost more pieces of himself.

"Please," Donny begged.

"Please what?"

"Please don't do this."

"Too late." I turned to Jacob. "Your turn, my love."

Muscular and strong, Jacob easily handled the bone saw and started cutting Donovan's legs off above the knees. Oh, what a masterpiece he would be by the time we were finished with him. With the amount of blood he was losing, I knew it was only a matter of time before he bled out. While Jacob worked away, I whispered in Donovan's ear, tickling the shell of it with my breath, "Bet you wish you never would've stepped foot in my office. I'm the devil in heels, baby."

Giving myself time to collect my thoughts, I stepped away and headed into the kitchenette for a glass of wine. With a last sip of Merlot, I heard my name called from the other room and followed Jacob's voice.

"Ready for me?" I questioned with a sly grin.

"Always, baby."

Donovan was dead. After Jacob put away the tools and hid the body parts, all that was left were the stains from what we'd done.

"You didn't have to hide it from me." Once again, he'd made sure I didn't have to do the heavy lifting.

"I'm more interested in other things."

"You'll burn in hell for this."

"Save me a seat, sweetheart." Plunging the blade into Donovan's chest cavity, I opened him up just as a hunter would with his prey.

Jacob headed toward me, his arm wrapping around my waist as he got close. "You're vicious."

"I'm yours."

"Promise me, Alana."

"I promise, Jacob."

Jacob reached up and caressed my cheek. The warmth of his hand spread through me as his eyes caught in mine. My body trembled with lust. With need. With want for Jacob. My breathing was heavy, my lips opening as his fingers drew closer to my mouth. He traced my lips with his tongue, leaving behind his saliva. I licked it off before sucking his finger into my mouth. Stepping back, I unzipped my dress and let it pool at our feet. Jacob's heated gaze took me in.

"You've been naked underneath this whole time?"

"I wanted to be ready for you."

Gripping my hips, he responded, "You sexy, evil woman. I can't believe you're finally mine."

"Believe it."

Looking down, I saw the blood on my hip where his hand gripped me. Remnants of what he'd done while I was drinking my wine. Jacob, me, and blood. This was meant to be. This was our destiny. We were turned evil by one man so we could save each other. So we could become one. Wrapping my arm around Jacob, I kissed him with all the passion built up in me. His tongue slid wetly against mine. His hands seared into my flesh, and I grew wetter.

Dropping to my knees in front of him, I unbuckled Jacob's pants and pulled the zipper down until the material fell down his legs. I licked my lips at the sight of the hard bulge under Jacob's boxer briefs. Pulling them down for him, I looked up as he threw his shirt on the ground. He stared back at me as I started mouthing his cock. *My* cock. Every inch of Jacob's well-defined body belonged to me. I was his and he was mine.

"So fucking sexy." His gravelly voice washed over me, and the growl I could hear in it caused an ache in me. "You look so fucking good like that." Reaching down and grabbing me by the hair, Jacob pulled me up to him. "I want to see every inch of you."

"Anything you want, Jacob. Anything."

He pushed me back on the floor and took his time. His gaze traced my skin, the heat pulsing over my nerve endings everywhere.

"I need you, Jacob."

Plunging two fingers into my hot, wet cunt, Jacob bit down on my shoulder hard enough that I knew his mark would be on me long after he took me. Moans of pleasure fell from my lips as my head dropped to his shoulder.

"Bend over, baby."

Doing as he asked, I bent over my medical table. Usually used to keep my captives tied up for the night, it was serving a whole new purpose as Jacob grabbed at my ass cheeks and breached me in one hard thrust. There was nothing to compare to being taken in the darkness. To unleash our mutual madness. Now one, I would forever be Jacob's and he was putting that claim on me with every thrust of his cock, every pull of my hair, and every bite to my neck. His hands caressed up and down my body before stopping to pull on my tits, leaving me to let out a loud gasp.

"I think my girl likes that," he whispered.

"Yes … Yes … More."

"Tell me you love me."

"I love you."

"Tell me like you mean it."

"I love you, Jacob. I love you."

He picked up the pace, his thrusts becoming harder, faster. My moans fell from my lips between loud pants.

"Touch yourself. Touch your fucking clit."

"Yes, Jacob. Yes."

Circling my clit, the sensations hit me. Right before the wave of pleasure overcame me, Jacob wrapped his hands around my throat, pushing the pleasure higher. Putting my trust in him not to kill me, I gave myself over to him, and as the pleasurable wave of orgasm overtook me, I could hear Jacob whisper, "I love you." With that, a second orgasm hit me.

As my knees shook, I told him I loved him too. And I meant it. With one last thrust, he filled me with his release, marking me.

I was, and always would be, Jacob's. His lover. His friend. His enemy. His own personal darkness.

I was everything to him as he was to me.

"You meant it, didn't you?" Jacob questioned in awe, still inside of me, face buried in my neck.

"I did. I do. I love you, Jacob."

He hardened within me. From the beginning, it was all he'd asked of me, and now I could give it to him. I could give myself to him without losing all of my control. Jacob was my equal. He always had been, even when he tried to pretend differently.

"I love you, Alana."

"I know you do, Jacob. You always have."

Pulling my head back by my hair, he positioned us so he could kiss me. And what a kiss it was. Jacob's kiss set every nerve on fire. As he deepened the kiss, I knew this was it. This was forever. Fucked-up and broken, we were a pair with a bond that could never be severed.

Thrusting inside me once more, Jacob carried me off into a nirvana of pleasure and pain, of darkness and light. For years I was dead inside, but in this moment, every sensation was overwhelming. His breath on my ear, his bloody hand on my thigh, his thick cock inside my pulsating core.

Everything we had been through had led up to this moment. And what a perfectly dark moment it was.

# Chapter Thirty-One

## Jacob

The dead started to blend together. I didn't think we knew how to stop. Over the coming weeks, we didn't kill only one. No, we killed many. Some we researched, others not so much. But we believed each and every one of them deserved falling under my blades. We took pimps and drug dealers. Gang members and patients—so many dark patients of Alana's who needed our sort of retribution.

And the darkness between us swelled.

But we should have been more careful.

"Reports are stating this is one of the worst epidemics in missing persons from the area in over three decades. Statistically—" I stopped listening to the newscaster as a knock sounded on Alana's door.

"You expecting company?" My voice was barely above a whisper. I slid on silent feet from the bed I was sharing with Alana and tiptoed to the windows. There was an unmarked car outside. "It's the police."

She was already getting up, tossing my black t-shirt over her naked form. I hated the fact I couldn't see my brand on her ribs but loved that she was in my clothing. She looked sexy and bed-tousled like that.

"Might be about the missing cases," she stated. "We've been a bit heavy-handed."

I shrugged. "It happens, but maybe they're not here for that. Could be routine if any of the missing persons show up on your lists of clients."

"I won't know until I've talked to them. Follow on the stairs and stay within earshot. I want to make sure we both hear what they have to say."

My heart thudded in my chest. We were a pair in this, always, and she trusted me. We killed, tortured, and loved together with no apology. For the first time, the hell of my past didn't seem so bad. At least with her I had a reason for living, someone to understand me and love me despite the fucked-up hell deep inside me. Maybe we would have been too different if my father hadn't snatched her, but I was selfish enough to see I would have never been free. I shouldn't have been happy she'd been taken, but I fucking was.

"Good evening, Ms. Winters, we understand it's late. I am Detective Monroe, and this is my partner Detective Jackson. Would it be okay if we asked you a few questions?"

"Gentlemen, this would have been better at my office. You've caught me at a time when I'm not exactly presentable."

"We understand," Jackson said, "and we hate to do it, but the boss is jumping down our necks about the abundance of missing persons, and we are trying to make heads or tails of things."

"Oh," Alana said. She crossed her arms and leaned against the doorframe, my t-shirt riding up her thighs. The pose was provocative, but her expression was all business and concern. Both detectives, though, didn't miss an opportunity to ogle her legs.

*She's mine, assholes.*

"My guess, since you're at my door, is that some of my clients' alleged victims are on your list?"

"Not quite. More like several of your clients. May we come in?"

Alana nodded her head, that same concerned expression on her face. "Please do."

She backed away from the door, and I slid back along the wall toward the bedroom. The stairs blocked me from view downstairs, but I could still hear. The open floor plan of her house could make this tricky though.

"I know it may be a crazy question, but are you on TV or something?" Jackson waited for Alana's answer with a calculated stare.

Alana shifted. "No, why?"

"You look familiar that's all. Like I've seen you before. Oh well," he said, shaking his head. Bu he hair on my arm rose. Who the fuck was he?

"I want to put something on. Can you wait here?" She pointed to her main living area. The detectives nodded and sat down obediently. I knew they wouldn't stay there once she left the room, but I could keep an eye on them, and I knew she had a reason for doing it. Besides, it helped that everything we did was kept at the warehouse. They wouldn't find anything here.

She padded by me quickly, put on a bra, pants, and came back out of the bathroom. She showed me our phones and put hers on record. Then she did the same to mine and laid it on the counter.

"Keep an eye out while this records. We don't want to miss anything," she said quietly. I didn't have time to do much more than nod before she was heading back downstairs.

"Thank you for waiting, gentlemen."

They hadn't waited. They'd pawed over her mantle, a bit over the books and magazines on her coffee table, and paced around the floor looking for things. Monroe had even tried the locked door of her library. But at least now they were back in their seats, acting like good little cops.

"Now, who do you have questions about? You do understand I am under client-doctor privilege and there are some things I may not be able to talk to you about."

"We understand that. This is more of a cursory investigation. We want to get to know these victims and see what we can find out about them."

I swallowed a snort. Those fucking bastards weren't victims, they were predators, like Alana and me. We'd been stronger than them in the end.

"Okay, ask away."

"What sort of client was Donovan Miller?"

*Shit.*

"Mr. Miller was a public defender, well put together, young but charismatic."

"That's all we can find out from his friends and family."

"Then ask the questions you want to know, Detective. I can only answer what I'm given, within the bounds of my code."

"He was seeing you after several allegations of rape from ex-girlfriends, is that correct?"

"That is correct." She didn't say more, and the way Jackson chewed on his lip, I'm guessing he expected her to.

"Who would want to hurt him?"

"Probably quite a few people, if you look at his record. But what makes you think he's missing? He sometimes takes long trips between cases when he can. He's attempting to start his own firm, from what I understand."

"Because he missed an interview with the prosecutor's office, and from what we have learned, he was obsessed with working there. He also hasn't shown up to speak with any of his clients, to his office, or contacted any of his friends."

"Hmm, that's not like him."

"Are you sure you've never been on TV?" Jackson pressed.

I didn't like that bastard at all. Why the fuck did he keep harping on that?

Alana was good. Damn good. She frowned appropriately and paced her room as if she were thinking. She answered questions and deflected them when she couldn't betray her client. She was magnificent and sharp, but there were three victims on her client list from our recent spree, and that made the cops think of something else.

"Do you believe this could have something to do with you, Ms. Winters?" Monroe's gaze was pointed, and I shifted.

"I'm not exactly sure what this has to do with me. I mean, with my sort of occupation, we deal with clients who lash out and make threats. It goes with the territory. But I haven't been attacked or faced anything threatening."

"Ah," Jackson interrupted, snapping his fingers. "I know

where I've seen you. It wasn't on TV, but your story was looked into it while I was in the Academy. You're Alana Masters, the survivor of Elliot VanDuyn, right?"

Alana tensed, the first time her mask of perfection had slipped. I saw the fear and rage flush in her eyes and the slow way she turned on him. Monroe didn't miss a thing. His keen eyes were measuring as she spun on Jackson and spoke to him with a coldness she hadn't had before.

"How would you know anything about that?"

I cursed under my breath. She was going to break if I didn't get down there. This was unexpected, and her time with my father was a touchy subject for her, no matter how long ago it happened. Thinking quickly, I put on a robe to hide my brands and snuck into the bedroom. Once there, I made noise getting out of the bed and heading to the restroom. A few seconds later, I flushed the toilet and headed out of the bathroom, toward the stairs, rubbing my tired face.

"Baby? Where are you?"

"I'm in the living room," she said, but the ice was still there.

*Fuck.* I padded down the stairs and stutter-stepped when I saw the police looking me over.

"Who are you?" Then I looked at her. "What's wrong?" I ignored them as I pulled her into my arms and kissed the nape of her neck. Then I dug my nails into her sides and nipped her skin. A reminder. A punishment. The only one able to hurt her, to punish her, was me. Fuck what these cops said. They didn't have the power to touch her.

"This is Detective Monroe and Detective Jackson. They wanted to ask a few questions about my clients."

"Is that what had you upset?" I looked only at her and thumbed her cheek. Fuck them. I could kill them right now for her if she asked. If they were bothering her, I would remove them. I think she saw it in my eyes. She smiled, her body losing some of the coldness as she sank into me.

"Brought up the past."

Finally, I looked over at them. "I'll be dealing with nightmares the rest of the night now. Is there a reason you brought up something so traumatic when inquiring about missing persons?"

Jackson had the nerve to look sheepish, but Monroe simply shrugged. "My partner didn't think before he asked about it. But Ms. Masters—"

"Winters," I interrupted.

"I'm sorry?"

"You called her Ms. Masters. You know she changed her name to Nila Winters. It's why you asked about it," I argued.

"My apologies, Mr ...?" Monroe's words trailed off.

"Daniels," I answered. I took his proffered hand and shook it. "Mason Daniels."

The detective stared at me a moment, wheels turning in his head. His partner's gaze narrowed, but after a moment, he shrugged.

"How long have you and Ms. Winters been dating?"

"I'm wondering about the relevance of these questions," Alana interrupted. "I do not believe my clients' missing status has something to do with them being my clients."

"No, but it could be *because* they were your clients," Monroe stated. "You know, there are a lot of angry groupies after the VanDuyn case. Many thought you deserved to face charges. Have you thought maybe someone from your past caught up with you and is doing things in retaliation for that?"

"It would be hard for someone to find about that. My name was redacted from everything because I was a minor when things happened originally, even though I was an adult when I escaped. Then, I had my name changed and was given a new lease on life to start over without all of that in my history. Most didn't know I had that in my past. Even background checks couldn't have pulled that up. Not without FBI clearance, as I was in a protection program," Alana argued.

"You're right," Monroe said. "We never said we were from the CPD. Perhaps reintroductions are in order. Special Agent Monroe and Jackson, FBI, Chicago field office."

"I think you gentlemen need to leave. You came in under false pretenses, as you stated you were local detectives and not FBI agents. You stopped asking me questions about the missing persons and focused on *my* past. Until you have a warrant, do not return," Alana said.

"That can be easily arranged. I've got Judge Sovern on speed dial. Should I contact him?" Monroe added.

"Sure, I'll be happy to speak to him," Alana returned.

"Call who you like, gentlemen, but tonight you are going to leave," I added. They stared at us a minute but finally made to leave.

Jackson turned at the door. "There are more than three patients you've dealt with, Ms. Winters, that have gone missing in the last few years. Expect to see us again."

"I have nothing to hide," Alana said. The door slammed as they left, and Alana spun on me in a rage. I let her leap on me and attack me. Let her anger sizzle over my nerve endings from the bite of her nails digging into my skin and her teeth muffling her screams. I let her get it all out of her system as I gripped her through it.

"I need to kill again," she whispered hoarsely into my throat.

"Alana, it might be too soon."

"I need it, Jacob. I need to get rid of the rage. I need to break something, to remind myself your father didn't break me. That I haven't fallen all over again."

How exactly was I supposed to deny the woman of my heart the chance to get what she needed? How could I tell her I wouldn't give her anything her heart desired, even if it sent us burning up in smoke together.

I couldn't.

I sighed and gave in. "They may look harder at you afterward."

"And we'll make them disappear if they do."

"A big flare-up, right there, killing cops."

"Jacob, I need it. Please."

Fuck me, I couldn't say no. Even when I knew it was fucking crazy.

"All right. Choose one."

# Chapter Thirty-Two

## Nila

I knew Jacob was right. We had to be careful before my thirst for blood and vengeance got us caught, especially with the cops on our backs. I couldn't help it though. The lust for blood was at its all-time highest, and with Jacob here, the act was even more intimate, more important. But we had to be smart about things. We couldn't risk what we had. There was no way we could be separated again. We wouldn't survive without each other.

As the sunlight streamed in on Jacob's naked form lying in my bed, I looked at him, examining all he had to offer. His muscular, toned chest on display with my brand proudly there. His firm, hard cock rising. His hands that held me gently but gave me punishment when I deserved it, when I craved it. The scars he bore from his father's hands. I loved every part of Jacob. Imperfections and all. That's why I knew exactly what we had to do.

Dressed in a dark Black Halo sheath dress and Louboutin pumps, I picked up my briefcase from the chair in the corner. With a kiss on Jacob's forehead, I headed for my library to grab a patient file before I left for the office.

Once at the office, I pulled out the patient file with contents full of secrets and lies. I knew if I were going to put my plan into action, this would be the last patient killed at my hands.

William T. Lee.

The man was a mogul. He made his living off shipping exports and imports, but what no one knew was some of those imports were girls from China. Girls who dreamed of a better life and instead found themselves auctioned off and sold to the highest bidder. The men would rape, torture, and kill them. And for the last few months, I had been hearing Lee's tales that sounded like a horror story once a week. He trusted me because he knew I was bound to listen, but he didn't know I could've dropped his name with the cops at any moment but chose not to because I was biding my time, waiting to strike. But his next shipment was coming in this weekend.

If Jacob and I were going to go on the run, I wanted to take out one last monster. And the little bit of Alana that remained in me, well, she wanted to do something good. As long as my plan worked out, I could nail Lee for his crimes, kill him, and fake my own death, leading police to believe it had been Lee all along.

"Baby, what are you doing here?"

Looking up, I saw Jacob in front of my desk looking down at me. I was so lost in thought, I didn't notice anyone coming in. I was really losing my touch.

"I couldn't sleep. I'm sorry if I worried you."

"Of course I was worried! I woke up and you were gone."

"I'm sorry."

Walking around my desk, I waited until Jacob was seated before making myself at home in his lap, my arm wrapped around him.

"What's on your mind?"

"We need to disappear. The cops are keeping tabs on me and now they know I'm Alana. We can't stay here. I can't lose you."

"You'll never lose me."

"You can't say that for sure. If we get caught, I'd have to live without you, and I've already done enough of that for one lifetime."

"So what's the plan?"

"William Lee."

"Hmm?"

"He's a client of mine. A sick son of a bitch. He sells girls for money and has a new shipment coming in this weekend. If we want to leave and have a clean getaway, we set him up to take the fall for my murder and the trafficking of the girls."

"You may be onto something here."

Arching a brow at Jacob, I replied, "Well, I'm not just a pretty face." With a short laugh, I relaxed into his body, letting my worries disappear for a few minutes.

William was scheduled the next day, so I called to tell him I had an emergency and offered him a late appointment that evening. Agreeable as usual, William's appointment was set. Telling my assistant to take off for the night because I had no other appointments on the books for the day, Jacob and I waited in silence. When the elevator dinged to let me know William was there, Jacob slipped silently into the closet, ready to strike when I needed him to.

*Patient Notes: William Lee. Dangerous, calculated, and respected. He uses his money and connections to stay out of trouble. He believes he has more power than he does, but he uses it effectively.*

"Hello, William. Thank you for making it on such short notice," I greeted him as he came in, already beginning to unbutton his suit jacket to get more comfortable.

"No problem, Nila, dear."

In his fifties, William had a head full of gray hair, a shorter stature than most men, and a paunchy stomach. Dressed in an expensive suit, the smell of money practically wafted off him.

"I had a last-minute conference come up so I was happy you were able to come in today. How have you been?" I asked William.

"Good, good."

"Wonderful to hear. Any problems lately? No side effects from the new medication?"

"No. Things are well. Doctor gave me a full checkup the other day and said I'm in tip-top shape."

"So what's on your mind this evening, William?"

"Well, to tell you the truth, I have an important shipment coming in this week."

"Oh?"

"Yes, yes. One of my special shipments," he replied with a wink.

"Ah, I see. And tell me, William, do you derive pleasure from this?"

"Oh, honey, if I'm making money, that's all the pleasure I need from life."

"Hmm ..."

"Look, I didn't have anything but the clothes on my back when I was growing up. I came from nothing and rose to the top on my own. If I have to blur the lines between good and bad sometimes, I'm fine with that. At least I know I'll have food in my stomach and a place to sleep at night."

"I see. We never really discussed your circumstances growing up. Care to share with me, William?"

"What's there to share? My mother was an addict who threw away our rent money on drugs, forcing us to live on the streets. I escaped her claws before she started selling me like she was selling herself. The crack whore died on the streets, a needle in her vein. My father was an idiot for marrying her. Met her in China on one of his tours. Navy man, you know. Brought her back to the States and that was how she repaid him. By becoming a junkie. When he died, it got worse. She didn't care about anyone but herself."

"I'm sorry to hear that, William. What about siblings?"

"She got knocked up a few times. Gave the babies away."

"Did you ever look to find them once you were older?"

"No. Why would I? They were just a bunch of bastards."

As William got out his last words, Jacob stealthily snuck from the closet, coming up behind him. Placing his forearm around William's neck, Jacob put him in a chokehold and William lost the last bit of his breath and his eyes closed.

"That should hold him for a while," Jacob's gravelly voice cut into the silence.

We knew better than to use any drugs with William. We didn't want anything suspicious coming up on an autopsy. As Jacob bound William's hands behind his back with a cloth, I ran downstairs to pull the car up to the elevator. Once Jacob and William were downstairs and William was safely put into the car without anyone seeing, we were on our way to the warehouse.

"Are you ready for this, Alana?"

"I'm ready for anything that lets me keep you."

With hands held tight, Jacob drove us into the night as I prepared for what was to come.

Jacob and I watched from the other room as William screamed at someone who wasn't even there.

"Whore! Whore! Stay away, you fucking whore!" came from the sound system.

We had a perfect view of William through the two-way mirror. Two days had passed since we'd taken him, and in that time we starved him, kept him awake, and made sure he was cold. Both Jacob and I were sure William was at his breaking point. Soon, he would give us the answers we so desperately wanted. In the meantime, Jacob hacked into William's accounts and managed to steal money from him. Half of his riches were now ours.

"You ready, baby?"

"Of course, lover."

Walking into the room where William was being kept, Jacob pulled his chair over to the metal wash tub. William's screams echoed off the walls as he begged for his life, for Jacob not to kill him. Jacob, on the other hand, was wrapping a cloth around William's mouth and leaning his chair back.

"Tell us what we want to know."

Pouring water over the cloth on his mouth, William gasped for air, head shaking side to side.

"Tell us what we fucking want to know!"

Once again, William shook his head, declining to answer.

"Please, please. Mother, let me go. Let me go."

*Ah, so that's who he had been referring to as a whore earlier. His mother, the prostitute.*

With a push over the edge of the tub by Jacob's hand, William went falling into the ice-cold water, chair and all.

"Help me. Help me. Please help me."

"Tell us what we want to know and you can be free," I whispered over his flailing body.

"Anything. Anything," he replied, voice quaking as he shook from the cold.

"When is the shipment coming?"

"F-Fri-Friday."

"Where?"

"The docks!"

"Time?"

"Midnight."

We now had the knowledge we needed. The girls would be arriving in hours, which didn't leave us much time to prepare. We had so much to do, and the world was suffocating us. If we wanted to be able to pull this off, we really needed to make sure everything was in order.

Tugging William from the tub of ice water, I took my blade and cut his clothes from him, leaving a sad sack of pathetic old man wilted in front of me. It wouldn't do to have him die from hypothermia before he could kill himself once the guilt became too much for him to live with. Throwing a plush blanket over his lap, I watched as such a proud man cowered like a sniveling punk. He was nothing. He was no one. A fuckup who thought he went on to do great things, but instead he ruined lives, one right after another, turning those girls into his mother.

Staring down at him, I cut the blindfold from his face, leaving him to see exactly who was behind his kidnapping.

"You!"

"Give me your confession, William."

"W-What?" he questioned, body still shaking from the cold.

"I want to hear your confession."

"You know it all."

"Do I?"

"Yes. Yes. Everything."

"I don't think so." I held my blade up for him. "Would you like to meet my friend here?"

"No … No."

"Then tell the truth. Give me your confession."

Shaking his head back and forth, he refused to admit his own truth.

"Jacob, grab William a clean shirt and a comb, please."

I couldn't help getting a look at his ass as he walked off to do my bidding. That man sure did have a fine one, and it was all mine. I intended to make sure it stayed that way. In order to do so, I needed William's confession, and this was the first I would make sure to get on tape.

"William, if you want to get out of here alive, you need to tell me why you started trafficking the girls."

"Then you'll let me leave?"

"Of course, darling."

"Okay."

"Glad to see you've come to your senses."

As Jacob returned to the room, I grabbed the shirt from his hand and pointed to the camera in the corner so he would get things ready. Making William somewhat presentable turned out to be a job with the bags under his eyes, but it gave to the story that he could no longer live with the guilt.

"Okay now, William, tell me."

"My name is William Lee. I was born Willy Martin, the son of a Naval officer and a Chinese immigrant. My father died, leaving my mother to raise me, but she was too hooked on drugs to do it. When I was eleven, she tried to sell me to her drug dealer and pimp, but I got away, running as fast as I could. I lived on the streets a while, taking handouts until I was thirteen and a man found me, took me in, raised me up, and taught me everything I know.

"Gave me his company when he died, even. But I c-couldn't get rid of my anger at my ma, at what she tried to do to me, so I started importing and trafficking little Ch-Chinese girls like Ma.

Selling them off to the highest bidder and profiting from their rapes and d-deaths."

Perfect. Just what Jacob and I needed in order to set things in motion. William was still so out of it, he didn't even realize he was being recorded. Head hung low, eyes closed, he looked one step away from death. How I longed to stick a dagger in his heart or gouge out his eyes, but alas, there would be plenty of victims to choose from in the future. This man was our way out.

As Jacob stopped filming, I blindfolded William once more to leave him in the dark.

"Think of all those girls, William. Think about what you've done."

With that, I swept out of the room, parting ways with Jacob so we could get everything ready.

Friday, I would spill my own blood and die, but for now, I had things to do.

# Chapter Thirty-Three

## Jacob

Alana's office was nothing like I thought would fit her. The place was all white and blue lines, all soothing and shit. Nothing black or red. No violence and blood splatter. Instead, classical music pumped softly through the speakers, wrapping the empty desk chairs in cocoons of safety. Whenever her clients came in, they had magazines and books to read while they waited, or drinks provided to soothe their anxiety.

I fucking hated it on sight.

But I wanted to see my girl. She'd been dutifully going to work during the day and spending her nights helping me with William while we planned our escape. She barely slept, but we'd get out soon. We had to. We'd already taken a hefty amount of money from William. Combined with the fortune my father had squirreled away in offshore accounts, we were set for the rest of our evil little lives. I had a proxy working on moving the stolen funds from William's empire to our accounts as I stood in her office.

What a difference a few months made. Alana and I had weathered storms, fought our way apart and then back together.

I refused to let it be soiled by these cops sniffing around her life. The sooner we got going, the faster things would move on. Today, though, I wanted to focus on who we were. On the fact that I could walk into her office and see her. Touch her. Have her if I wanted to.

That was all that mattered.

As I stepped up to her receptionist, I smiled a charming grin. Vanessa Rodriguez, her nameplate said. The last time I talked to her, I was hunting Alana, hiding who I was just to see her. Now I could be myself, at least as much as I was able to in public.

"Can I help you, sir?"

"Yes, I'd like to see Ms. Winters if she has a few minutes."

"Do you have an appointment, Mr. …?"

"Daniels. Mason Daniels. And no, I don't, but she will see me."

Vanessa frowned at me, then turned a delightful shade of pink when I winked at her. "Hold on a moment."

I shrugged and paced to one of the chairs and sat down. No use looking threatening to the help.

"Ms. Winters? Yes, you have someone here to see you. A Mr. Mason Daniels?" For a few moments Vanessa was quiet, listening on the phone, and then she smiled.

"Not a problem, Ms. Winters. Mr. Daniels? She'll see you no," she said, directing me to the door on the left.

"Thank you."

Alana smiled at me as I walked in, tilting her head slightly to the side. Dressed in a simple, mauve pencil skirt and a golden, silk blouse, she looked classic and timeless. I loved her like that—in her mask, waiting, a predator more dangerous than I. I liked that I could see the mask slip, view the messy inside of her, watch her as she satisfied the darkness. I loved that her eyes went soft, and, only for me, she was Alana. The girl who'd crawled through hell and survived it in her own way. The girl who'd found me and brought me enough light that I could love her.

"You're beautiful." I closed her door behind me.

"The feeling is mutual," she returned. "Why are you here? Like this?" She gestured to the door, and I picked up her meaning.

"I wanted to see you," I replied, and then quietly I added, "and fuck you."

She swallowed, her graceful neck muscles showing the movement. "Right now?"

"No time like the present. And it might do good for your assistant to see the man you're dating in case the cops come calling."

"Ah, is that the reason?"

"No, I told the truth the first time. Get up and lay your chest on your desk. Press your cheek on all those pretty papers."

She hesitated only a moment before she stood and did as I asked. Framed in the sunlight, I wished I had waited until dark, to have her in the right element, but this suited me. The chance for her assistant to hear her, for her next client to come in. It made it hotter. Sexier.

"I have an hour before my next case."

"Then I'd better make sure I hurry, shouldn't I? Lift your skirt to your waist."

Alana's fingers were delicate instruments as she did as I had instructed. I'd seen them wrapped around a blade, a whip, and chains. I'd seen them curled to rake my flesh. And now I knew them to be soft, pliable. So many sides, like the woman of my heart. I stepped up behind her and pressed my jean-clad lower body against her exposed ass. She had on a black G-string, and it peeked around the globes of her ass. Fucking vixen. A sexy, wildcat belonging to me. I palmed her ass, testing the firmness of her skin before I leaned forward to whisper in her ear.

"How thin are these walls?"

"They are reinforced to protect client confidentiality, but if you're loud enough, you can be heard on the other side."

"Hmmm." I looked over her desk and found a slim tome, something about the ravaged minds of mental illness, and pressed the spine against her lips.

"Better bite down."

The leather slid between her sharp, white teeth as I stood back up. Her ass was too white; I wanted it red. To add color to this sane place. I wanted to see her cry, sweat, and her body beg.

"Grab the desk, baby. This is going to fucking hurt."

She moaned around the book in her mouth as she gripped the edge of the desk in front of her tight enough to make her knuckles go white. As she breathed under me, I removed my belt and laid it next to her. The clink of the buckle hitting the desk was loud in the silence. I opened my jeans and pulled my stiff cock out of my boxers. Her skin was smooth and warm against the underside, but I wanted her hot. I angled myself downward, so it was protected between the globes of her ass and our bodies.

I grabbed the belt and was swinging. She grunted, taking the hit. A fine, red welt instantly raised on her ass. So fucking perfect. More. There needed to be more. I swung again, hitting the other side and making a matching welt. With each swing, the leather wrapped around and kissed her hips, extending the heat and the pain. She twisted and turned but never let go of the desk. And her ass was nice and red. So fucking hot. My dick slid wetly against her cleft, my pre-cum and her arousal easing the way.

"You're so hot, Alana."

She didn't respond, but I didn't need her to. Instead, I needed *her*. It took less than a few seconds to pull her G-string to the side. The puckered hole of her anus tensed in the cool air, and my mouth watered. I fucking wanted it. Using my saliva as a lubricant, I massaged it into the hole and pressed my thumb in. She gasped but didn't move away from me.

"That ass is so tight. Will it choke me, Alana? Will it make me come so fast my head will explode?"

Tears were falling from her eyes, and her face was flush and red, but she bucked against me, begging for me. Needing me.

"I'll be there soon," I whispered and slammed into her pussy. Her scream was strangled against the book as I pounded her. The pleasure bit at me as her walls clenched, milking me and pulling me deeper inside. I lifted my foot up on the desk and sank in further.

"Fucking take it all, dammit. Every last inch."

I knew I was big, that my girth would stretch her out, and I'd bump her cervix with every stroke, but she was so wet, so hot. She melted against me and wet my balls. They slapped her clit with each stroke, the rasp of her pubic hair edging me higher. A grenade detonated in my ears, leaving a ringing behind as I fucked her. I needed to be closer.

"So good. So damn good."

I gripped her hip with the hand holding the belt and pushed my thumb into her ass with the other. She bucked, keening. Her office smelled like hot sex, and I sucked it in.

"Fuck," I cried. Jerking her against me as I thrust hard, I pulled my thumb from her ass and stuck two fingers deep inside. Her back arched as I fucked her. I opened and closed my fingers to loosen her ass, to let me in when the time came. I was going to come in that tight fucking ass. But first, I wanted her to come all over me. I pulled harder on her waist, bending my knees slightly to change the angle. I hit the top of her insides with every roll of my hips. She stopped, went silent, and froze.

"There you are, baby." I released her hip and reached around her body to find her swollen clit. It was fat and hard between my fingertips. With my next shove inside of her, I pinched it, hard. She screamed into the book, jerking and shaking as I rode her through it. She clamped down like a vice and I could barely move, but I held on, stretching her orgasm until she turned to molten lava. Pleasure pulsed in my balls, drawing them up tight. My stomach clenched as a tendril of need coiled there and angled lower. So good. So fucking good. I needed this. Needed her.

I pulled out of her, removed my fingers from her ass, and slammed inside. Everything froze for a precious moment. Her tight sphincter muscles tried to push me out, the warm space past them closed around me, and I thickened. I'd never come before without nutting. It throbbed through me, the pleasure. I couldn't breathe, couldn't see. I was stiff, held captive by the pleasure in her body.

And then she tossed her ass back on me, pushing me deeper, and I exploded. I didn't remember gripping the belt tighter and swinging, but the burn seared my flesh. The ache as the tail end slapped against my groin, even as the shaft struck her ass. I swung again, punishing us both, adding that sharp bite of pain we both needed. Pushing us higher.

"Fuck me!" she cried. It was muffled, but I heard her.

We rocked in opposite motions, coming together hard in the center, accented by the strike of the belt. It was a vicious, dirty way to fuck. Her ass wide open, her pussy wet from release, her clit throbbing in my hand, and our bodies straining with each leathery strike. It was perfect. It was us.

"I want you to come, Jacob. Deep in my ass. Fuck, I need it."

The book was gone, and her hurried words were mere pants, but they hit me like bullets. Pressing through my bloodstream and ripping their way into my balls. As my scrotum tightened, her buzzer sounded.

"Your next client is here, Ms. Winters."

"Fuck them, Jacob, fill me with your seed."

I fucked her harder, pushing through her tight muscles and hitting us harder with the belt. She rocked with me, twisting her hips in a circle. The change hit me. Spiraled outward until I was on the balls of my feet, trying to get closer. I gritted my teeth, sweating and huffing like I was running a fucking marathon.

"Ms. Winters?"

Alana's hand slammed on her speakerphone button. "Tell them to wait a moment."

She sounded enraged and controlling, and I loved it. Loved even more that she left the speakerphone on. That our movements were broadcasted into the shocked silence on the other line. She looked over her shoulder at me and winked. My fucking crazy-ass woman winked, and then slapped her own ass.

"Make it yours," she said.

"Please hold on, sir, she'll be right with you."

I was lost. Totally fucking lost. I came, balls-deep in her ass, shaking and groaning.

# Chapter Thirty-Four

## Nila

Jacob was right. The heat was on, and killing another victim should have ruined us, but William Lee was going to be our way out of here. For now, we needed to remove every trace Jacob and I were ever in my warehouse. William was back in his music blasting room, begging for his life to end. I listened to Jacob when he told me I needed to disappear—to make it look like there might have been foul play—so we cleaned out any incriminating evidence in my home, even wiped his prints from the house.

And then I let him beat me.

His fists marked my flesh and made me spit blood. He dragged me from my bedroom, down my stairs, and then into the front hall. He slammed me against walls and dragged me out the front door. Then, with gloved hands, he tossed a massive rock through a window on the bottom floor, the one my assailant would have gone through. He drove me to the warehouse and dragged me through it. Right up to the room where I killed my victims.

It made sense. My body ached, though, as we went through the warehouse. I kept lye and bleach in the kitchen area in case I

LeTeisha Newton

needed to ruin DNA evidence as best I could. We spread it in places where there wouldn't be an easy explanation why I was there, even if I'd been kept here. My phone was destroyed, and I was now a missing person if the cops came looking for me. I knew they would.

As Jacob and I finished with the last of the evidence, Jacob shredded patient files I'd collected over the years and placed them in a plastic bag to take with him. I headed in to face William once more. For the plan to succeed, William must die. He was the last victim I would take as Nila Winters, but for the first time there would be no cuts, no torture. No, William would die at his own hand, with a little help from Jacob.

Reaching William, I paused to look at him, an almost fond grin stretching across my face. William was the one who would give the light that was left of Alana Masters's one last good deed. I would make sure each one of those girls he had in this shipment would be freed. None of them would be sold or traded. Killed or raped. As Alana, I faced the cruelness of having my freedom taken from me. I was raped, beaten, and marked, but like the Phoenix, I rose from the ashes with new life ahead of me. Once more I was starting over, but this time I was not alone. I was with Jacob. I would forever be with Jacob. Two Phoenixes born from a cruel, unjust world. While apart we were strong, together we were unstoppable, and the way this plan was unfolding right before my very eyes proved it.

Turning off the music, I began speaking, drawing William's attention to myself.

"Are there any other dirty little confessions you have, William? Anything you need to get off your chest? I *am* a therapist, you know." I mocked him, disgust radiating from every pore of my body.

"You're a fucking psycho."

"Oh, you say such sweet things. Too bad the fun must come to an end."

"What are you talking about?"

"Come now, darling. You didn't really think you were going to walk out of here alive, did you?"

"You promised!"

"Yes, so I did. I guess I lied."

"Bitch," he spat.

"You see, you've seen my face. You know who I am. Who's to say you wouldn't go running to the cops and give me up? Give my love up? I can't have that."

"What are you going to do to me?" He glared up at me, hate evident in his eyes.

"Simple, really. You're going to turn yourself in to the cops."

"Why would I do something like that?"

"You're going to die either way, William. The choice is up to you. Would you rather have the painful death you'll receive if you refuse to do as I say? Or would you rather have an easy, painless death? Personally, I would choose the painless one if I were you."

"You can't tell a man to decide how he's going to die!"

"I think I just did. Tick-tock. Tick-tock. Time is running out. What's it going to be, William?" Looking him over from head to toe, seeing what the last few days of psychological torture had done to him, I couldn't help but continue, "Although, you *are* pretty insane to me already."

"I wonder why, cunt."

"Now, now, darling. Did your mother teach you how to treat a woman at all? Because surely, sweetheart, you know it's not right to refer to a lady as a cunt."

"Fuck you, Winters."

"Not my type, dear, but thanks for the offer. Now either take mine or leave it. But I'm telling you, you'll regret it."

"Fine, I'll do it," William said as he spat at my feet. "Bitch."

"Good boy," I murmured, stepping away to prepare.

Unlike before—when I would torture for hours, drawing every ounce of pain from my victims, taking their guilt and madness along with their blood—I had no blade to use against him. I had no torture devices to call upon. No, instead I was left with a gun. How … common. But it would serve its purpose.

Last year, the suicide rate for middle-aged men began to skyrocket. Coupled with the guilt of having trafficked so many innocent, young girls over the years, it would easily be believable he finally had a breakdown.

The plan was we would make it look as if he had been stalking me for a while, thinking I had caught on to him. In turn, he began to go crazy, taking out my clients to get my attention until he finally snapped and took me. In the end, once I was gone, he realized I was the one person who could have helped him and now I was dead. The guilt drove him to have a complete breakdown and take his own life but not before confessing to the police what he had done.

"It's done."

I turned to find Jacob standing in the door. "Good." I picked up the phone and Jacob grabbed the video recorder once more. Turning to William, I began speaking directly to him, making sure to keep eye contact with him the entire time.

"I need you to do one last thing."

"Why would I do anything for you, you crazy bitch? You're about to fucking kill me and you want me to do you a favor? You're out of your mind!"

"Possibly. But still … I need you to look at Jacob and his trusty camera and admit to murdering me."

"What?" Caught off guard, William floundered, not knowing what to say.

"I need you to admit to murdering me."

"You're right in front of my face."

"I won't be for long. Jacob here is going to kill me."

"What the hell? Are you people *insane*?"

"Yes."

"Pretty much."

Jacob and I talked over one another.

"Fucking crazies."

"William, focus! Look into the camera and admit to my murder so we can get this over and done with. Otherwise, I'm going to go get my blade and start cutting off fingers and toes to get your attention."

With that, William snapped into action, mouth closing before a retort could form on the tip of his tongue and his eyes centered on the camera.

"And why did I kill you?"

"Because I got too close to blowing the lid off your trafficking ring and taking you down. By the way, you took me from my house."

Focusing directly on the camera, William began speaking.

"I took Ms. Nila Winters, my therapist, from her home in order to hide my crimes after she got too close to discovering the truth. I killed her to protect my secret, but I no longer can."

Jacob put the camera down and came closer, pulling the gun off the table beside him. Holding it to William's head, Jacob cocked the trigger.

"Any last words?"

"I hope you burn in hell, the both of you."

Grabbing William's hand in his, and being sure it was his dominant one, Jacob placed William's hand around the gun to be sure his fingerprints were on it and the gunpowder would show if tested. With one bullet, William was dead.

"Okay, do me."

"With pleasure," Jacob smirked.

"Oh, hush. You know what I meant."

Trusting Jacob, I put my life into his hands, literally, as I handed him the needle. Filled with the drug we'd chosen, there was a good chance that once this needle entered my skin and the drug worked its way through my system, I may never wake again.

Scary as it was, it was the only way our plan would succeed. The cops had to really believe I was dead, and the only way to prove it was to produce my body for them.

Staring into Jacob's eyes, I thought of all the things I never got a chance to say to him and all the things I wish we could've shared together. I committed his image to memory, hoping it wouldn't be the last time I saw his handsome face staring back at me, eyes gazing into mine, drinking me in as if I were a cool drink in the middle of the hot desert.

"I love you, Jacob," I whispered as I grabbed his hand, pulling him into me. "Hear me? I love you. Even if I don't wake from this, I need you to know that. I need you to realize I will always love you, in life and in death. You're my soul mate, my other half. Without you, I am not complete. Thank you for saving me. Thank you for loving me. For showing me who you truly are, who *I* truly am, and thank you for sharing the last few months with me."

"Baby, don't talk like this."

"I don't want anything left unsaid. We spent so many years apart, and now that we are together, I want to make sure you know the truth."

Tears came to my eyes for the first time in a long time. I tried to brush them away, but Jacob held me tighter, planting a kiss on the top of my head.

"I love you. And I know you love me. If you didn't, you wouldn't be doing this."

"I do love you, Jacob. And I trust you."

Safe in Jacob's arms was the only place I wanted to be. It was funny how my captor's son would save me, only to one day become my captor himself. But instead of fearing him as I did his father, I grew to love him. Immensely. My love for Jacob was indescribable. Despite how fucked-up most people would find our story, it was ours. It was our love story filled with pain, blood, and tears. We'd both survived a monster by working together to put an end to him. Now, eight years later, we ended another monster's life together. As a team, we were unstoppable. We had overcome so much in our lives, suffered so much in the years spent apart. Now we were here, in this moment. In love, happy, ready to start a new life together.

I only prayed once the drug wore off, I would wake up.

I couldn't bear for Jacob to be left alone. Knowing Jacob as I did, I knew he would self-destruct and become a shell of himself until he killed himself or was caught. I couldn't have that.

For the first time since I was a teenager, I prayed.

I prayed to live. I prayed to love. I prayed to be Jacob's forever, to stay with him.

Reaching up and grabbing Jacob's face in my hands, I made sure he was looking at me.

"I love you, Jacob VanDuyn." With that, I kissed him.

"Don't you leave me, Alana. Don't you dare."

"I can't promise you that, Jacob. We both know the risks. But I'm sure as hell not going to say goodbye to you, my love."

"No goodbyes. Only see you soon."

"I can't wait to start our life together."

"Neither can I."

"It's going to be a good one, isn't it?"

"It's going to be amazing," Jacob said, kissing the tip of my nose. "I love you, Alana Masters."

"How many times do I need to tell you that it's Nila?" I smirked.

"You'll always be Alana to me."

Losing myself in his eyes, I whispered one last I love you to him.

"Do it, Jacob. Do it now."

His hand moved, tightening around the needle, and the distress played across his face. Agony and despair filled his eyes as he plunged the needle into my arm. With a sad smile, I whispered, "I love you."

And then my body was sinking, sinking, sinking until I was no more.

# Chapter Thirty-Five

## Jacob

My hands were shaking. Fucking shaking. There was nothing worse than seeing the one person in your life who made you even marginally human stop breathing. I fucking swear my heart stopped as I kissed her still lips and left her in that fucking warehouse to finish the rest of what we needed to do. The drug was supposed to keep her out for nearly twenty-four hours, but that would be dangerous for her system. I needed to get her out of the morgue as soon as possible and administer the antidote.

"Fuck, this is worse than I thought it would be."

There was no one to talk to, and no one answered me when I called out. She was always there after I finally found her. I had to walk away from that warehouse. I was right outside, up on the roof of a building, waiting. It was dangerous, but I didn't want to leave her there alone. The cops were swarming around, lights blazing red and blue. I heard the buzz of their radios as they talked back and forth and figured they'd found a fucking gold mine of information.

And I guess they did.

It was all there for them. Random, scattered patient notes we'd saved and placed in good places. Pictures of torture and the camera that was set up to record William's confession. We made sure we never moved it and William hadn't been tied down. It all looked like a serial killer's suicide. And I didn't give a shit about any of it. The one thing I needed out of that fucking building hadn't been loaded yet. Instead, they poked a fucking thermometer to her liver to test for the time of death. But I was worried fucking sick. She could be dead right now. Gone. No oxygen to the brain. Losing herself. Even if I could bring her back, all of it could royally fuck her and she may never come back as the woman I loved.

I'd paint the fucking world red if that happened.

For now, I stayed on my perch. With all sort of darkness going through my sick mind, I could come up with a lot of fucking mess in that head of mine. I waited and waited, until two black bags on gurneys were wheeled out of the warehouse and loaded into ambulances. I didn't care about the scene at the warehouse. All I cared about was getting to Alana and getting out of there.

It took a while to get down from the roof and get to my car parked a good distance away. Those minutes made me grit my teeth, but they were part of the plan. If they found the car, it would have been suspicious, and that would have messed up a lot of shit. Hearses weren't lying around, especially ones emblazoned with a local business on it. Once I reached it, I was out of the old district and heading toward Mercy Hospital, obeying all the street signs like a good little driver. I resisted the urge to press the gas pedal to the floor and focused on making sure I gave the cops no reason to stop me.

Once I reached the hospital, I slipped on the shirt I'd stolen from the funeral home. I then put a timer on my phone. I wanted to be out of there in fifteen minutes. Anything more than that could be dangerous. Tucking it into my jeans, I made sure I was parked in the proper location to load a body and entered through the morgue entrance. An older gentleman, Frederick by the name on his nametag, looked up from his desk when I limped in, a bit hunched over.

"Can I help you?"

"Hey, I'm sure hoping you can. I got a call about a Nila Winters, scheduled for cremation? Can I go ahead and pull her?"

"That was quick, and I don't remember making any call. The police just brought her in a little while ago, and the body is tied to an investigation. Until the M.E. gets hold of her, they won't be releasing the body."

"Really?" I frowned and scratched my forehead under my hat, taking a few minutes to look off into space like I was confused. "Then who would call us? Somebody going to pay for the mileage with this? From what I got, she had explicit wishes, per her will, to not be tampered with, and she wanted to be cremated within twelve hours of death. Some sort of religious thing her family has."

"Family? We don't have any listing of family."

"Maybe the police didn't let you know. You know how these things go sometimes. They want to do things the family doesn't agree with, so they push some buttons. I've got the paperwork right here."

"Let me see that."

I pulled out the Will and Testament of Nila Winters, born Alana Masters. Alana had it drawn up a very long time ago, maybe in case she didn't make it out. The will had her remains to be immediately cremated and sent to her mother and father. In the event they were deceased, her remains would then be buried alongside them. It was ironclad and legal, no matter that it was going to be used incorrectly. Of course, I only handed him a copy, printed over with the paperwork from the funeral home. I was cold, hoping steady hands and quick talking would get me through this. My hat was still pulled low over my face to shield it, and I'd padded my stomach to make me appear like I had a pot belly. Last, I'd added a bit of makeup to my face to make me look much paler than usual. Anything to throw the cops off if they looked my way.

"Damn, this paperwork is all in order. But I'm not going to have Agents Monroe and Jackson breathing down my neck on this."

"No problem. Stick to what they tell you and I can go home and not have to do anything the rest of the night. I've got a hot piece waiting anyway." I forced myself to turn and walk away. Then I stopped and snapped my fingers.

"Almost forgot. Can you sign that you aren't accepting the transfer? I don't want to have her family coming after the home with some sort of legal shit and suing the pants off the company. I don't want to lose this job."

"Sue?"

"Yeah. You don't recognize the name? That psychiatrist is pretty big shit around here, and her family has a lot of money. They can afford to do it."

"Now, wait a minute. I didn't say I would stop the transfer, I want to call it in to make sure it's okay."

"No problem. How about this, since I know it's a formality once you tell them what I've shown you, I'll start getting her set up, and if you hear anything wrong, you tell me to load her back in. I really don't want to mess with this or have my boss up my ass."

"All right, hold—"

My phone buzzed in my pocket, the alarm going off after my allotted fifteen minutes. *Fuck.* I had to be quick. "Dammit, that's him. Can I get in and start loading?"

Instead of waiting for him to answer, I pulled my phone out of my pocket and acted like I was answering a call.

"Schultz, here. Yeah, boss, I'm here now. I have to wait for things to get approved. What? Are they there? Why?" I pulled the phone away from my mouth and covered it with my hand. "The family is there waiting to view the cremation," I whispered to Frederick. "Yes, sir," I said back into my phone. "Tell the family Mercy has been extremely accommodating and is helping me get her taken care of now. They even made another home wait to take care of her first."

I shrugged at Frederick, faux apologizing for the bullshit lie I was making up. Finally, he turned toward the morgue entrance, waving at me to follow.

"Gotta go, boss. About to get on the road. See you in about thirty."

I didn't have to wait long. Frederick went right to the slab Alana was on and told me to take her. I didn't ask twice or even turn to thank him. I carried her out of there and placed her in the back of the hearse. I drove until I was out of sight of the morgue and got in back with her. Pressing the needle into her arm, I administered the antidote. I took a few more minutes to dress her and trade cars for the unmarked one I'd parked in preparation.

Then I drove my sleeping beauty into the night and to the ship that would take us away.

"Jacob?"

My eyes were gritty as I forced my eyelids open at the sound of my name. Sun filtered in and stung, but I didn't care. Suddenly, everything was white-hot and in complete focus. Alana was tucked against my side on the bed in our cabin, her eyes open but dazed.

"I'm here, baby. I'm here."

"My head …"

"It might hurt for a bit. You need water." I got out of bed and grabbed a bottled water from the mini-fridge, helped her sit up, and fed her the water slowly.

"What happened?"

"We got things to go the way we wanted. The cops took a bit longer with you than we expected, and they stuck you to fucking check your time of death, but you're healing. The drug did its job, but you were out for some time. I was afraid there might have been some lasting effects."

"Like my memory?"

"Are the days hazy around the end?"

"Um, last thing I remember is you taking me on my desk in the office."

"Good memory to have."

She slapped my shoulder, and I laughed. She was here, awake, with me. I squeezed her to my chest, not wanting to let go.

"As good as that is, Jacob, my bladder is about to burst. Think you can let me go to the bathroom?"

"Yeah, I can do that." She smiled at me and kissed me softly. *This* was the best in the world—a beautiful moment that stretched until she pushed at my chest with pointy nails.

"After I pee, you can have your way with me, got it?"

I smiled and helped her out of bed. It took a few moments for her legs to stiffen under her, but she did it and padded to the bathroom. I waited until she was finished.

"Where are we anyway?"

"On a yacht."

"A what?"

"You know, a yacht, sails in the water. Goes pretty fast. All that."

"Why are we on a yacht, Jacob?"

"Because it's ours. Free and clear. We go where we want, when we want. No one has to know us, and we fly the flag we want to when we reach their waters. But mostly because it was the easiest way to get an unconscious woman out of the country. Soon, we are going to hit an island in the Pacific and port."

"We're in the middle of the ocean?"

"Not exactly middle, but yeah."

"We're free? Really free?"

"Yeah. We made it. No one has come after us. And as far as the world is concerned, Nila Winters, the woman who was once Alana Masters, is dead. We can be whoever we want. Go wherever we please."

"You told me the truth, Jacob."

"What?"

"That you would set me free. It was the truth. God, I love you. So much."

"I love you too."

She fell into my arms, all gangly limbs and hot skin. Nearly ten years ago, I fell in love with a toy—a girl who didn't know how to fight but had the drive to. Now she was a woman of deadly beauty, powerful, and riddled with scars. I knew them all. The taste of them, the weight of their pain. Some I'd placed there, others I'd taught her to love, as much as I loved her.

And as I laid her down on the bed and climbed between her legs, I wanted the fibers of those scars to cut through me. Make me bleed and remind me she was alive. That she was mine. And no one would ever take her from me again.

They'd die first.

# Epilogue

## Jacob

*One Month Later*

"One of the worst crime sprees in American history has finally come to an end. The sad tale began nearly ten years ago, with the abduction of high schooler Alana Masters. Though the teen was able to get away from her captor, it was a nebulous situation that left her assailant murdered and his son put away in a mental facility. Alana Masters, later to become the renowned psychiatrist Nila Winters, was later killed by one of her crazed patients who'd become obsessed with her case. Her killer, William Lee, has now been found to be the perpetrator of nearly fifteen deaths, along with slave trade ..."

I closed the webpage, smirking at the news footage. The news always got shit wrong. Always. But whatever. They had taken the bait—hook, line, and sinker. That was exactly what we wanted.

After placing my wipe disk in the hard drive, it only took a few clicks to wipe everything off the computer until there was nothing left.

Alana's hair was now layered around her shoulders and dyed a warm brown with golden highlights. There were times I missed the blonde, but it made her stand out no matter where we went. We stuck to countries with no extradition laws with America just in case, and we lived on our boat when we needed to get away for a while.

"Find anything?"

I turned to find Alana bending over, holding out a cold brew by the neck of the bottle. She wore a half-shirt over the top of her bikini, hiding the identifying mark of my brand on her.

"They took the story we left behind, as much as they could piece together. There wasn't any mention of inquiries or how you got out of the morgue. I think we are officially cleared."

"I like the sound of that."

I grabbed the beer and took a long swig as she sat on my lap, facing the people milling around the hotel lobby. It wasn't the most high-end place, but enough tourists were there that we blended nicely into the background. It was a safe place to be, and Alana and I liked that.

"So when are you going to marry me?"

"Hmm?"

"You know, make an honest man out of me?"

"You'll never be honest or good, Jacob, and that's what I love about you."

"I am for you." I took another mouthful of beer, and she kissed me before I could swallow. Our tongues danced over the flavor of hops, and she sipped some out of my mouth before swallowing.

"Now?"

"What?"

"Aw, come on. Don't chicken out on me now."

She jumped from my lap and grabbed my hand. Dragging me through the hotel to the front desk, I couldn't do anything but laugh.

"Concierge, you know where we can find a priest?"

"A priest?" The heavily accented words were sweet and lilting from the small woman.

"Yes, someone who can officiate over a marriage?"

"Married. Ah!" The woman clapped her hands and chatted rapidly in her native tongue as she picked up the phone. After a few moments, she hung up and gestured for us to follow her.

I followed behind Alana's swaying hips, mesmerized by how they moved. I followed her frame all the way outside to a fountained area where a man in a bright-yellow robe was standing. In a blur, I was married. Saying words of honor and everlasting fealty to a crazy girl in a bikini. A scarred soul as dark as mine. It shouldn't fit the fucked-up souls we were, but it was one last thing that made her mine.

"Now I'm Mrs. Jacob VanDuyn," she said, her tone bouncing with laughter.

"I suppose we'll have to get rings."

"Might get in the way. How about some tattoos?"

"I like the sound of that."

And so our wedding rings became a crown of thorns tattooed around our ring fingers with pricks of blood. Us. Dark. Everlasting.

"But I want a honeymoon present, Jacob."

"Demanding little thing, aren't you?"

"You'll like it."

"I bet I will. What is it?"

"You see that man over there? With the dark hair and Hawaiian shirt? He's here alone, and he's been taking really young girls into his room at night."

My gaze swept to where she pointed, seeing the older man glancing up at Alana's slightly bared form as she leaned against me.

"He's at the hotel?" I was already making plans.

"Yeah, the floor beneath us."

"How badly do you want him to hurt?"

"Enough that we'll need to head to another country."

I chuckled. "So be it. I'll get the yacht ready and then we can take him."

"Thank you."

"Anything for you, Alana. Anything."

# Thank You

Thanks for reading *Whispers in the Dark*. I really hope you enjoyed it!

Want to know when my next book is available? You can keep in the know by signing up for my new release newsletter at

http://darkreaders.leteishanewton.com/

Reviews help other readers find books. I appreciate all reviews, whether positive or negative.

# About the Author

**W**riting professionally since 2008, LeTeisha Newton's love of romance novels began long before it should have. After spending years sneaking reads from her grandmother's stash, she finally decided to pen her own tales. As many will do during their youth, she bounced from fantasy, urban literature, mainstream, interracial, paranormal, heterosexual, and LGBT works until she finally rested in contemporary romance.

LeTeisha is all about deep angst and angry heroes who take a bit more loving to smooth their rough edges. Love comes in many sizes, shapes, and colors, as well as with—or without—absolute beauty and fairy tale sweetness. She writes the darker tales because life is hard … but love is harder.

www.leteishanewton.com | @LeTeishaNewton

# Coming Soon

## Scathed

### Coming Mid 2018

The anticipated follow up to *MIDAS*

### Nathan

I should have been dead, but Midas saved me. He gave me the weapons to seek revenge on my enemies and family to love again. It should have been enough ... but it wasn't. I needed to feel their blood on my hands, hear their screams in my ears, and mark their passing on my flesh.

Then I found her.

### Chiara

My father taught me what was most important for a woman of La Cosa Nostra: to be silent and worth what power I could bring. But I lost my place, because I hated him for what he'd done. Scorned my father for breaking the one I could have ever given myself to.

Then he found me ...

*I loved him, he broke me ...*

# LeTeisha's Bookcase

## The Lost Series

The way to love isn't always paved in sweet words and roses. Sometimes it's hard. Other times it's violent. More often than not, it's filled with heartache before the healing can come. Read three stories of the struggle to find love in the darkness. Call girl Celeste is addicted to sex and dangerous situations, the chance to love never factored in One Hour Girl. River searched for a way to learn to kill, instead she fell in love with a killer in Scarred. Aeryn only know how to take a punch and fall down, but when he found the woman of his dreams beaten and tossed aside, he learned to stand up and fight in Phenomenal.

## A SEALed Fate Series

All is far in love and war. Seven SEALs. Seven stories of blazing romance amid action. The intelligence community is facing an epidemic--someone wants them dead. It's up to an elite group of SEALs to find out just what's going on. Everything becomes personal when their loved ones are attacked.

Someone should have told the enemy, SEALs don't back down. They fight back, and destroy.

# Claimed Trilogy

All three Claimed Series novellas in one full-length work.

Follow Zelina's struggle with Tarquin and Centurion in *Theirs to Claim*, a menage novella.

Jezzie must decide whether or not to submit to Andrzej in *The Fire of His Claim*, a BDSM piece.

*Accepting Their Claim* is the final work in this series, an MMF story of Sonja, Hideki, and Tobias.

# Taken Trilogy

Now, all together in one location, The Taken Trilogy is here.

Selene fights to accept the creature she has become while Pietr attempts to earn her love and trust in *Taken by Lust*.

Sasha and Cirro have a connection which can't be denied in *Taken by Desire*.

Can Maddy allow Connor back in her life after he's hurt her so deeply? Find out in *Taken by Need*.

Follow the leopard shifters through stories of romance, murder, and suspense and fall in love with the characters in this series you just can't put down.

# Corporate Hitman Trilogy

Welcome to the world of Corporate Espionage and dangerous liaisons …

The Corporate Hitman trilogy features three men, GLITCH, SCRATCH, and JACK; each plucked from a different path in the life of crime. They've led lives of trauma and full of illegal activity, forced to use their talents to aid in the bidding of a rising corporate conglomerate.

Pierce 'Eagle' Eaglemor is the CEO of Hawk Global Industries and the mastermind behind the hitman crew. He searched far and wide to find the best of the best to do his dirty work. Now, instead of crime for play, these men commit crime for pay. But the old adage "there is no honor amongst thieves" rings true.

When the crew realizes their days are numbered, and the plans Eagle has for them are void of a happy ending, the three decide to get even. Together, they devise a plan to beat the master at his own game. In their quest to stay alive and bring Eagle down, love plays an unexpected role when Araceli, the Hacker, Monica, the FBI Agent, and Pristine, the Russian Sex Slave, enter the mix.

Three men, one common enemy, and one story that will blow your mind.

LeTeisha Newton

Made in the USA
Las Vegas, NV
15 April 2021

21463692R00174